ALLEGORIES
OF THE
TAROT

ALLEGORIES
OF THE
TAROT

EDITED BY ANNETTA RIBKEN

Word Webber Press
Fairview Heights, IL 62208

Allegories of the Tarot © 2013 Annetta Ribken
Cover image © 2013 Kris Austen Radcliffe based on photographs of artwork by Pamela Coleman Smith
Copy edited by Jennifer Wingard
Book design by Valerie Bellamy, Dog-ear Book Design
Tarot symbols © Clive Ayron Arnold. Used by permission.

2013 Word Webber Press Trade Paperback Edition
Published in the United States by Word Webber Press
Fairview Heights, IL
ISBN-13: 978-0615899008
ISBN-10: 0615899005

CONTENTS

THE FOOL

ON THE ROAD
TO DEVIL'S GULCH

By Peter Giglio

WHEN MAX LOOKED UP AT ME WITH THOSE SAD EYES OF his, I smiled, trying to be reassuring. "A car will come along soon, boy," I said, "take us to the next town and more good times."

Max's dry bark said he wasn't buying it.

"I'm not your owner. Run away if you think you can do better without me."

A blast of prairie wind rolled across Highway 23. Tumbleweeds tumbled.

Although Minnesota was said to be land of 10,000 lakes, the slogan clearly didn't carry to this remote corner of the state. The way I figured it, every land left their armpits and assholes out of the brochure. But it was fine by me, even if Max was having one his many moments of doubt.

You see, I was looking for experiences that couldn't be found any other way. The land must be felt, smelled, and touched to be truly under-stood and that wasn't a thing you could do thirty-thousand miles above the earth. Even in the air-conditioned comfort of a car—though Max and I often counted on the kindness of travelers to bridge wilds like these—it was hard to appreciate the complex beauty of the terrain.

Max and I met many kind people along the way, and we had a lot of fun. Trust me, that dog knew he'd found a good thing, even if he chal-lenged me from time to time.

A hopeful bark sounded, one I knew well, causing me to turn. From the north, a Lincoln Towncar approached. I stuck out my thumb, flash-ing an enthusiastic smile, and the car slowed before pulling to the shoul-der. Yanking the heavy pack from my back while Max ran in excited circles around me, I strode to the open driver's side window. There, a wizened man took my measure through his squinted gaze.

"What're you doing out here?" the man asked. "Did your car break down?"

"No, sir."

"Funny, you don't look like a homeless. Don't smell like one, either."

I smiled. "I'm not. I'm just looking to get a little further down the road. I'll gladly pitch in for gas."

"So you have money?" The man's tremulous voice rang with disbelief. "Yes."

"Haven't you ever heard of planes and buses, young man?"

It wasn't particularly funny, but I chuckled. I guess that's a natural reaction when you've heard the same thing too many times to count. Maybe not. Repetition seems to anger or annoy most folks. Perhaps my parents were right—I'm just wired wrong.

"I like to experience the land and meet new people," I said.

Shaking his head, the old man reached down. A click sounded as the trunk lid popped open, then the driver hooked his thumb toward the back of the Lincoln and said, "I'm going as far as Garretson, South Dakota, about twenty miles from here. Will that work for ya?"

I nodded eagerly then started around the car. For a moment, I was struck by the emptiness of the trunk. Most travelers carried some kind of luggage. But it didn't seem like a worry worth dwelling on. After all, the car had Minnesota plates. And, as the man said, we were only headed twenty miles down the road. I stowed my pack and slammed the trunk.

Despite the age of the Lincoln, the interior sparkled. Clean and fresh, like a car just driven off the showroom floor.

How will he react to Max, I thought, worried poor eyesight had caused the old man not to notice my traveling companion. As Max jumped onto the leather passenger's seat, I said, "He's a good boy, very well-behaved."

The old man laughed and threw me a dismissive wave. "Oh, I can tell he's a good boy. I used to have a Jack Russell just like him. Best dog I ever knew." Then he scratched Max's head, and Max's big doggy smile widened with approval.

I slid into the car, and Max made himself comfortable in the backseat.

"How long have you had that dog?" the old man asked.

"Max joined me at a rest stop in Pennsylvania."

"A stray?"

"He must have been abandoned by a family. Maybe forgotten. I just couldn't let him fend for himself. Besides, it's nice to have a friend along for the journey."

"A journey, huh? Well, where are you headed exactly?"

I shrugged as the old man steered the car slowly back onto the empty highway.

"You know," he said, "a journey ought to have a destination. Or are you some kind of rambling man?"

"I guess that's what I am."

"Fellas like you were around a lot in the '60s, but I suppose you're something of a rarity these days."

"That's what I hear."

"Don't think I'm hassling you about it. Fact is, it kinda takes me back a bit."

I didn't know what to say to that.

"So," he said, "what are you hoping to gain from all this? You ain't one of those kids who's trying to find himself, are you?"

"No," I said. "I'm just looking to broaden my horizons, gain experiences that I can write about someday."

"Ah, so you're a writer."

"Hope to be, but I think I need to do some living first."

A moment of silence followed as the car sped down the road at ten miles above the posted speed limit. That rate of travel, counterintuitive to how I'd seen most elderly folks drive, surprised me. Although I wasn't in a hurry to get anywhere, a glance at Max told me he approved. Panting, he stared at the blur of yellow through the window. I'd treat his patience with a big fat burger when we reached the next town.

When I shifted my gaze to the world outside the car, a sign welcomed me to South Dakota. "Great Faces, Great Places" the marker assured, and the iconic countenances of Mount Rushmore hung above that slogan.

"South Dakota," the old man whispered. "Hell, I haven't been here for thirty years."

"Is it a long drive from where you live?" I asked, my mind flashing back to the empty trunk.

The man shook his head. "Nah, I'm from Mankato, not too far from here. I just haven't had a reason to come back for a long time."

"Why are you returning now?"

"The wife and I honeymooned here. We didn't have much money in those days, so we couldn't afford a fancy trip. I'd served my country in Vietnam, so I'd seen a good bit of the world. But Ellen, God rest, had never left the state. She was tickled to see something new, even if South Dakota ain't much to brag about." The man pointed up through the windshield and smiled. "There's a reason why they call these the fly-over states."

"I understand how she felt," I said.

"Yeah, I suppose you would. Guess you're just looking for something different, too, huh?"

"Something like that."

"Maybe you're just hunting for a good place to settle down?"

"Maybe. Eventually."

"Well, you ain't gonna find it out here. I'll tell you that much."

"So why are you coming back now?"

The old man, who'd dodged my question the first time, wasn't quick to answer. His sad stare lingered on the road, and it was clear I'd hit a nerve. I hoped he wasn't offended.

Finally, he said, "I'm coming back for one last look, a trip down memory lane. Ellen, you see, she passed away last year, and I know my own time on this rock is winding down, too. She always wanted to relive our honeymoon by coming back, but I kept putting things off. There's always enough time, you tell yourself. Always enough time...'til there isn't."

"I'm sorry to hear that," I said.

"Oh, don't be silly." The man's outward mood seemed to shift in a more positive direction. "You're on an adventure. I guess I am, too."

"Is that why you didn't pack any bags?"

The old man nodded then he fell silent again. I feared further questions would only spark more painful memories, so I kept my mouth shut. Able to see for miles, I took in the flat landscape and tried to enjoy the scenery, but those bleak environs failed to inspire my attention.

Then the trouble started.

The old man took a deep, consumptive breath, and the car swerved into the oncoming lane.

My heart thundered.

Max growled.

I grabbed the steering wheel and guided the car back into the proper lane. The old man shook his head and sucked another lungful of air. Exhaling slowly, he gazed at me, his eyes misty and distant. Then, turning his attention back to the road, he gripped the wheel.

"What's wrong?" I asked.

"Nothing's wrong," he said with a grin. He added, "I bet you're excited to see Devil's Gulch again, aren't you?"

Now I was confused. "Like I told you, sir, I've never been here before."

The old man laughed. "Now you're just pulling my leg, you old kidder."

"No, I—"

"Forty-one years ago," he said in a wistful, faraway voice. "It's been a long time, but certainly you must remember."

"I don't understand," I said. "I'm only twenty-three."

He turned to me, and I readied myself to grab the wheel again. "Oh, Ellen," he said, "you'll always be twenty-three to me."

I backed against the door, putting as much distance between me and the old man as I could. "Stop the car," I shouted. "I want out! Now!"

Sadness swept the man's parched face. "Don't act like that, Ellen."

"My name's Bill," I said. "I'm...I'm not your wife." I reached for the door handle, calculating my chances of survival if I leapt from the moving car. Not good. And then there was the matter of Max, who was still growling at the driver. Like most dogs, Max granted trust with graceful indifference, but at the first signs of trouble, he didn't hesitate about changing his position.

Perhaps it was best to just play along, I told myself. Max and I would make a run for it in Garretson. "I'm sorry," I said. "I don't know what's gotten into me."

The old man smiled. "Ah, nothing to worry about, dear. Happens to the best of us. You'll be glad to hear we're almost there."

"That's good," I said. "Very good."

"I wonder if the old tales of Jesse James and Devil's Gulch are true, don't you?"

I nodded as if I understood what he was talking about.

"I just don't see how a man could jump that ravine on a horse and live to tell the story."

"I don't, either," I said.

"Well, I guess we're gonna find out in Garretson, aren't we?" He patted the dashboard. "This old girl has far more horsepower under the hood than Mr. James ever dreamed of."

I felt the sudden jerk of the engine in the pit of my stomach. Faster... faster...we sped down the highway. My gaze became frantic. Where was the state patrol when you needed them?

"I don't want to die." I wheezed. My pulse thrummed, running a race it couldn't win.

The old man laughed. "Oh, Ellen, we're already dead. Why not go out in a blaze of glory?"

I yanked the seatbelt over my chest and fumbled beneath the leather bench for the locking mechanism. Snapping the restraint in place brought no comfort. I glanced at the speedometer. The needle vibrated just south of one hundred.

Numb with panic, I hadn't realized Max jumped onto my lap until I looked down. Trembling, he stared at me, clearly trying to determine if I had a solution to the mess of ours. When he seemed to come up empty, he turned his attention to the driver.

Hunching low, Max growled.

The events following that diminutive—though predatory—warning happened fast.

Max sprang at the old man, biting and scratching. The man's eyes widened as he released the wheel to defend himself, but he was slow and Max was fast. Sharp canines sank into the man's neck as we careened off the road.

The car somersaulted, the world around me spinning.

Then the embrace of darkness.

When I opened my eyes, Max sat in my lap and looked up No longer was he trembling. I patted myself, looking for injuries, then pulled the sun visor down and studied my face in its mirror. Other than a terrible case of dizziness, I felt fine. I wiggled my fingers. I moved my legs. I rubbed my stiff neck and groaned. Yeah, I was alive.

Blood trickled from a gash above Max's brow. Concerned for his well-being, I felt his limbs, then pressed two fingers into his belly. When he didn't whimper, I assumed he'd live, too.

The same couldn't be said for the old man.

Jagged lines spiderwebbed across the windshield, and in the center of that bloody mosaic, the old man hung suspended. The lower half of his body was still in the car, but his front half draped across the Lincoln's blue hood.

I heaved my breakfast onto the floorboard, unsnapped the seat belt, yanked the door handle, then staggered from the car. With Max at my side, I stood in the deep ditch that stopped our fall, waiting for balance to find me. After a few baby steps, testing my ability to walk, I ambled to the driver's side door and leaned through the window. Doing my best to ignore all the blood, I reached down and pulled the trunk release. Sliding on my pack, I trudged up the steep embankment to the highway. Max followed at my heels.

Short of breath, I stood on the shoulder of the road. I looked left then right. No cars. A sign staked in the barren earth read, Garretson 3 miles. Max and I started walking.

The afternoon sun blazed, and my mind became as empty as my stomach. Max's head hung low as he panted, but he kept pace with me.

A few minutes later, an engine roared behind us. But no hopeful bark erupted from Max.

Without so much as a glance at the approaching vehicle, I stopped walking and stuck out my thumb.

Max gazed up at me, titling his head quizzically.

"Don't worry, boy," I said. "The next one will be all right. I promise."

⊕ ⊕ ⊕

A Pushcart Prize nominee and an active member of the Horror Writers Association, Peter Giglio is the author of five novels, four novellas, and he edits a successful line of books for Evil Jester Press. His works of short fiction can be found in a number of notable volumes, including two comprehensive genre anthologies edited by New York Times Bestselling author John Skipp.

THE MAGICIAN

THE INTERN'S STORY

By Lon Prater

HANSOM HADDIX NUDGED THE ANTIQUE PICKUP'S THREE-on-the-tree column shifter back into third. The transmission shrieked like a circular saw cutting through knotty wood. The big truck shuddered, but somehow kept right on zooming down the red clay Georgia road. We were on a mission, the infamous white-haired photographer and I.

I just didn't know what it was.

"So why this location, Mr. Haddix?" It was my first day interning for the aged photographer. I wanted him to know he'd made the right choice, picking me from all the applicants. I hoped no one from the college had called to let him know I had dropped out soon as I finished my photography elective.

"Someplace lucky," he said. "And call me Hansom."

Hansom won awards and worldwide fame for his body of work. Many believed he crossed the line from technical skill into Fine Art with his Faces of the Fallen photo essay on homeless vets. Having just turned eighty-two at the end of 1982, he wasn't getting any younger, nor was he expected to do too many more shoots. Which is why I applied the moment I heard about the chance to spend the summer working with him on his next project in the boonies of Southwest Georgia.

What I hadn't expected was to spend the first day of summer trundling out to a bingo parlor in the boonies with a man so far off his rocker he made that Pink Floyd movie seem positively sane by comparison.

"Fairies," he told me for the fifth time, "love to be around enormous swings of luck. The moment someone's fortune changes, good or bad... It's like candy to them."

"Uh-huh."

"But they don't like a lot of flashing lights and fuss, so you'll never find one in a casino or a dog track. You have to stay small time. Au naturel is the only way to catch one."

I made a face as I considered that.

Hansom's laugh brayed out like a big horse. It was jarring to hear that robust laughter pealing out from such a narrow-framed old man. "Not naked." He brayed again. "Just in a natural state. Do I look crazy enough to go around shooting pictures butt naked?"

I grinned back at him, not as relieved as I'd hoped to be. "Sure hope not."

Around dusk, we pulled up in front of the Hoot 'n' Holler Bingo Parlor in a little farming town too small to mention. I kicked as much of the red dirt as I could from the soles of my shoes and carried the tripod and other gear inside while Hansom spoke with the staff.

He apparently did not mention fairies to them. That must have been a special flavor of crazy he was only sharing with me. Had to admit, other than his weird Tinkerbell fixation, the old guy's faculties were sharp as a tack.

"Where do you want me to set up?"

"Back there." Hansom nodded his head toward the far end of the parlor. He leaned in close enough that I could smell the Chicklets gum on his breath.

"Fairies can't see into corners," he breathed.

"Of course not, Mister—I mean, Hansom."

The regulars poured in between six and seven. They greeted each other with loud, rattling coughs. Ordered greasy food from the short order grill in back. Set up their pink-haired Troll dolls and colored daubers in meticulous arrangements.

We waited most of the night. There were plenty of missed shots that would have been fine for any of the human-interest slicks. A palsied woman with a scarf on her head and her teeth in a glass of water glared at us over an Olympian selection of thirty-two different bingo sheets. The jowly caller taking off his cowboy hat and wiping sweat from his brow on one sleeve. A black man in patched jeans and a pressed shirt, disappointed that he didn't have a good bingo after all.

Not Eisenstaedt's photos of V-J Day in Times Square or Sophia Loren, but solid stuff, real humanity distilled onto film. Hansom Haddix wanted none of that.

Bored, I wandered to the snack bar and got a bottle of Coke and a MoonPie. I really didn't have the money for either. My ex-girlfriend had wiped out my account to pay my share of the overdue rent and then dumped me. (All of which had been about four hours after I told her I'd dropped out of college to pursue my dream of being a photographer. You're giving up a marketing scholarship for THAT? I never got a chance to answerI walked back to the corner, realizing for the first time that marshmallow could actually go stale. As I approached, a woman rasped out "BINGO!" like it was her last breath.

Hansom thumbed the shutter release button.

He only shot one roll of film that night, just winners and losers. No flash at all. Contrary to his usual habit, he took a single picture of a scene before moving on to the next composition. "After each shot, they hide. You have to be real particular and give them plenty of time to forget you're there before you take the next picture."

"Hmm." I was too young and maybe too worried for his sanity to engage him on this.

Around eleven that night, we piled into the Chevy and rode back to the motel we'd set up in. We drove under streetlights that had been shot out, past boarded-up stores and three different First Baptist churches, a slaughterhouse and a Rexall drugstore advertising two-for-one paper towels.

We'd rented two adjoining rooms. One of them we rigged into a darkroom. Soon as we were inside, Hansom made sure the heavy black fabric he'd stapled along the window frame and over the doors was still intact and lightproof.

Meanwhile, I got the temperatures right by floating the gallon jugs of developer, stop bath, fixer, and clearer in a tub full of 68° water. He came over to watch my work long enough to be sure I did things correctly.

I asked him again why we weren't going to make any prints.

He dismissed the thought with a wave of his hand. "No point."

"Then why did we take the pictures in the first place?"

"Make prints later if you want. What's important to see is only on the negative."

Like so many of the things Hansom had told me today, this made no sense at all. I let it go.

Hansom took a quick inventory of where things were in the room and switched off the light. I waited, smelling the vinegar stink of the stop bath, feeling for the scissors and timer I'd placed on the motel's bureau.

He had me withdraw the film, cut it, spool it onto the reel, and put a lid on the developer tank. The lights blazed back on and we both stood there blinking while I agitated the developer bath. Hansom kept track of the time.

"All the fancy new equipment we could be using, and we might as well be making daguerreotypes. Is that what you're thinking?"

"Sir?"

"I've seen the way you've reacted today. You think the old man's gone batty, don't you?"

"Not at all, I—"

"Say it!"

"I'm glad to be here, I'm not going to question your—"

"Stop."

I stopped.

"The stop bath, I mean." His voice held an edge now. A desperate tone had crept into his words. Something impatient and very close to manic. I hurried to obey.

Hansom didn't speak another word until we'd finished with the fixer, clearer, and distilled water wash. He snatched the strip of film from me before I could hang it up to dry.

"I started seeing them in my Las Vegas shoots," he said, inserting the still damp filmstrip hurriedly into the projector. His wrinkled hands, so steady on the shutter release just hours before, shook like the palsied bingo lady's had. "They waited in big packs, tribes almost, in the dark corners outside the casinos, attracted to all the fortunes being won and lost, but repelled by all the noise and neon."

He pointed the projector at the wall and turned it on. I said nothing. "Get the lights."

I stood there blinking in confusion and dismay for a split-second, then swiped my hand over the light switch.

Hansom waited til I was looking directly into his rheumy eyes. "When you first see them, you have to allow your eyes to commit immediately, or your brain never will. If you don't see them on the very first glance—if you blink instead—then you never will. Understand?"

I nodded, but it was a lie.

Hansom slid the film into the projector and hurriedly focused the image on the wall. He grunted. "None in this one."

He went through three more then stopped.

A man wearing a "Disco is Dead" t-shirt who'd won $200.00 for a Cover-All materialized on the wall in all his magnified, negative-image, toothy glory. The shutter had caught him in mid-jump. Hansom jerked a finger at the projected image. "See there! Just behind his right shoulder?"

I'd become pretty good at converting negative images to positives in my mind. Most photographers get the hang of it eventually. Even so, I couldn't be sure what I saw. It might have been a tiny face, dragonfly eyes and slits for a nose. There might have been some out-of-focus bit of background there that resembled a scaly wing and limber little arm.

There might have been, but I didn't have time to decide. It could have just as easily been water spots from not letting the film dry.

Hansom advanced the strip of film quickly through several more frames until coming to a stop on the image of a thoroughly depressed-looking woman who had missed a big pot by one number. Cigarette smoke wreathed around her face like a surreal picture frame. He scanned the blown up negative and shouted, "There!"

I looked where he was pointing. It could have been a black butter-fly wing by her earlobe, but it could have just as easily been part of her earring, too.

The old man moved the film again and again, grunting mostly, but occasionally pointing at things too fast for me to really keep up with him. When he reached the last image, he rushed up to the wall and pounded on it with one angry, shaking fist. "Do you see them? Five in one shot! Five!"

It was a picture of me, coming back from the rest room near the end of the night. I had talked to someone in there, the older black man in the patched jeans and pressed shirt.

"You with the photographer." It was more an accusation than a question.

I nodded.

"Seems kind of sad, a man such as himself wasting time snapping pictures at Hoot 'n' Holler."

"It makes him happy," I replied, wondering if the man had recognized Hansom out there at the camera.

"What do you think makes him happier? Taking pictures of people gambling money they ain't got—or being taken seriously by a young man such as yourself?"

By the time I found my words he had already zipped up and walked out.

I peered at the enlarged negative of myself on the wall. Hansom stood at the edge, his knees pressed into the cheap mattress and bedspread. He waved a frantic finger at something blurred into the foreground. Specks of dust spun in the projector's beam like tiny angels in search of a pinhead to dance on.

In that negative, I had just decided to try my best to learn what I could from Hansom. No matter how senile he might be, the master photographer still had plenty he could teach me. It wouldn't hurt to humor him about the fairies, would it? It's not like anyone would ever have to know. Maybe there was an explanation besides the one involving straightjackets and rubber rooms. Dust or water spots on the film or something.

"Do you see them?" Hansom pleaded. The projector shone in the old man's eyes, making them glisten.

I squinted. Took a step forward into the projector's beam. Hansom tugged at my shirtsleeve like one of his homeless veterans asking for spare change. "Do you?"

For a tenth of a blink or less, projected on the wall of a dingy southwest Georgia motel room from a bingo parlor negative taken by a Pulitzer-winning photographer, I saw something I can hardly describe, much less believe. In the foreground, almost too fast for the mind to commit, but not the eye—

—A trick of the light?

Lithe arms, holding hands. Blur-frozen wings.

Eyes like tiny sequins that faded too fast.

I hadn't felt any difference the moment my luck changed, but I felt different now. Ecstatic. The hairs on my arm stood on end. Electrified with wonder.

"Yes," I breathed. My eyes watered a little at the ache of what they'd glimpsed and lost. I would spend the rest of my life trying to see them again, one split second at a time.

Lon Prater has worked in the Reactor Compartments of USS Enterprise, edited the military's textbook on arms deals, and kept things safe in the produce and laundry industries. He lives, writes, and plays a lot of board games in Pensacola, Florida.

*Visit **lonprater.com** to find out more.*

THE HIGH PRIESTESS

DEADLY SON

By Billie Sue Mosiman

THE LAND OF SOLOMON NEAR THE EDGE OF THE SEA
shook with thunder and lightning. Bold silver rain poured in shiny
sheets, turning cobblestone streets to rivers. The people of the city
closed their doors and windows, took in their goats and chickens, and
prayed for the sun.

Katrine, high priestess for the great Solomon, sat before a parted veil
embroidered with palm leaves and pomegranates. She kept her window
open so she could see the roiling sea beyond her home. Her sister, the
empress, had come to visit earlier, but warned she might not be able to
return because of rising waters.

Katrine had sent her servants home to parents and mates rather than
ask them to stay in her palace to be stranded. She was alone now, subject to the whim of weather, but she could far-see and knew she'd per-
severe. As for others in the city, she worried for their safety, petulant
in interpreting the visions plaguing her. The sights she saw playing out

in thin air before her disrupted her sleep. Many would die. That's what she saw in the visions. Bodies piled like cord wood, fires set to consume flesh. There were too many for burial in the underground crypts.

Far-seeing was Katrine's gift. With her help as his main confidant, Solomon made the kingdom happy and prosperous. The land was a Mecca for trade, with ships coming from foreign shores like South India, Ophir, and Tarshish. Camel trains from across the vast deserts, from Arabia or Egypt, sometimes Tyre. The crops grew in fertile ground so the granaries were full each fall to feed the city's citizens. Do this, she told Solomon, and he did. Do that, she advised, and he never refused. In this way Katrine felt she served both the Spirit and her country. Solomon was known far and wide as a good king, a fair and caring ruler over his people.

At least he had been a fine man and king until he met Sheba, the queen of a land in Ethiopia, a country none of Solomon's people had ever seen. When Katrine first met Sheba, she'd been highly impressed. The young girl's hair was braided with gold threads all across her scalp. She wore a gold bodice that sparkled in the sun and a long, body-hugging, diaphanous scarlet skirt worked with streaks of gold thread. Her skin was even darker than any of Solomon's people, so dark it was like stony night. The contrast between her color and her clothes made her look like a waltzing, ribald angel. She came to Solomon bearing gifts— barrels of fragrant olive oil, tankards of rich, heady wine, dried mango and coconut, barrels of gold nuggets. She bowed to him and when she smiled the audience was swayed to love her.

It was the first night of the queen's visit when Katrine saw the vision of downfall. The next morning she hurried to Solomon's chambers. He sat, immersed with writing on a scroll, perched on a cane chair before a table inlaid with chips of abalone. He paused in his work, looked up, and frowned.

"Something is wrong, isn't it?" he asked. "I don't have to far-see to know from the look on your face."

"Master! The woman from over the sea! She brings dissolution and catastrophe with her."

"Are you speaking of Sheba, our latest visitor?"

"I am, Master. I saw a vision wherein she...she..."

He waved at her with his quill pen. "Katrine, isn't it too early to make these kinds of pronouncements on a stranger? Shouldn't we give the girl a small chance to show herself either good or evil?"

"But, Master, she'll manipulate you. She'll bring down the tem..."

He spoke a word meaning the whole idea ridiculous and returned his attention to the scroll. "She's just a girl. I'm not afraid of a girl."

Katrine, dismissed, bowed low and backed from the room. She had failed to warn him, to make him understand the seriousness of her vision. She would have to approach him again when the girl began to work her magic. She mustn't let her master and her country be brought to ruin.

That evening the empress sent carriage bearers to the palace where Katrine lived in a room separate from Solomon, asking her to come. When Katrine told her sister of the dire warning, the empress laughed, for she was sometimes amused by the idea of far-seeing. "You don't know that for sure, Kat. The girl's so clever and generous. She's such good company. She even brought her own dancers for our evening's amusement."

"You're seeing the outward person," Katrine insisted. "It's the inner one of which I speak. The inner one is dark purple as the rind of shriveled valley grapes. I tell you, she'll bring down Solomon."

The empress laughed happily at the idea of dried grapes and sent her maid servant to fetch a platter of them. "Since this gift has befallen you, your worries have mounted, my sister. You know yourself sometimes they are for nothing."

It was true some of Katrine's visions failed to materialize. She believed it was because she'd waylaid the chaos by turning the people involved another way, speaking a different phrase, or praying a new prayer to some old deity. How could she explain some visions remained unfulfilled only because her advice had prevented them? She couldn't prove it.

⊕ ⊕ ⊕

Solomon took Sheba to his bed. The whole city knew it and none more intimately than Katrine. She rarely moved beyond her quarters in the palace, but during the times she did, she heard the two of them cavorting, laughing, and sometimes grunting like animals in rut. Katrine spent more time consulting the Great Spirit that moved her, and asking for intervention. The girl seemed no threat. She was the king's plaything at the moment, but in time he would be mad for her. He would be willing to die for her. He would be so snared in her golden tendrils of mystery, he'd never waggle free.

Katrine barely saw her master as his time was taken up with Sheba. Therefore, Katrine watched for the woman when she went for her ablutions. She was a fastidious woman and bathed daily, surrounded by her dark handmaidens. Katrine intruded, walking toward the pool set in the floor and taking a low position on a turquoise cushion. She smiled innocently at the worldly girl. "Your skin is so beautiful," she said

Sheba eyed her carefully. She said, "I bathe in goat milk as you can see. It keeps my skin soft and pliant. Are you the king's witchdoctor?"

Katrine, taken off-balance, laughed then covered her mouth. One should not laugh at a personage as great as a queen. "I'm sorry, I was startled. No, I'm a friend of the king and his advisor."

"But you cavort with spirits," Sheba insisted.

Katrine's spine straightened. "I do no such thing. I'm a far-seer. I see in the distance of time."

"Do you, now? That's very interesting." Sheba inclined her head to the side and studied Katrine while the maidens washed her neck and shoulders with soft sea sponges. "Tell me, then, what do you see in time for me?"

Now Katrine felt uncomfortable. This strange woman didn't abide by any of their customs and her courtesy was at a minimum. She spoke her thoughts, no matter what they might be. She seemed to have no fear of reprisal or of censure.

"I...I have not looked," Katrine lied.

"You far-see for the King then?"

"And the kingdom," Katrine added.

"What do you see for this great land, my little friend?" Repulsed, she was being grilled and insulted. Katrine was neither little nor was she the girl's friend. Just the opposite. She saw Sheba as the enemy to both her master and her country.

"I see on your face your thoughts," Sheba said, pushing away her handmaidens. She stood regal from the milky water and let a maiden wrap absorbent cotton cloth around her nakedness. "You think I'm some sort of demon, don't you? Some dark lady here to bring harm."

Katrine jutted out her chin. She rose, fists balled but hidden behind her skirts. With great control, she lowered her head and backed from the room. She would not answer for it would force her to lie to the girl's face again and she'd know. The girl already knew.

⊕ ⊕ ⊕

Finally, Katrine had another audience with Solomon and this time she insisted he take her seriously. "You know I've been right before. You know I kept morale up when I saw rains were coming to save the crops in drought. You know I told you we would be a central spoke for commerce from foreign lands and that event would make you wealthy and your kingdom would increase. You know..."

He raised his palm for her to stop. "I'm grateful for you, High Priestess. I've always listened to you. But if this is about Sheba, you can save your breath."

"But why, Master? Why must you travel down this road to perdition? She is greedy, she'll have your..."

He stood, bellowing, "ENOUGH."

Katrine's gaze lowered to the floor where she stared until tears came to her eyes. He had never spoken to her so harshly.

"I'm sorry, but I won't have anyone speaking against her. She's my lover. She will be my queen. Never speak again her name connected with a negative word if you value your position in this palace and beneath my shelter."

Katrine now sat before the blowing winds, the blanket rain, the rising waters, the tossing sea, and she mourned the falling of both her king and her land. This was the man to whom God gave wisdom. In one instance, two women came to Solomon arguing over a child, each claiming to be the mother. The Great and Wise Solomon decreed they divide the child with a sword. One of the women leaped forward and said she'd give up the child, do not kill it! That was the woman Solomon gave the child, calling her surely the true mother. How could such a wise man be so clouded in judgment by a mere girl-queen?

Sheba goaded him.

He stood in Hiram's hall entrance between two massive columns housing the Ark of the Covenant and his legendary strength put to test.

Crowds gathered and looked on as Sheba bade him, "Bring them down, Solomon! Bring down the walls!"

She had turned the king to idolatrous gods and away from the god of his father. Sheba told him his strength was given him by these foreign gods and to show them his gratitude he must tear down the temple of his old religion, burying the Ark beneath rubble.

While Katrine stood on the lower steps watching, her heart sunk in despair. It was the vision she'd earlier seen coming to fruition. Solomon pushed until sweat broke out on his massive biceps and shoulders and back. His mighty head hung down, like a lion about to roar, and the columns trembled, the stone ceiling shook, blocks of marble crumbled and fell inside to crash on the floor, and still Sheba screamed, "Bring it down, bring it down now, Solomon!"

When it fatally cracked, the walls and ceiling giving, Solomon walked placidly down the steps and away, his queen's arm linked in his own, as the temple fell behind him into a monstrous cloud of gray dust.

People wailed, some danced with joy, and Katrine wiped the tears from her eyes and followed behind her Master to the palace.

It was only months later the girl tired of her plaything and left the kingdom, her belly swollen with Solomon's seed. Katrine went in search of her king and found his locks shorn, his head bald, his face sagging with age. "She left me," he said simply. "She talked me into shaving my hair. She left with my son in her womb. She took away my heart and my heir."

Katrine wanted to remind him of her warnings, but said nothing. She walked to him where he sat on his throne, a diminished man, and placed her hand on his shoulder. "I'm sorry, Master," she said. "I am so sorry."

The high priestess lived out her days with the king as his kingdom divided and dwindled and grew dim. He never found his former self, nor his wisdom. He took too many wives, gathered too much gold, and fell into greed, lust, and gluttony.

This day, with the storm raping the land of Solomon, and the sea threatening to swallow the city's edges, the king lay silent somewhere in the dark depths of his palace. Katrine had been banned from that sacred place years in the past, never enjoying the king's protection again after she'd spoken against his dark Ethiopian beauty. More walls would fall. Armies would invade. The lands would be split in two under the reign of Solomon's Israeli son. After this natural storm came another, one unnatural, one cleaving the kingdom in two and murdering thousands. The nature of those wars were kept secret from her beyond the deaths.

⊕ ⊕ ⊕

Sheba's son was born with the strength of his father Solomon, yet he died one long night when the moon was full and the stars were bright. Despite all they could do, nothing could save the little boy from a sudden onset of illness.

By morning he was dead.

Sheba dispatched her attendants from her chamber and sat with the body. As she thought her dark thoughts, she heard a rustling and glanced up to see a viper curling over her son's chest. She stood, horrified his body was being defiled by this evil creature. Even as she tried to think what method to use to remove the snake from him, its triangle head snaked into the boy's open mouth, between the chalky lips, and slid down the cavern of his throat.

Sheba raised her hands in the air and screamed.

The boy sat up and blinked.

He swallowed noisily and said in a snake's rasp, "Mother, I'm back."

From that time on, he was possessed of darkness, his hungers deep and unrelenting, his violence renown throughout the nation. He was King ruling with a dictatorial hand. When his people starved in their villages, he laughed. When his mother grew old and lacked wit, he sneered and kicked at her. When she died, he lit her funeral pyre on fire and danced around it naked, striking terrible fear in witnesses

This was the man-thing that came galloping into Israel where his father's other son reigned. This is where he split the country, pushing part of it close to the sea.

Over succeeding years, as Solomon grew old and of no use to anyone, even his many concubines, he heard his son with Sheba was a demon possessed of a magical snake. He called for his old high priestess, Katrine, to ask her for the truth. She lived in a small palace he'd given her long ago.

"My son, the one born of Sheba, is said to be of the devil and that's how he split my country. What do you know of him?"

Katrine sat still, hands in her lap, dressed in a blue gown. She regarded her master, noticing the passage of time in the face of the once-mighty ruler. Outside the storm raged as she waited for another vision. The far-seeing came seldom these days as if it was only really needed when she was in the employ of Solomon.

She closed her eyes and she saw evil, the Son of Solomon, the dark one. He was not even a living being. He was infested with the wriggling of black snakes as venomous as any that ever lived. Animated by their squirming, even his brain was coiled with them, and his thoughts poisoned by their venom. Katrine, deep in her vision, saw he made more like him, thousands more. He brought them snakes in their sleep and dropped them into their open mouths. His army of the undead grew and that's why they won their battles. Nothing could kill that which did not live.

Katrine opened her eyes wide, fear spilling out as a flood. "Oh, dear God, Solomon, he's the greatest demon and he's come with abandoned souls to turn the soil and the water to blood."

This time Solomon believed her. "I'll send out troops to find him."

Katrine knew this wouldn't matter. They'd never find him. He was as destined to be on the earth as was Solomon, and Sheba, and...Katrine herself. They were the three shafts of the trident, but Solomon's son was the rain of floods, the fire of devastation, and the chaos of the universe.

She bowed to Solomon and slowly backed from the room for the last time. She'd never see the king alive again. At least she wouldn't live long enough to taste the worst brunt of the coming apocalyptic wars and neither would her sister, the empress. Their generation was fading and the new one—remorseless, conscienceless, and thoroughly evil—was on the way to power. Those without souls would rule the new world.

At the thought of such a thing, Katrine felt a tug on her heart and a pain shot through her chest to double her over. She tried to catch her breath, to calm herself, and she couldn't. She went to her knees expecting she would die even before her king. She tried to cry out, but darkness invaded her tongue until she lay on the marble floor in death. It had taken her abruptly, without warning, sending her into the great beyond.

From out of the shadowy hall, a servant approached the dead seer. He turned her onto her back to see she was indeed dead. He slipped a black snake from his pocket and dropped the head into Katrine's mouth to let it wriggle down into the body.

The servant trotted away so she might come awake on her own. He knew she would give the death-gift to her king within days, maybe within hours.

The deadly Son of Solomon would rule all the world one day, they all understood this truly—all the entire living world.

⊕ ⊕ ⊕

Author of more than 50 books, I am a thriller, suspense, and horror novelist, a short fiction writer, and a lover of words. In a diary when I was thirteen years old I wrote, "I want to grow up to be a writer." It seems that was always my course. My books have been published since 1984 and two of them received an Edgar Award Nomination for best novel and a Bram Stoker Award Nomination for most superior novel. I have been a regular contributor to a myriad of anthologies and magazines, with more than 150 short stories published. My work has been in such diverse publications as Horror Show Magazine and Ellery Queen's Mystery Magazine. I taught writing for Writer's Digest and for AOL online, and gave writing workshops locally in Texas. I was an assistant editor at a Houston literary magazine and co-edited several trade paperback anthologies with Martin Greenberg.

Recently I've sold short stories to the anthologies **Better Weird** edited by Paul F. Olson from Cemetery Dance, **Fresh Fear** edited by William Cook, and **Someone Wicked** edited by Weldon Burge. My latest novel, **The Grey Matter**, will be published in May 2014 by Post Mortem Press.

I was born in Alabama and live now in Texas on a small ranch.

News of my e-book publications can be found at: **peculiarwriter.blogspot.com**

My Facebook page is: **facebook.com/billie.s.mosiman**

I'm on Twitter as **@billiemosiman**

THE EMPRESS

FLESH IN FRAME

By Spike Marlowe

THE ARTIST BITES INTO THE APPLE, BREAKING ITS FLESH
with her teeth, easing the fruit's meat into her mouth with her lips,
full and rouged.

Her model lies on a bed of grass, her body entirely white except
for her tiny nipples, two pink blushing bumps beneath the sun's
rays. She lies exposed to the world as if newly born—open and vul-
nerable and cold. An aspen quakes near her head.

The artist closes her blue eyes, and drops her apple to the dirt;
clumps of mulch and shards of bark stick to its red and yellow striped
flesh, white meat. She raises her hands to the sky, and tips her head
back, exposing her face to the sun. She inhales, breathing in the
scent of wildflowers, the dirt, the grass, the nearby sea. And then
she relaxes, faces her model as before, and opens her completely
black eyes.

She begins to blink, and with each blink, there is a click. She stares at her model, blinks faster and faster, and soon the clicks run together until the meadow reverberates with the sound. Click. Click. Click.

The model lies still. She has done this before; she knows the artist will not be pleased if she moves.

Finally, the artist closes her eyes. When she opens them, they are once again blue. She opens her mouth and releases a stream of photographs of the model from which the artist will birth images into wood.

The artist sits on a pile of pillows—red, orange and gold—before a white table, surrounded by the lemon-colored walls of her studio. To her right is a corkboard covered in photographs of her pale model, to her left sits a myrtle wood bowl of oranges, before her lies a square of cottonwood. She lifts her right forefinger and runs it across the cottonwood, stripping away wood, as if peeling away a layer of skin.

She works through the night, into the morning, applying fingers that form themselves into knife, gouger, chisel, fluter. When she is done, her model stares back at her from the wood, her body trapped beneath the roots of a tree, twisted and tangled.

When the artist takes photographs, she eats apples. When the artist carves, she eats oranges. When the artist makes love, she eats pomegranates.

Her model lies in the plush bed the artist has provided for her, snuggled in a nest of sheets and blankets so white they almost seem to have hints of pale blue.

The artist sits down on the bed, half a pomegranate in each hand. She whispers to her model, murmuring soft promises, if the model will wake.

When she finally opens her eyes, the artist feeds her model

pomegranate seeds, dropping them onto her delicate tongue like nectar from the gods. But the artist knows she is not a god, no matter how much the model calls her goddess, no matter how much the artist tells her her name is not goddess but mother.

Mothers are so much more powerful.

When the pomegranate is bare of its seeds and the model's mouth is red from its juices, the artist kisses her, licks her lips and then pulls away, smiles. She walks to the kitchen, retrieves a sea green clay bowl brimming with pomegranate seeds.

The model sits up, bedclothes as pale as her skin falling to her narrow hips, revealing the perfect breasts and belly of the young. The artist shakes her head. The model reclines on the bed and kicks the sheets and blankets away from her body.

The artist pours the pomegranates onto the model's body, covering her flesh with red seeds. The artist removes her clothes and sits astride the model, crushing the seeds into the model's torso with her hands, red pomegranate seeds gushing their juice, soaking the model's skin, staining the artist's inner thighs, steeping into the sheets.

Hands on breasts, blood-red sex against blood-stained belly, the artist lowers her mouth to the model's chest and laps the pomegranate juice up like a kitten laps milk. The model shudders.

It is then that the artist asks, "Would you like me to birth you anew? Would you like to be immortal?"

She sits up and reaches behind her, rubs the model's mound until the model cries, "Yes, mother!"

And so it is done.

⊕ ⊕ ⊕

Over the succession of many nights and mornings and afternoons, the artist impregnates her model, fills her with pomegranate seeds from which the model's immortality will grow.

Finally, the model's belly quickens. Weeks later she births a butternut tree.

The artist is never sure what type of tree her models will birth. No matter—she knows how to carve them all, knows how to carve all woods to immortalize her models, each one in turn.

After the quaking aspen is birthed, the artist sends the model on her way. The model's body is still ripe from her pregnancy. Her cheeks are plump and rosy. Her eyes luminous. Still, she doesn't want to leave the artist; she doesn't want to leave this home.

"You are woman now," the artist says. "It's time to go into the world and make your way. It is time for me to carve another into your wood." With that she pushes the model out the door with a basket of food and a bag holding the model's worldly goods.

The room, wide and white as the tundra in winter, is empty. The artist walks in, followed by a man in an expensive gray suit. He pulls a large wheeled suitcase behind him. He stares at her body's curves beneath her long red dress.

The artist surveys the room, walking along the walls, studying the matte black floor, the matte black ceiling that rises into forever.

"Open the suitcase," the artist says.

The man lowers the suitcase to the ground and opens it. Inside are dozens of carved pieces of wood with girls' images staring at him.

The artist picks up four of the carvings. In one, a girl is bound to a tree with moss, gagged with flowers, blindfolded with giant leaves. In another, a girl hangs from a tree's branches, strapped to the branches by thick strips of bark, cherries spilling from her ripped open belly. In another, a girl is trapped beneath a tree's roots. In the last, a girl has a tree growing from the center of her chest.

One by one, the artist nails these carvings to a display wall. She studies the wall from different directions, from different distances.

Finally she says, "This will work. This will be a fine place to house my daughters."

The man nods his head.

"I will send the rest tomorrow. And leave one space empty—I have one more piece to add."

⊕ ⊕ ⊕

The artist stands naked in the forest. Her breasts and belly and hips full, yet supple. She props a large, full-length mirror framed in ebony against an oak. She takes several steps back, and closes her eyes. When she opens them again they are black. She stares at her image in the mirror, and she begins to blink.

⊕ ⊕ ⊕

Spike Marlowe has held a number of odd jobs, including working as a detective, a Bigfoot researcher, a writer for an internet content farm, a busker and as a performer in a wild west show. These days she's a writer, blogger and bizarro editor for Eraserhead Press, with a focus on the New Bizarro Author Series. Her first book, Placenta of Love, *is available at all the usual locations. You can stalk her online at her website **spikemarlowe.wordpress.com** or on Twitter at **@spikemarlowe**.*

THE EMPEROR

DMITRI AND THE MAD MONK

By Kris Austen Radcliffe

"YOU HAVE BRAINS ON YOU, GRAND DUKE." THE SPY sniffed the air and lifted an eyebrow, proud of his vocal inflection.

The Englishman's need to state the obvious and then pass it off as wry humor annoyed Dmitri more than the gore on his greatcoat. He watched the body on the floor of the prince's flamboyant estate, ignoring both the spy and the metallic stench of blood mixing with the pathetic notes of fear wafting off the other men. The pistol in his hand, he still aimed. Now was not the time for distractions.

Ten minutes inside the palace and Rasputin had bled out onto the extravagant rug. They'd tempted the vile fornicator with breasts and the promise of a cock sucked by a woman of the royal court. Clubs, a knife strike, and Dmitri now tasted the acrid smoke rising from the English spy's pistol.

The prince danced about flapping his arms and whining some nonsense about "destroying the unkillable prey." He stopped, stared wide-eyed for a long moment, then babbled more about cyanide and his own brilliance under the pressure of the deed.

The politician watched the prince's melodrama with dull fascination, one hand on an elbow and the other stroking his chin like some stage villain. The doctor and the lieutenant whispered, heads close, a plan for burning clothes and disposing of the body forming between them.

The spy held out his hand for the pistol.

Dmitri Pavlovich Romanov, the only true patriot among them, opened the chamber and dumped all but one bullet onto the man's hand, not once pulling his gaze away from Rasputin's corpse. "Go home. Tell your superior you did this job." He waved the pistol at the body.

The spy's eyebrow arched with an almost audible crinkle, even as his lips frowned.

"If you interfere again in the affairs of my homeland, I will kill you. Do you understand, Englishman? Now leave." Dmitri pointed at the door.

International whining would start as soon as the Tsarina realized her pet monk had vanished. The whore would blubber like the Hessian spawn she was. Cries of "The boy! The boy!" would ring through the cold halls of the Tsar's winter palace as she pleaded and pawed over the irrelevant Tsesarevich and his blood disease—the disease she brought into Dmitri's family.

The disease Rasputin was supposed to control. Dmitri bounced the pistol against his thigh, his grip so tight his fingers ached. No woman incapable of giving the Empire an heir should be allowed the title Tsarina.

The spy backed away, his step muffled by the garish weave of the prince's imported rug. The others milled about, nattering about alibis and consequences. Dmitri glanced at each, assessing, in turn, the level of intervention necessary to assure the success of this plan. The politician would need to be dealt with. The others, with the exception of the prince, would show caution.

Wild idiocy at this point would make the murder worthless, and Russia could no longer afford idiocy.

Dmitri kicked the body. His boot, crafted of fine leather specifically for his Romanov foot by Moscow artisans, had saved his toes on many a winter evening. Now it sank into Rasputin's shoulder as if Dmitri had struck clay.

Clay—not meat. He frowned and stepped back.

He'd sensed Rasputin's abilities the first time they were within sight of each other. Dmitri had entered the grand ballroom behind his cousin's guard. Blinking away the morning sun, he'd been more focused on some forgotten foolishness of the court's women than on the possibility of another like himself walking the halls of the Tsar's palace.

Yet there stood Rasputin behind the Tsarina, unwashed and oily, grinning at Dmitri with a skull's teeth. Rasputin, another like himself. A fellow *Oboroten*—a Shifter. And one with the special touch, the same as Dmitri. A man who could heal.

The body at his feet did not move, yet Dmitri had heard tales of other Shifters who had survived bullets to the skull. They'd gasp awake, disoriented, but still dangerous. The probability could not be ignored.

He tossed the prince's tasteless rug over Rasputin. Blood had seeped to the floorboards and the prince wheezed, pointing, his lips twittering once again.

Even with the brain splatter on Dmitri's coat and the marks on the wood under the carpet, the monk had not bled enough.

Another reason to be concerned.

The quicker Dmitri threw the body into the river, the better. He didn't want to smell the shit in the prince's trousers when he realized his ramblings about "the unkillable prey" held truth.

⊕ ⊕ ⊕

One of Dmitri's men stayed behind. A Shifter with a special voice, he'd whisper enthralling words into the ears of Dmitri's co-conspirators and fix the prince's mad ramblings into their minds as "truth." Then they'd all scurry away with the same preposterous tale of bravery and shored-up masculinity.

Dmitri drove his Romanov vehicle through St. Petersburg unmolested by sentries and guards. The body rolled against the rear seats, thudding with a vibration Dmitri heard as well as felt. Each time the tires slid on the frozen cobblestones, or the inky night caused Dmitri to slow, he compensated a bit more, one small inching of his fingers farther to the left or to the right, to deal with the bulk he hauled.

He gripped the steering wheel tighter, waiting for a gnarled hand to reach over the seat back and take hold of his neck. Or a howl to rip through the interior of his car—rasping and violent, shrill, like the monk himself.

Or for a healer's touch to snake around his neck and deal death, forcing Dmitri to taste his own guts.

Dmitri stopped in a small stand of trees at the head of the Petrovsky Bridge. The shores were even and offered good footing, the mud frozen smooth and the slope flat. A narrow wood bridge above creaked in the winter wind as it crossed over the Neva River. This part of the city lay blanketed by both darkness and poverty.

Dmitri glanced into the back seat. When a bullet was not enough, he'd been told, extreme measures were needed. Freezing until limbs broke off. Drowning. He'd carry the body down the bank and dump the bastard below the ice.

Incineration worked best, but there would be no evidence. And in the spring, when the ice melted and all other evidence had washed away, that Hessian tart needed to see the consequences of her handiwork.

So did Dmitri's cousin. The Tsarina wept and Nicholas licked her tears from the floorThey destroyed his nation. His family. They'd birthed weakness and named it "Alexei."

Dmitri flung open his door. The night's air slapped hard and he tucked the edges of his scarf into the collar of his greatcoat. Christ's birthday had brought with it true cold this year—the kind that freeze mens' feet into their boots and their hands into blackened claws.

The cold prickled but Dmitri lowered the scarf and sucked it in, fixing it to himself. He looked at the river, fixing that, too, into his vision. Even in the darkest hour, the burning fire of the Motherland's crystal ice danced on the solid waters and through the stillness of the air.

He, unlike the Hessian, would do what Russia needed.

Dmitri yanked the body through the rear door of the vehicle. His Shifter ability to change himself took time—considerable time, since his morphing was much weaker than his healer's touch—but he'd learned early how to maximize his body's potential. He'd kept himself small for a Shifter male, concentrating his mass instead to increase his strength and athleticism. Hoisting Rasputin onto his shoulder took little effort.

The air smelled clean only because the cold made all scents crystallize and drop to the ice. The monk flopped as Dmitri slid down the slope, and the rustling of the rug combined with the scrape of his boot's heels in a whispered cacophony. The sensations of the world popped against Dmitri's face and burst on his tongue, a wild integration of perceptions that could only happen in a place where nothing moved.

If the monk breathed, Dmitri did not feel it, nor did it fog the air. Perhaps the shot to the head had been enough.

He dropped the bundle where the mud met the edge of the ice. The carpet muffled the thud but moved too easily on the frozen ground. Dmitri kicked at it again, angling the body into the river so it wouldn't roll away.

Snow swirled over the river's surface as miniature winter faeries full of twinkle and malice. Dmitri stared, his gaze following the only movement in the stillness. He heard the sparkle, felt the slight brush to his cheek of the breeze, as the little whirlwind moved downstream.

He'd commission artwork when this was done—a painting, perhaps, depicting living snow singing bright and high and as strong as he'd now made his home. Or maybe he'd compose something himself, a tune for the new, stronger monarchy. One capturing this surreal moment

Down river, the sun pushed upward along the horizon. Red seeped into the edge of the night, along the curve of the ice, and Dmitri stood, breathing it in. This was his nation. This red—the cold fire of the northern sun. The blood of the land flowing under the ice and his boots. An Empire that had spread wider than Rome herself.

Threats to the stability of his home loomed—threats the pathetic Tsar needed help to prevent. Threats that could no longer be ignored. But with the—

The carpet twitched. Dmitri stomped, his body responding with long-practiced precision. His foot aimed for where the monk's head should be, but the bundle rolled and his boot caught only the carpet's edge.

Rasputin unfurled onto the ice, stink and the slapping crackles of freezing blood following his body as it slid sideways off the rug. A wicked gasp blew from between his blue lips. Dmitri lurched backward, but the monk's hand moved faster and latched onto his ankle.

The world tilted—Dmitri's sense of the horizon no longer matched what he saw as the line of the river. He buckled onto his knees, the leg held by the monk twisting away from his hip. Agony fired into his belly. He kicked again, but the monk moved with him, sliding closer to Dmitri's side instead of away.

The gun was in his pocket. He still had a bullet. Dmitri reached but the monk's rancid breath hit his nose. He'd used his momentum on the ice and now he grinned like Death himself, inches from Dmitri's face.

A guttural, angry roar ripped from Dmitri's throat. This peasant did not understand his station. He'd destroyed the monarchy. He dare touch another Romanov? Dmitri kicked but Rasputin's calloused hand squeezed the exposed skin between his hat and scarf.

Disorientation slammed his balance hard. Dmitri dropped onto his back, suddenly and completely unaware of what was up and what was down.

The touch of a healer could also harm, and Rasputin was a better healer than him.

Dmitri's arms flailed, as disoriented as his vision. The bridge should hold horizontal, its supports vertical, but his gut said the opposite. He pitched to the side, staring across the river and praying for straight lines.

Dmitri tasted the upward draft of the cold—it moved vertical, instead of across, as it should, and siphoned away his strength the way a chimney siphoned smoke.

Rasputin's touch set fire to every nerve and muscle in his head. A rancid fire, one as ugly as the man, oily and slick and pawing. Dmitri opened his mouth to yell, to call to the bridge's sleeping sentry, but no sound escaped.

No breath curled into the cold air kissing his lips.

The monk stole his life.

Rasputin withered away his body. The sky was under him, the river above. The stars were nothing more than layer of frozen faerie dust, twinkling like a harpsichord but as thick as the river's ice. The red of the sunrise bled onto both and crept over Dmitri's skin.

His healing ability fought—he wasn't yet dead—but the night wrapped around him like the carpet had wrapped around the monk.

On the downbeat of his blink that should have been up, Rasputin's face came into focus. Flat, dead, gray still, the bullet hole in his forehead open as it was the instant after Dmitri released the shot, he attacked as a corpse. Yet Rasputin was stronger, more practiced, more in control of his abilities. Strong enough to cheat death.

But he did not carry the blood of a nation in his veins. Rasputin, unlike Dmitri, did not work for the good of his land.

Across the edge of the river, the sunrise red turned to orange, which then turned to gold, and his country brightened, his home gleamed. He pulled his fingers free of his glove, raking his hand across the ice to dislodge the leather. The blistering chill stole his skin's warmth and the shock screamed into his wrist, a blazing sensation as sharp as the first rays splitting the ice.

This piercing reality, both sweet and blinding, cut his perceptions away from the fog of the night. Dmitri Pavlovich knew clarity in his Romanov bones.

He twisted his fingers into the snow, his enhanced strength gouging the ice, and dug deep. Strength sliced into him, sliced into his body and cut with his voice. "Dog!"

Rasputin gurgled. Bone crackled as the monster's skull knitted.

His face showed the first hints of animation—a twitching cheek, some reflection in an eye.

Dmitri swung his hand toward the monk's head, feeling the give of skin and the grease of the peasant's hair.

Pressure pushed against the walls of Dmitri's veins. It shaped his healer ability into a bullet like the one lodged in the monk's skull, a solid force the squish of a man's brain could not counter.

Rasputin grunted. His mouth opened and closed but only a high-pitched wheeze escaped. The breath he dropped onto Dmitri tasted of filth. Let him whine. Let him whimper. This thing with its hand curled around his cheek was nothing. And he would no longer infect all that Dmitri held dear.

Air rushed into the monk's lungs. The wheeze dropped into a gasp. Then words: "Why do you want the boy to die? He will be Tsar! Not you."

The boy? This was not about the boy. The Tsesarevich would be dead by his eighteenth birthday. The family knew it. The world knew it. The boy's blood made him immaterial. Only the Empire mattered—only the Empire glowed so bright in the morning sun that the rest of Europe dared not look upon it. The Empire would not bend to the whims of a German whore.

"Stay dead!" The words croaked out of Dmitri, still strained but louder than the monk's.

All Dmitri's anger—all his will and his ability—moved from his fingers into the monk's scalp. He'd seen that woman's influences from the beginning. Only Dmitri had the will to deal with her lapdog. She had no right. And she let this obscenity touch the Tsesarevich? A growl escaped, a deep sound that bounced across the ice to the other shore before it echoed back to Dmitri.

"You want to be Tsar?" Grayness returned to Rasputin's skin as he spoke—it crept from Dmitri's fingers toward the fiend's revolting eyes.

Dmitri did not want to be Tsar. No sane person wanted to be Tsar. But if called, he'd serve. He'd do what was right.

Rasputin panted. Dmitri's power flowed through the fingers he cinched around the villain's head. He'd end this.

"Be the Tsar!" Rasputin's suddenly paled to ash. A bolt ripped from the monk's temple into Dmitri's fingertips as Rasputin's eyes rolled back into his head. His snarls bubbled away.

He stiffened one last time then dropped, lifeless, onto the ice.

Dmitri pushed against the body. His jaw cinched closed—the skin of his face burned as if he'd washed with acid. As if the twinkling, malicious snow faeries had returned and now slashed at his cheeks with their ice wings.

Agony flicked on an off as it moved from his face, across his tongue, and down his neck. It spread like slush into his joints. He'd need days, perhaps weeks, to heal himself from this. He'd claim a winter's chill, retreat to his estate, and await his cousin's gratitude. Then perhaps he'd propose to the other daughter—the prettier one. They'd make a proper Tsesarevich.

The dawn's cold bit into the oversensitive skin of his bare hand. The same agony that burned his face fired up his forearm.

He reached for his glove. A fingertip pushed out of his sleeve, followed by another, then another. Then the back of his hand.

He stared. His flesh swelled. His fingers would not move, all as bloated as sausages. His hand and wrist had turned the dark purple-green of a bruise and now it spread up his arm like some horrid poison.

Blood. He bled inside, under his skin, and he knew that if he cut himself, if it opened, it would not stop flowing until his veins ran dry.

The monk had forced the boy's blood disease into Dmitri's hand.

Is this what he meant by "Be the Tsar?" Dmitri scoffed, staring at his hand as the cold numbed his bruised flesh.

Enough concentration and his fingers would be strong again. How often had he healed himself? The knife wound in his shoulder after that fight with the French emissary, the broken leg when he fell from that damned horse as a child—this injury meant nothing.

He stared at his fingers and willed the numbness and the blood back to their places. His flesh would not riot. He would not have an uncouth and ill-mannered hand.

Except the healing did not happen. The blood pulled back only a fraction.

Dmitri sucked in the morning's frozen air, his foot lashing out at the corpse. He'd bound Dmitri to the boy. To irrelevance. To the Tsesarevich.

Thunder rolled under Dmitri as the ice cracked. The sun flooded over the river, the red hitting the floe's edges. He flew backward, crawling up the bank, as the river took the body and the rug.

A prick and he clutched his swollen hand. Nothing bled. He stared at his flesh, thankful for the mud's smoothness.

Thankful that his blood stayed where it should be.

Dmitri glanced up at the rising sun. The cold of the world burdened Russia, but she controlled it. His nation's strength knew no bounds.

He looked down at his hand. This burden would not kill him. He was Russian and he'd control what that peasant did to him. He'd keep it in his fingers, make it obey. Dmitri would carry this burden, because he could. He would not die before his next birthday. He had the strength needed to be the Emperor.

He stumbled to his car. The Tsar would not send him to the Prussian front. Or worse, banish him to the decadent west of Europe. Nicholas would see the truth. They'd clasp shoulders.

Dmitri Pavlovich Romanov would now and forever do his best for the Tsar's family. For Russia. Because Dmitri Pavlovich Romanov could be Tsar.

⊕ ⊕ ⊕

Read more about Dmitri in the Fate ~ Fire ~ Shifter ~ Dragon series:
Prolusio
Games of Fate
Conpulsio
Flux of Skin
*For more info, visit **sixtalonsign.com***
As a child, Kris took down a pack of hungry wolves with only a hardcover copy of The Dragonriders of Pern *and a sharpened toothbrush. That fateful*

day set her on a path traversing many storytelling worlds — dabbles in film and comic books, time as a talent agent and a textbook photo coordinator, and a foray into nonfiction. But she craved narrative and a richly-textured world of Fates, Shifters, and Dragons — and unexpected, true love.

Kris lives in Minnesota with her husband, two daughters, Handsome Cat, and an entire menagerie of suburban wildlife bent on destroying her house. That battered-but-true copy of **Dragonriders?** *She found it yesterday. It's time to pay a visit to the woodpeckers.*

THE HIEROPHANT

On the Shoulders of Muses

By Jessica McHugh

THE BELL CHIMES, AND RICO DROPS HIS SANDWICH.

"Every damn time," he grumbles, sighing at his lunch before he switches on the transceiver. "Bridge here. Go ahead, Dispatch."

He hasn't eaten a meal in fifty years. Although he doesn't derive energy from food anymore, he still enjoys tasting it, chewing it, even the faint memories of when something worked in his interest. His work for others is monumentally more important, but that fact no longer satisfies him. A bite of turkey wouldn't change that, but the treat could lessen his melancholy for a day or two.

"New kid's here. Want me to send him in?" Dispatch asks.

"Can it wait until I've eaten?"

Dead air. Whispers.

Rico leans in to the speaker, his bones aching. A resounding "no" barrels into his ear, and painful static crackles through his brain. He uncoils the terminal cord from his ear, twisting the pin in the canal and blowing on the other end. His mind fuzzes over for a few moments before clearing with a squeak. He sits down at the terminal and switches on the teleporter.

"Go ahead, Dispatch. You're clear to transmit."

The teleporter's silver platform blinks as a huddled figure materializes, shivering. Rico tosses him a blue jumpsuit, but the young boy is too blind to catch it. He squints, rubbing his silver eyes in panic. Rico knows he resembled this boy once, but he can't remember looking so young, or his eyes being so faint. Not that the memory matters. Unlike the thousands of creatures whose stories he collects and delivers across the Spectrum, Rico's memories will die with him.

He helps the boy stand and slides a pair of goggles onto his face.

"Give your eyes a decade to darken," he says. "After a while, you'll forget the light in the Bridge ever pained you—until you deliver this speech to someone else."

After zipping his suit, the boy extends his hand. "I'm pleased to meet you. Balar, of Jupiter5," he says.

"Jupiter5, you say. Quite a ritzy piece of the Spectrum. Did you train for this, or are you a blood-muse?" The boy clenches his jaw, and Rico apologizes. "That was rude of me to ask. All that matters is you're here. My name is Rico, and I'll be your trainer."

"Thanks," Balar says, his gaze traveling around the circular chamber. The lights of the terminal are reflected in his goggles, reds and blues and whites flashing beneath the two concave screens covering more than half of the Bridge. "Can you really see every world on these?"

"Every version of every world in the Spectrum."

"You must love this job."

"It's more than a job. The Bridge, the Graveyard, the millions of minds I visit every day—it's my life, and it's exhausting."

"You don't look too worse for wear."

"I'll take your word for it. I haven't seen my reflection in almost a thousand years."

Spotting Rico's sandwich, Balar shudders. The bread is dark green, the meat inside crusty and shrunken.

"You're not going to eat that, are you?"

"Not anymore, which means I'll have to wait another fifty years to file a meal request. The window for organic freshness on the Bridge is tiny. Time passes differently here, hence your jumpsuit and goggles. They will protect you for the few years it takes for your body to adjust."

The bell chimes again.

"Spec just called," Dispatch says. "We've got a live one. Earth7-1587 to Earth2-2013."

"Live one?" Balar asks.

"He says that all the time, don't ask me why. I think millennia of working Dispatch has driven him a little nuts."

"I heard that."

"He means we have a story to transmit. Dead guy, live idea."

"It's a woman, actually," says Dispatch.

Rico ignores the comment. "He also likes to waste time. All we need from him is the origin planet and destination planet," Rico says to Balar.

"And your explanation does what, create time?"

"I'm training someone, Dispatch."

The speaker murmurs. "Not to talk back, I hope."

"You guys have a weird relationship," Balar says.

Rico and Dispatch answer together, "Anything to pass the time."

The bell chimes again, and Rico groans. "I get it, I get it. Thank you. We'll take it from here."

The caption "Earth7-1587" appears on the left screen and "Earth2-2013" on the right. Balar gasps in awe, and Rico chuckles. He's aware it's the first time he's laughed in ages. The new kid's excitement kindles some of his old verve, but sorrow remains strongest. Like Rico's verve, Balar's awe won't survive the centuries. Balar himself might not even last.

Most new recruits drop out after the first delivery to their home world. Standing in the past has a way of making one look to the future. When faced with a future of hard work with little reward, it's easy to run.

Unless there's nothing to run back to. Those are the ones who wind up like Rico, with a heavy case of Muse's Malaise.

Rico can't imagine Balar is anything like him. Having grown up in Jupiter5, one of the richest worlds in the Spectrum, he's the very definition of a flight risk. But Rico has learned to keep his mouth shut about such things. A man must discover his aversions in his own time.

Rico unwinds his cord and plugs into the terminal. The left screen zooms in on a pale planet with ice spreading across land and sea. It's small and dense, surrounded by a thin, frozen shell.

"What is that place?"

"Earth, Version 7. Time, 1587 AD," Rico replies. "The origin planet can be from any universe in the Spectrum, during any time in its existence, but deliveries can only be made to worlds in their present time. The past provides the stories. The present, the storytellers."

"How do you decide who deserves to tell a story?"

"I don't decide anything. Spec notifies Dispatch, and Dispatch notifies me. It's fairly common practice, Balar. If you want to dig into Spec's motivations, maybe you should apply to become a god instead of a muse."

"No way. I don't want that kind of responsibility."

"We have our fair share, believe me. Some take it more seriously than others, though."

"Like you?" he asks. "I thought muses didn't work longer than five centuries, but I heard you've been working for ten. Are you a blood-muse?"

"Now who's being rude?" Rico snaps.

He's not ashamed of his heritage. Embracing it was better than the alternative. An orphan from Earth33, he came into the world alone and remained so until he came of age. Many blood-muses turn from their fate. There are better lives, with better payoff, but after learning what he was, Rico saw no reason to fight it. The mere prospect of leaving the filthy streets of Constantinople was better than anything else he'd encountered there.

Rico presses the entry button on the terminal, and the left screen bulges into the room. Elongating to a tunnel, it spirals open for the muse and his trainee.

"We're going in there?" Balar asks as a frigid breeze rushes out from the opening.

"You'll be safe, I promise. Until you get a terminal cord, your suit will allow you to enter the Graveyard and travel between worlds."

"After we've done the job, do you mind if I take it for a spin by myself?"

"A spin would be the most you could do. Suit or not, traveling without me could earn you a place on the other side of the Graveyard, with a very short story to tell."

Balar's eyes widen. "You're joking." "Not at all," Rico smiles, and pulls the trainee into the tunnel.

The wind blasts them as they push through. Balar's suit frosts over, and Rico grumbles, "Damn Earth7" as he flicks the icicles from his cord, but the chill is less abrasive upon their exit. The passage opens into an ivory flatland. There are no animals, no plant life, only millions of small onyx pools stretching as far as the eye can see.

"Where are we?"

"The Earth7 Graveyard. Each of these pools represents a sentient being whose has lived between the beginning of time and 1587. There are significantly more plots in this version of Earth because it happens to exist in an eternal Ice Age. But the person we're looking for didn't freeze to death. She was beheaded for allegedly conspiring to kill her cousin, the Queen of England."

"Did she really do it?"

"That's not our question to ask or answer. It's our job to deliver the story, with all of its possibilities, to the proper artist. In this case, someone who lives on Earth2."

Rico scans row after row of black plots until he sees a blue pool winking in the distance. He heads toward it, and Balar holds onto his cord as he marches behind.

"Here she is," he says, gazing into the azure pool. "Everything Mary is, everything she did or said on Earth7 exists in this plot."

"You mean her plot is in this plot?" Balar snorts.

"You're new, so I'll forgive that archaic quip," Rico says. "Anyway, it's inaccurate."

He removes a syringe, uncapping it as he kneels beside the pool. Piercing the surface, he draws up the shimmering liquid.

"This," he says to Balar, "is fact plus possibility. Mary Stuart, residing on Earth7, was accused of treason. She was imprisoned and executed. She was born and died in an eternal winter, the blood of her beheading freezing before it could hit the ground. Those are facts. There are more, but few compared to the spaces between. Those spaces are the realms of possibility, to be filled and filed and fit into any shape the artist wishes."

"And it's different every time?"

"Usually, though there are exceptions. Some minds can only stretch so far and will settle on similar storylines."

"It sounds confusing."

"This is the easy part, kid."

The pool fades back to black, and the field is uniform again. When Rico was Balar's age, the sight broke his heart. He knew he would be back for more collections soon, but he hated the moment when he'd look out upon a Graveyard lacking stories to tell.

He doesn't feel that way anymore, especially on a busy day when the fields don't darken. It doesn't happen often, but complicated deliveries cause their fair share of delays, and missions can pile up.

"The job of a muse is twofold: deliver inspiration, and protect the artist," Rico tells him. "Except for sleepwalkers, safeguarding a slumbering artist isn't difficult, but if they're flying a plane, or scuba diving, or performing a high-wire act, they'll require closer attention. Inspiration can be a dangerous thing, Balar. It can strike all at once, or it can appear in the periphery, a glimmer awakening other glimmers that eventually become solid ideas. But no matter how it comes, inspiration is always a distraction. You must prevent it from becoming a fatal one."

"Have you ever lost an artist?"

Rico answers with silence, his head bowed, and turns back to the tunnel. Dozens of sad memories bloom as he walks back to the Bridge, but he forces them to disappear with the Graveyard. Back in the Bridge,

"Earth2-2013" fades from the right screen, zooming in on the planet, greener than Earth7. The image enlarges until the screen focuses on a window into a cluttered room.

Then, there's a girl. The laptop beside her is open, but the word processor is blank, the cursor blinking like a sleepless tease. But the girl dozes, hunched over at a desk with her head resting on folded arms. With a sigh, Rico thanks Spec for an easy delivery.

He plugs in to the right side of the terminal, presses a button, and the screen bulges again. The tunnel stretches out to meet him and Balar, who smiles when a summer breeze eases from the entrance. The destination is brighter than any Graveyard, but it's nearly as silent. The only sound comes from the oscillating fan in the corner of the teenage girl's bedroom, and the fluttering posters of baby-faced boys with side-swept hair.

Whispering, Balar asks, "What now?"

"You don't have to be quiet. She can't see or hear us." Rico removes the syringe from his pocket. "And she can't feel this." He injects the blue liquid into the girl's neck, saying, "Watch, Balar. Tell me what you see."

Rico pushes the plunger, and inspiration rushes in.

"I see it, bright blue in her veins," Balar says. "It's charging down her arms and up to her brain."

"Put your hand on her shoulder."

Balar obeys, gasping when he makes contact. "She's flying through cotton candy clouds. How is that possible?"

"You're looking into her dream. Keep watching."

"She's shivering now. The clouds have turned to ice, and she's floating toward the courtyard of a frozen castle. There are hundreds of people there, wrapped in filthy fur. They cheer as she lands, but not for her. There's something happening ahead of them, something exciting."

Rico smiles, remembering the thrill of the first time he watched inspiration seep into someone's dream. He wonders if he looked like Balar, with a smile testing the limits of his cheeks.

"The crowd is chanting. It gets louder as she gets closer to the front. 'Mary, Mary, quite contrary, how does your treason grow?' She's singing along and clapping," Balar says. "There's a queen nearby. Her face is white as snow and her hair red as fire, but the girl ignores her. She wants to get to the front. She can't see what's up there yet, but I can. I see a man in a black mask holding an axe. He's standing next to a blood-drenched block of wood. There's a body on the ground beside it, but I can't tell whose it is. I can't see the head."

"Nor will you," Rico says, unclamping Balar's hand from the girl's shoulder. "It's her story now. Let's leave her alone to explore it."

Balar pouts his lip, pleading, but Rico shakes his head. "You have to let go. Even when you deliver inspiration to a dangerous place, you can only take artists so far. Keep them inspired, keep them safe, but know you are nothing to them."

"But she's going to wake up and write a story, isn't she? Won't she wonder where it came from?"

"Maybe, but she'll never guess right. Artists stand on the shoulders of muses to see the expanse of their imaginations, but they can't see far enough to be grateful for our stability. We don't exist to them, Balar. Our memories do not survive death. Our own stories will never be told."

Rico exhales, feeling his age. "It's time to get back to the Bridge."

Holding onto Rico's cord, Balar follows the muse out through the tunnel. Once they're back in the chamber, Rico reaches out to unplug his cord from the terminal, but it's not there. Not in the terminal, not in his ear.

"What's going on? Where is it?" he asks frantically.

"You don't need it anymore," Balar replies. "You have done well, Rico. For thousands of years you have given the living world reasons to create, and in turn, reason to live. I am proud of you for all you've done, but it's time for you to rest."

Balar removes his goggles. His eyes have changed, become deeper. Rico has never seen those eyes before, but he knows them in an instant. He sinks to his knees, tears welling as he whispers, "Spec?"

Balar's hand is warm against Rico's face, but Spec's words are warmer.

"I know your lifelong loneliness, child. I've seen your malaise and how you've set it aside to inspire joy in others. Because of that, I will not let you fade."

"But that's the fate of blood-muses. We don't go to a Graveyard. We fade from the Spectrum's memory."

The screen fills with the image of Earth2. As Rico watches in awe, it zooms in on North America, America, Maryland, Frederick County, Taney Avenue, a townhouse, and a cluttered study.

"For your service, for your sacrifices, your memory will endure. With the entire Spectrum as my witness, your stories will be told. And she," he says, pointing to a woman with curly hair, scrawling in a notebook, "will be your storyteller."

Weariness hits Rico like a sledgehammer, and Balar helps him lie down. From the beginning of his lonely life to this moment, Rico felt the weight of responsibility. There had been moments of pleasure, but none comparing to the sensation of a slowing pulse. His life will end, but Spec's gift grants him the chance to live better ones. The facts of his existence won't change, but the spaces between are endless now. For the first time, he knows the weightlessness—and joy—of possibility.

Rico's eyes close, his breath ceases, and the storyteller lowers her pen.

⊕ ⊕ ⊕

Jessica McHugh is an author of speculative fiction that spans the genre from horror and alternate history to epic fantasy. A member of the Horror Writers Association and a 2013 Pulp Ark nominee, she has devoted herself to novels, short stories, poetry, and playwriting. Jessica has had thirteen books published in five years, including the bestselling Rabbits in the Garden, The Sky: The World *and the gritty coming-of-age thriller,* PINS. *More info on her speculations and publications can be found at* **JessicaMcHughBooks.com.**

THE L⊕VERS

A M⊕DERN AFFAIR

By Eden Baylee

STRANDS ⊖F JET-BLACK HAIR BRUSHED HER FACE AS SHE tilted her head from side to side. I guessed her to be no more than thirty, but her bad skin aged her by at least a decade. Even with her face hidden in shadows, the lines around her mouth revealed she smoked. Her intensity frightened me a little as I watched her eyes narrow. I swallowed hard and cleared my throat, fighting the urge to say something.

"I see a man," she said, finally breaking the silence. Her husky voice reverberated off the walls of the tiny room. She continued to stare intently at my cards. "Is there a man?"

A tiny smile curled my lips. "Yes, there is."

"Is he a lot younger than you?"

"No."

"Hmm…" She pressed her fist to her lips. "Perhaps he is less mature?"

I couldn't help but laugh as she fished for information. My husband was twelve years older than me, the furthest thing from immature. I remained silent to avoid offering any clues.

"I see a man who is either biologically younger than you or sexually less mature."

I nodded to show support, just because I felt bad she was so far off the mark. "And what does this card mean?" I pointed to *The Lovers*, the card in the middle of my Tarot spread.

"It can mean many things. The five apples on the tree behind the woman represent the five senses, indicating sensual love is very important to her. The snake suggests the temptations of the world, perhaps a love affair."

I chuckled but quickly regained my composure. "Are you saying I will have an affair with a young, immature man?"

She shook her head, leaned back in the chair. "Not necessarily."

I massaged my temples. "Okay, what does it say about the man?"

"The flames behind the man represent the flames of passion, his primary concern."

I don't think so.

"Your card is upright," she continued, "an indicator of harmony, trust, and mutual attractiveness. On a more personal level, it represents your own belief system, staying true to who you are."

"Staying true? About what?"

She looked me square in the eyes. "Just be aware of the difference between love and infatuation."

My face tightened. Her words made no sense to me. "Thank you for your time."

"You're welcome." She offered a sympathetic look before sweeping the cards off the table. "One more thing. If you find yourself at a moral crossroads, consider all consequences before acting. The Lovers card is about making choices, and they are not always easy or obvious."

I walked out of the dimly illuminated apartment following the thirty-minute reading, thankful I had only paid twenty dollars for it. Though I could relate to what the Tarot reader said about my career choices, her implausible thoughts on my love life merely amused me.

I filed the experience away until a week later when I recounted the highlights to a friend over drinks.

"You're the most grounded person I know, Ellen. I didn't think you believed in stuff like that."

I shrugged my shoulders. "I did it on a whim."

"So, you think there's something to it?"

"To what? To Tarot cards?"

"No, to what she said about the young man and an affair."

I scoffed. "Of course not. I love Patrick. You know that."

"Yes, but..." she leaned in and lowered her voice, "it's been awhile, hasn't it?"

My cheeks reddened and I took a sip of wine. Marilyn was my best friend, and I had confided in her about my situation. Still, I flinched at the honesty of her words. "Like you said, I'm the most grounded person you know."

⊕ ⊕ ⊕

The alarm woke me in time to make breakfast for Patrick every morning at 6 a.m. sharp while he showered. I knew I wouldn't see him again until late that night.

"Don't eat so fast," I said, placing a mug of French-pressed coffee on the granite countertop.

"Can't help it. Staff meeting." Patrick reached for another almond croissant. "They expect me to arrive first."

I sighed. "Will you be home for dinner?"

"I doubt it. I'll call if I'm able to leave early." He kissed the top of my head and headed for the door. "Have a good day writing, darling."

"Wait." I handed him the travel mug. "Don't forget your coffee."

"Thanks, love, or should I say, Electra?"

I shrugged my shoulders. "You still like the pen name?"

"I think it's perfect for you." He pulled out the key fob from his jacket and started the car remotely. "Now I really must run or I'll be late."

Thanks to his prestigious job as Director of Obstetrics & Gynecology, I was able to pursue my dream of writing. But at what cost?

After Patrick left for the day, I sat down at my computer and attempted to rework a pivotal chapter for my debut novel. The book revolved around a May-December romance and for some reason, I struggled with the sex scene. I chose the storyline based on the old adage of "write what you know." The rest of the story came easily, so it concerned me I could not hammer out a short sex scene.

As I re-read the manuscript, words from the Tarot reader hijacked my thoughts. How could she be so wrong? A young, sexually immature man was the exact opposite of who Patrick was. It annoyed me I was giving it another thought.

Memories of our tenth wedding anniversary in Paris came to mind. The city of love. Though we didn't make love once during the entire week we were there. It wasn't that he was not affectionate; he just wasn't particularly sexual anymore. At fifty-three, his sex drive waned as mine was ramping up.

The ding of an incoming email vibrated in my ears. I plucked out my earbuds and hit the mute button on the laptop. *Fuck.* I'd forgotten I inserted the headphones to drown out the sound of the summer roadwork down the street.

Since my writing wasn't going anywhere, I toggled to my email program and opened a message from someone named J.D. Ellsworth. I hit the link and his face appeared on screen. His name sounded familiar, but I'd never seen him before. Clean-shaven, boyish, big blue eyes—nice. His mouth spoke to me. Lips were my thing, something about imagining how they moved when talking, eating food…eating me.

My mind jumped back to the sex scene I was writing before thoughts of the Tarot invaded; I immediately squeezed my eyes to recapture it. Slow drifting human shapes writhed in my mind's eye. A smile crossed my face as letters formed words. The image merged with potential sentences and I repeated the words in my head so I would not forget them.

Fluid, sensual, union, motion, all great words colliding and trying to fall into place. Only moments away from cohesive structure, the picture blurred. In what seemed like an instant, dark shadows replaced the shapes and faded to black. I remained still for several seconds, desperately hoping the scene would return. It didn't. The words had evaporated too.

My eyes shot open in frustration. I suddenly remembered how I knew J.D. Ellsworth.

⊕ ⊕ ⊕

J.D. Ellsworth was part of an online writers' group I belonged to. Helmed by an ambitious young woman who updated regularly, I found the group supportive of new writers, a forum where one could connect to someone who might like us; I mean, really like us.

At the time, J.D.'s profile picture was a horse, as pretentiously regal as I thought his abbreviated name and haughty surname sounded. I had a slight complex about my name. Ellen Lee was perfect if I wrote children's books, but I didn't write for kids. I wrote for adults only, and I needed something punchy and original. It took me a few days to settle on Electra—just Electra, writer of eloquent erotica. The one name gave it a diva-esque quality, and the tagline explained what I did.

I never saw J.D. post to the group until about a month ago when he appeared saying he'd released a book of poetry and short stories. He included a link to a sample and requested the group give it a read. He even said "please" and added a happy face emoticon. His polite demeanor seemed genuine enough, so I made a mental note to come back to it later if I had time.

That was my one and only interaction with J.D. Ellsworth...until today.

I touched the mouse pad to bring my computer out of sleep mode. J.D.'s face brightened the screen. As innocuous as his request was, his timing sent an odd chill through me.

No one so good-looking could possibly be a poet. He must have substituted the horse picture with some male model. Most poets I met looked like Bukowski in his later years. They had no sense of their appearance because they didn't care about it. Their hair was a greasy mess, and they had bad skin from too much drink and cigarettes. I clicked on J.D.'s website and found more photos. It was him all right, not a model. He looked unbelievably hot in each picture.

I sent J.D. a note, not revealing too much about myself. Some people had funny ideas about writers of erotica; maybe he was one of them. As much as I considered it important to make friends in the writing world, I didn't care to expose too much of my private life.

I wrote him a brief message, conveyed I had a fan page specific for my author friends. I invited him to visit it and connect there if he was interested. He responded immediately and extended a polite invitation for his page as well. From there, we discussed the merits of self-publishing and found out a bit more about each other as writers, then J.D. injected a tidbit, which surprised me.

I've written an erotic short story and I'd love your thoughts on it, the message read.

It was a favor authors asked of one another all the time. Why then, did I find myself hesitant to say yes?

I'd be happy to read it, I finally typed.

He said he looked forward to hearing my comments. Nice, polite, sweet—all words swirling around my brain as I stared at his picture and started burning up. Springtime in Toronto was not yet above freezing, with one more snowfall predicted for later in the week. There was no reason for me to feel so hot.

My fingers strayed between my legs as I sat stretched out on the couch with the laptop on my thighs. When I slid my hand down my panties, the sticky wetness of my excitement did not surprise me. Lifting my ass slightly, I inserted a finger inside, clenched the walls of my pussy, and stroked myself for several seconds. I knew I wouldn't be able to write another word until I found release.

Reluctantly pulling my hand out of my panties, I caught a whiff of my juices and it only aroused me more. What the hell, I thought to myself. With a few strokes of the keyboard, I found my way back to J.D's original email. Using the same finger I had just used to play with myself, I accepted his request.

J.D. Ellsworth and I were now officially friends via the social network.

⊕ ⊕ ⊕

Two days later, he popped up on my chat program.

J.D.: good morning, how are you?

Electra: hey, good, yourself?

I was going to message you

J.D.: oh? Is it okay if we chat?

I prefer the immediacy of this over email.

Electra: sure, just wanted to tell you I read your story

J.D.: what did you think?

Electra: in a word—delicious

J.D.: really?

Electra: yes

J.D.: glad you liked it

Electra: I did, it was hot

J.D.: you found it hot?

Electra: very much so

J.D.: hmm…may I ask what turned you on about it?

Electra: I like stories with masturbation, particularly men masturbating

J.D.: oh yeah, I'd forgotten about that part

Electra: you have a unique way of writing

short choppy sentences that move the story along

kinda like the act itself

J.D.: true, good way of putting it

Electra: well written for someone who doesn't usually write about sex

J.D.: Yeah, I guess it's a fantasy of mine to be discovered while masturbating

Electra: you're a bit of an exhibitionist then

J.D.: I guess I am…and you?

Electra: what about me?

J.D.: you write erotica, you have a favorite fantasy?

Electra: I have many, that's why I write

it's a release

J.D.: release?

Electra: hmm...I guess we're back on the topic of masturbation

J.D.: ha, I guess we are

Electra: I think I'd better do some vacuuming, chatting with you is...

J.D.: yes?

Electra: stimulating...to say the least

J.D.: I like the thought of stimulating you.

Pause.

J.D.: are you still there?

Electra: sorry, yes, I'm here, just thinking

J.D.: about?

Electra: vacuuming

J.D.: you mean hoovering?

Electra: ah, yes

J.D.: you enjoy that?

Electra: hate it, but it kills the sex urge

J.D.: Brill! Will you be online later?

Electra: unlikely, going out for lunch soon

J.D.: I forget I'm five hours ahead of you

Electra: true, how's the weather in London?

J.D.: it rained earlier but warming up, and in Toronto?

Electra: we are finally above zero

it's been a long winter

J.D.: nice, I hope you enjoy your day then

Electra: and you, have a great evening

I quickly went offline and felt myself hot and wet—yet again. Who was this man, and why did he have this power over me?

Flushed, I shut down my laptop and contemplated vacuuming.

⊕ ⊕ ⊕

Electra: So, what does JD stand for?

J.D.: James Daniel

Electra: James Daniel Ellsworth, that's a mouthful

J.D.: it's not the only part of me that's a mouthful

Electra: ha, you're terrible!

J.D.: *grin*

how did you come up with Electra?

Electra: my real name is too boring for erotica

J.D.: Ellen is classic

Electra: I suppose

I don't mind it

thankful I didn't have a phonetically translated Asian name like some kids I knew

JD.: Like what?

Electra: Hmm…let's see

there was Gee Sook Fat, Lee Ho Tam, and the worst one of all…

J.D.: yes?

Electra: Hung Toc Lo

J.D.: No way!

Electra: Yup, geeky boy I met in fifth grade

poor guy spent his years introducing himself as

"I'm Hung Too Lo, but call me Toby."

J.D.: Poor bugger, hope he got it legally changed!

Electra: Yeah, me too!

Pause.

J.D.: I like talking to you

Electra: I like talking to you too

Our online conversations continued daily over the next two weeks. Harmless flirtation, though I couldn't say they were entirely innocent. J.D.'s voracious sexual appetite aroused and amused me. More than anything, he infused youth and excitement into my days.

The fact that he had no qualms expressing how I turned him on didn't hurt either.

I limited my time with J.D. to the morning hours, convinced myself our chats were for research purposes only. After all, I had changed my story around because of him. My older man-younger woman story experienced a role reversal. Penning two thousand words daily suddenly became easy and I no longer struggled with the sex scenes.

On occasion though, reality hit when thoughts of the Tarot reading surfaced. Each time, I shook the words out of my head.

Just be aware of the difference between love and infatuation.

I didn't love J.D.

I loved my husband.

I was a grown woman.

I knew better.

⊕ ⊕ ⊕

J.D.: oh, there you are

Electra: hey. i'm here but just got out of the shower, brb

J.D.: i've missed you

Electra: Aw, that's sweet

J.D.: I'm serious

Electra: I know, I'm dripping

J.D.: Yeah?

Electra: From the shower, silly

J.D.: Are you naked? Oh god, i could really use that today

Electra: you're incorrigible

J.D.: the thought of your wet skin, licking you, tasting you

Electra: James…let me dry off and come back in an hour, ok?

J.D.: you're killing me

Electra: James, please…

J.D.: I'll be waiting

Pause.

Electra: I'm back. Are you there?

J.D.: yes, i'm here and ravenous, just to warn you

Electra: you should be ravenous, part of being so young

J.D.: 26 is not that young

Electra: don't say that to someone who's almost 40

J.D.: I want you

I want you, an older woman, dripping on top of me

begging me for my young, thick cock

Electra: Wow...you are ravenous

J.D.: Bloody well right

Electra: you really like that I'm older than you, don't you?

J.D.: LOVE it

Electra: why?

J.D.: I don't know why, truthfully

I dream of seeing my cum leak out of you

Electra: oh god

J.D.: I want your pussy so badly

Electra: you want so much. You're insatiable

J.D.: I constantly crave and need

Electra: I see that

J.D.: It turns you on, doesn't it?

Pause.

Electra: yes, shows me you're alive

J.D.: I'm alive for you

Electra: Charmer, how did you get to be so cute?

J.D.: haha, lots of world-weariness, travel, love, heartbreak

Electra: you're adorable

J.D.: so are you, and...

Electra: yes?

J.D.: and fucking sexy as hell

Electra: *blush*

⊕ ⊕ ⊕

I awoke in a cold sweat, breathless. The digital clock beside me read 5:22 a.m. Rolling over, I bumped up against Patrick who stirred and then draped an arm around me.

Willing him not to wake up, I took several deep breaths and nestled against him.

J.D. immediately popped into my mind.

Fuck.

What the hell was I doing?

I only had a vague memory of the dream—an angel in a purple cloak watched as I cried. I wanted forgiveness from the man near me, but he refused to answer. I demanded he say something; he wouldn't or perhaps he just couldn't. He moved away from me, slowly, until I could no longer see him. That's when I woke up.

I grabbed Patrick's arm and wrapped it more tightly around myself.

⊕ ⊕ ⊕

Electra: hi you

J.D.: hello

Electra: did you have a good trip?

J.D.: yes, it was good to meet up with some old mates

got pissed every night though

I'm exhausted!

Electra: Ha, serves you right.

I think I know every place you ate at from your updates

J.D.: yeah, I'm a foodie

takes a lot to feed this six feet frame

Electra: I don't doubt it

happy you had fun

J.D.: I missed you though

thought of you lots

Electra: I thought of you too

J.D.: really?

Electra: yes

J.D.: I like knowing you think of me

good thoughts?

Electra: Of course, only good

J.D.: I came five times this morning thinking of you

Pause.

Electra: now what can I say to that?

you're a semen machine

J.D.: I know

cum everywhere

it was a mess

Electra: you're a baby

J.D.: Ha, I'm no baby, but I could be your baby

Pause.

J.D.: You still there?

Electra: Yes, I'm here

J.D.: crossing the line?

Electra: if only I knew where the line was

I'm afraid it's been blurry the past few weeks

J.D.: Does that make you uncomfortable?

Electra: A little, only because our connection is surreal

J.D.: it doesn't have to be

Electra: what do you mean?

J.D.: Skype? I want to see you

Electra: no

J.D.: I want you, and I can't help it

Pause.

Electra: I know but…

J.D.: but what?

Electra: we need to take a break

J.D.: why?

Electra: James, what we have between us

all this sexual banter

It's….

J.D.: what?

Electra: It's a fantasy
you know that, right?
Pause.
J.D.: what are you saying?
Electra: I need to end the fantasy
please don't hate me
J.D.: I could never hate you
Pause.
Electra: Still friends?
Pause.
J.D.: Always.

⊕ ⊕ ⊕

I shuffled the deck as instructed and concentrated on what I wanted to know. The tiny, familiar apartment now comforted where it once spooked me. The Tarot reader nodded as I handed her the cards.

"Nice to see you again," she said.

I offered a sheepish smile. "Nice to see you too, happy to be back."

"Good." She started pulling cards from the deck. "Let's begin."

⊕ ⊕ ⊕

Eden Baylee left a twenty-year banking career to become a full-time writer. Incorporating some of her favorite things such as travel, culture, and a deep curiosity for what turns people on, her brand of writing is sensual, sexual, and literary.

Spring into Summer is her second collection of erotic novellas and the companion piece to Fall into Winter. Her latest release is a book of flash fiction and poetry called Hot Flash.

She is currently writing a psychological mystery novel scheduled for late 2013.

*Eden's laptop is attached to her hip and she rarely sleeps, so connect to her via her website, **edenbaylee.com**, and other virtual homes.*

THE CHARIOT

SQUASHFEST—
A SALLY MAE RIDDLEY
ADVENTURE

By Annetta Ribken

THE ONLY THING SAVING MY BEST FRIEND FROM MURDER was the fact it was illegal and I din't want to go to jail.

"Come on, Sally Mae. It'll be fun."

"Becky Jo McFee, I been to a hundred Squashfests and there ain't nothing fun about 'em." I zipped up my hoodie, grabbed the milk pail, and dashed toward the barn behind the trailer, hoping Becky Jo got the hint. But no, she was right on my tail, even though I knowed for a fact she hated the smell of cow shit.

"You ain't been to a hundred Squashfests. They're only once a year and you ain't but sixteen. Quit bein' a drama queen. Oh, come on. I don't want to go by myself. Think of it as a girl's night out."

Her voice sounded muffled and I turned to see she'd pulled her sweat-shirt over her nose and had to laugh despite my everlasting irritation. Downright comical, that girl.

"What's so funny?"

"You, with your sweatshirt. You look like a damned fool."

Becky Jo pulled the sweatshirt higher over her face. "I can't stand it, Sally Mae. In science class, Mr. Slater said there's these partic-u-lates in the air from the cow shit and I ain't breathing them in. Now quit tryin' to change the subject."

"Particulates. That's what you're worried about?" I pulled the stool over next to Molly and started milking. "Jeezum crow. You're gonna nag me until I say yes, ain't you?" The barn felt warm compared to the autumn chill outside, and the familiar hissing of the milk into the pail sounded a mite comforting.

Becky Jo shifted from foot to foot, although I knowed the stubborn thing warn't about to give up. "Yep. Sure am. You need to get out for a night."

My face flushed when she said that. She was talking about my mama, who'd been drunk every damned night for the last two months, even if she din't say it right out loud. Ever since my daddy done run off, leav-ing me and my sissy, Sue Ann, to make sure Mama din't kill herself drinking by choking on her own puke or settin' the trailer on fire with her cigarettes.

"You just let Sue Ann take care of business for once and keep her hootchie ass to home. Do her good to let that thang cool off a little."

I couldn't help it. First, I snorted, then Becky Jo giggled, and that was it. We busted up.

Poor Molly mooed and turned her head, looking at us as if we were crazier than Mad Hattie, the swamp witch. That just made me laugh harder, and next thing I saw was Becky Jo rolling around in the hay like she was having a fit, howling and holding her tummy.

"All right, all right." I wiped the tears of hilarity streaming down my face with my sleeve and got back to milking, while Becky Jo finally sat up with hay sticking out of her hair. This almost set me off again, but

I was afeared if I laughed any more I'd pee all over the milking stool. "I'll hightail it out after supper and meet you by the creek."

Becky Jo grinned and I had to grin back. Maybe this Squashfest wouldn't be so bad.

⊕ ⊕ ⊕

"This sucks."

Becky Jo swallowed a bite of her battered and fried butternut on a stick and said, "You know, Sally Mae, you got yourself a real bad attitude. I can't say as I blame you, but damn, girl."

Celebrating the wonders of squash was a tradition in Dinksville every fall. Although the array of large zucchini might be fascinating to some people, especially Mabelline Townsend who probably had something else in mind for the vegetable besides what's for supper, it din't impress me much. Neither did the Smash The Hubbard With Your Head competition, which Beau Miller won most every year. Seein' as he had the hardest head in town, that warn't no surprise.

We pushed through the crowd down the midway between booths of Pitch-Til-You-Win and Ring-Around-The-Spaghetti Squash with people lined up for a chance at a giant stuffed cucurbita, passing food trucks lit up and probably teeming with all kinds of bacterial life forms. *Here's this girl so worried about breathing 'particulates' of cow shit, and she's eating fried squash out one o' these death traps.* O'course I din't say this out loud on account just thinking about it made me want to urp.

"Get off my grits, Becky Jo. You'd be a mite irritated your own self if your daddy up and left with your mama so drunk every night somebody's gotta babysit her." *Two months now. Two months since my daddy took off and nobody knowed nothing 'bout where he went. I never thought my own daddy would do us like that.*

She finished off that butternut on a stick in two bites and said, "Hey, you just need somethin' to take your mind off your troubles. What about the Tilt O' Whirl?" and followed up with a belch worthy of one of them no-good delinquents who hung out at the pool hall and were currently whooping it up at the beer tent.

"You sounded just like Beau Miller with that belch. And your snack there is likely to make a reappearance if'n we go on a ride right now."

She nodded and looked a little green around the gills. I knowed how she felt. The stench of fried summer squash mixing with cotton candy was making me feel a bit queasy my own self. "I think you might be right. I know! How 'bout we get our fortunes told?" She pointed to a ratty tent set up yonder from the squash festivities with a hand-lettered sign, which read, FORTUNES TOLD.

I sighed. "You know that ain't for real. It's your Aunt Tilly in there and she's knowed us since we was babies."

"Nuh-uh. Aunt Tilly's back in Stillwater."

I looked at Becky Jo, whose eyes were full of tears. "The crazy house? Oh, sweet pea, why din't you tell me?"

She just shook her head. "You got enough goin' on with your own, Sally Mae. I don't know who's in there, but it ain't Aunt Tilly. You never know. Maybe you can find out something 'bout your daddy."

I grabbed Becky Jo's hand and squeezed. I knowed Becky Jo was scared stiff of ending up like her Aunt Tilly. The Sight was strong with the McFees, bein' related to the air elemental and all, but the bloodlines were so muddled in some families those with a gift sometimes din't run true, especially if somebody along the line hooked up with the wrong elemental. Then you had people like Aunt Tilly. Or Beau Miller with his hard head protecting nothing inside. My family, the Riddleys, could trace back the fire line direct quite a ways. The McFees warn't so lucky.

I felt a little glimmer of hope. Maybe Becky Jo was right and I could find out something about where my daddy was and why he took off. "If'n it makes you feel better, we'll go in," I said. "But you come with me, okay?"

She smiled. "I wouldn't let you go alone."

The best friend ever.

⊕ ⊕ ⊕

Inside the tent, the stank of fried squash faded in favor of some fancy incense stuff. Smelled pretty good, actually, especially compared to outside. I kept a hold of Becky Jo's hand and peered into the dimness. It looked a lot bigger on the inside. Made me feel right dizzy. A beaded curtain dangled in the doorway to what seemed like another room, and while the candles on a low table glowed, the darkness beyond the doorway was pitch black.

I couldn't tell if it were Becky Jo's hand sweating or mine. "Maybe this warn't such a good idea," I muttered, trying to swallow past the lump in my throat.

Becky Jo backed up a step and I was right willing to go with her when a woman emerged through the darkness, pushing aside the beaded curtain.

She warn't nothin' like I'd ever seen before. What I expected…well, I din't really know what to expect. She was lovely, with long dark hair shot with gray, a curvy figure, and pouty red lips. All decked out in colorful fringed scarves, showing a flat belly and tinkling bangles all up and down her arms like she was some kind of fancy-schmancy belly dancer or something Big hoop earrings I knew Mabelline would kill for.

But it were her eyes what caught me. Big, black as night, fringed with the thickest eyelashes I ever did see. *Sue Ann would slit her throat for those eyelashes.*

"Hello, girls," she purred. "What can I do for you?"

I exchanged a quick glance with Becky Jo. Sure warn't Aunt Tilly…but I din't recognize this woman a'tall. I figured it'd probably be a townie, but she din't look like anyone I knowed, and I thought I knowed everyone in this damned town.

I cleared my throat. "Well, ma'am, I'd like to get my fortune told. Like it says on the sign."

The woman nodded and gestured toward a pile of pillows settin' next to the low table. "Of course. Have a seat, ladies." From the twist of her lips I gathered the last thing she thought we was were "ladies", but at this point I din't care. I felt a burning need to sit and hear what this here fortune teller had to say.

She settled on one side of the table and me and Becky Jo flopped to a seat on the pillows. The woman's eyes never left my face, which I found a bit disconcerting. Like she was studying a bug on a pin. She reached out toward a covered object and moved it away. "Not the crystal ball," she said. Squinting her eyes, she pulled out a deck of old, worn cards and placed it in the center of the table. "No, for you it will be the cards."

I shivered. Becky Jo sat all quiet-like, her hands clasped in her lap. I wondered what she was picking up from all this.

"But first," the woman continued, "there must be payment."

Oh, hellfire. I hope Becky Jo din't spend her last dime on that butternut. "How much, ma'am?"

"Give me what you have in your pockets. Both of you. Because I can see you're closely tied together."

I warn't too impressed by that, considering we'd come in hand-in-hand. *She's probably nothing but a big faker.*

She tsked. "I assure you, I'm the real deal."

I pert near swallowed my tongue.

I turned to Becky Jo who looked white as a sheet. She pulled out a dollar from her pocket without even looking at me. With trembling fingers, I took it then dug for what I had in my own pocket. *Sixty-two cents. Pitiful.*

I handed it over and the woman snorted. "For this, you get one card."

I nodded. "I'm right grateful, ma'am." And I was. Mostly.

The money disappeared and her long, delicate fingers wrapped around the cards. "I will shuffle, and you will cut. Then we'll see what fortune has to tell you. Think hard about your question."

After her little demonstration about the faking thing, I felt a bit nervous, to be honest. Becky Jo pulled on my pants leg and when I looked at her, she shook her head ever so slightly. But in for a penny, in for a dollar and this weirdo already had my money. *Besides, it's only a card.*

I watched as Miss Fancy Pants Fortune Teller shuffled the cards so fast all I saw was a blur. I thought about my daddy and where he might be. That was my question. After what seemed like hours, she plunked them in the middle of the table.

"Cut."

The word seemed to hold so much weight it kind of hung in the air. Becky Jo's hand twisted on my pants leg, and I almost smacked her one because it pinched. I reached out and separated the cards into two piles.

The woman's gaze was as keen as a hunting knife. "Are you sure?"

"Yup."

She flipped over one card. Her face blanched.

I peered at the card but all I seen was a strange looking figure riding in what seemed to be a donkey cart.

"What in tarnation is that?"

"You need to leave. Now." I coulda sworn I heard a clap of thunder and Becky Jo 'bout jumped out of her skin. The woman gathered up the cards and got to her feet. Her face din't look so pretty anymore. As a matter of fact, she seemed right pissed off."Go on. Git."

I scrambled to my own feet, feeling a bit of righteous anger. "Hey, I paid you good money to answer my question." Becky Jo hung on to my arm for dear life, her fingers digging into my arm. Girl was about to get a slap.

"You don't want to mess with me, Sally Mae Riddley," the woman said, her face twisting. "You want to remember that. Now get out of my tent."

I opened my mouth to give this cheating bitch a piece of my mind, when Becky Jo practically dragged me outside, panting like a huntin' dog. She pulled me along until we was next to the beer tent. me sputtering the whole way. I was so plumb mad I wanted to kick something hard, and even seein' Beau Miller puking up his guts full of beer and summer squash just outside the tent din't make me feel better.

Well, maybe a little better.

"You just shush now, Sally Mae," Becky Jo huffed. "You was about to get yourself in a mess of trouble."

"Girl, you want to just let go of me right now," I huffed back. "That faker took our money and I got nothin' out of it but a pure case of I'm Gonna Kick Your Ass. That's stealin' where I come from."

I turned to stomp my way back to the ratty old tent and then stopped, my breath catching in my throat.

The tent was gone.

⊕ ⊕ ⊕

Back in my room with Mama snoring like a truck driver and Sue Ann out cattin' around, Becky Jo and I curled up on my bed. I was still fuming.

"That cheatin' bitch. If I ever see her again, I'ma kick her ass good and proper."

Becky Jo just shook her head. "I don't think you want to do that, Sally Mae."

I peered at her face and said, "What are you talkin' about? She stole our money. For nothin'. Say, you look a mite peaked, Becky Jo. Like you almost got hit by a bus."

She pinched my arm. I didn't punch her in the face because what she said next stopped me in my tracks.

"Girl, for real? *The tent disappeared.* She knowed your name! What more would it take to get through your thick skull?" She sighed. "There is somethin' right strange 'bout that woman, and I don't think you want to know any more than that."

"Well, when you put it that way…" I tried to let go of some of my anger, a difficult thing for a Fire Child, and tried to think things over. I flopped down and stared at the ceiling. "She was strange. First thing is she knowed I thought she was a faker. I don't know how she guessed my name, but I woulda told her if she asked. Polite-like."

Becky Jo snorted.

"She din't get real scary 'til she flipped over my card." I looked at my best friend. "Did you see it? Do you know what it was?"

Becky Jo nodded like she din't really want to. "Yeah. I knowed it. It were the Chariot."

I thought about this. "What, like I'm goin' somewhere?"

She shook her head. "No, Sally Mae. From what I know, the Chariot means you're in for a tussle."

I sat up. "A tussle?"

"Yup. A tussle." She played with the edge of my tattered blanket. "You'll have a heap to get over, but in the end you'll be on the winning side on account you're ornery and stubborn."

I groaned and let the ornery and stubborn thing pass for the moment. "Like I don't have enough on my plate as it is. Huh. Life is nothin' but having a heap to get over, but why did she get so pissed off 'bout it? And what does it have to do with my daddy? Because that was my question."

"I don't know. All I know is she was one scary woman."

"Not as scary as eating fried butternut on a stick."

Becky Jo giggled. "Hey, at least I din't spew like Beau."

We busted up, and I plumb forgot about the Chariot.

But the Chariot never did forget about me.

⊕   ⊕   ⊕

A professional editor of over eighty novels, Annetta Ribken has also been writing since a tender young age, when letters were chiseled on stone tablets. A precocious student, Annetta earned her Ph.D in the School of Hard Knocks, with honors, in the early Age of Disco. She lives and works just outside of St. Louis with her evil feline overlord, a rescued shelter cat named Athena.

Annetta has big plans to release the sequels to Athena's Promise (Book One of the Aegean Trilogy) *and* The Trailer Park Tiara and the Goat Incident (a Sally Mae Riddley Adventure) *in 2014. She is not too proud to bribe her muse with chocolate.*

*You can find out all about her at **about.me/annettaribken** including a link to her fiction on Amazon and all other fine online book stores.*

STRENGTH

A Promise in the Dark

By Rochelle Maya Callen

I COULDN'T REMEMBER WHEN I FIRST DREAMED OF THE boy. We sat on the cliffs above Zorilah in silence, the wind whipping at us, threatening to tear us apart. His black hair tickled my cheek as he leaned in close whispering in my ear. At first, I couldn't hear his words, but his breath was a warm caress against my cheek so I never leaned away.

One night, his voice was as clear and real as the cold nipping at my toes through my torn boots. He spoke of death, of ashes, of blood, but his words never frightened me. They were a comfort, a promise in the dark so I always snuggled down onto the wet concrete and stayed in dreams—dreams where Zorilah was free, beautiful, and ours.

I haven't dreamed in a very long time.

I pulled my thin shirt over my nose, trying to block out the smell of rot and human waste. I sighed loudly, but the whimpering down the tunnel overpowered my exasperated sound. I closed my eyes and tried to remember the angle of the boy's jaw, the pale smoothness of his features, the warmth he offered me every night. The memory slipped away from me and I clung tightly, because it was all I had left. I couldn't remember...anything. I choked down a sob building in my chest. No more quiet comfort or dark promises. Just cold, wet tunnels, hungry faces. Just danger lurking in the shadows and gruff voices of the King's Hoarders roaming at night. My palms tingled. So many desperate, weak souls quivered in the tunnels. They needed strength. My strength. But I just rolled over and faced the mouth of the tunnel and the blackness outside feeling like I had nothing left to give.

All the Arcana were marked with a brand on their back when they were brought into the King's Circle. I remembered the ceremonies: incense, candles, a night of fruit and cheese. No one went hungry on the induction night of an Arcana member. I knew I was Arcana before I felt the small mark etched on my hand between my thumb and index finger. I felt souls, felt when they trembled, felt when they needed my touch. Souls were tender blooms within a person, but sometimes fear or anxiety or sorrow choked them. Sometimes the bloom needed a little strength to break free.

I remembered sitting beneath a rickety roof and looking over at my Mama as she tried to smash berries in a bowl. I stared at my mother's hunched shoulders and shining eyes and saw the petals of her soul drooping. I asked her, "Mama, why is your soul tired?" She stiffened and jerked toward me in alarm. Her eyes searched my face, neck, shoulders, until they settled on my right hand. She fell to her knees, the bowl splintering into a hundred shards. She lunged forward, snatching my hand in her own.

That is when I saw the twining symbols decorating my skin. Arcana. I nearly hiccupped with laughter I was so excited. Mama yanked me to her chest and smothered my sound. She wailed to the gods to take my gift away. I felt her soul then, her strength withering away into sorrow and fear. I caressed it, whispering, *I am Strength, Mama. Lean on me and yours will not wilt.* But fear already had its hold on her. She wouldn't let me be taken.

She lit a fire and dragged me over to the flames. With desperation breaking her voice, she whispered "I'm sorry," and shoved my hand into the fire. I don't remember how long I screamed, but I do remember every tear that slid down Mama's face.

⊕ ⊕ ⊕

I ran my fingers over the gnarled flesh. It had been eight years since my mother burned off my mark. Mama told me the Arcana would steal me away, torture me. Ruin me. I didn't believe her until the day I disobeyed her...it was the last day I saw her alive.

I crouched in the alley away from the crowds. I wasn't near the procession, but I knew the Arcana were here. I felt them, like a prickling on my skin, an ache in my bones, a phantom limb throbbing, a scream scratching at my throat. The procession had begun, but I didn't want to see it. The streets were riddled with broken and bruised faces, reaching into the path of the Arcana, towards the pristine red robes flapping in the wind—as if the gods themselves knew who marched through the city. The Arcana glided through the streets without even a passing glance to those who worshipped them, those who reached with scarred, withered arms in hopes of salvation. I knew the scene, knew it so well. Because there was a day, when I stood reaching too. I gritted my teeth and shook the memory away.

The hum in my palms vibrated within me. I clenched my fists tighter. *No.* I bit my lip, those heartless bastards were no part of me. I was classless. Outcast. Just another lost and broken soul waiting to die—hopefully, before one of the King's Hoard raped or tortured me, or threw me into the arena for the king's sport of Lion Fighting. I sneered at the word "fighting". A weak, starved person facing a lion in the arena as the city watched cheering. I never knew if the crowd cheered to give the "fighter" hope, or because they were crazy with bloodlust. But as

I heard their twenty-one distinct calls whisper in my mind, and my own reaching up to reply, I knew I was lying to myself. I was not just another citizen of Zorilah. I was Arcana. The last one unfound. Pain shuddered through me as I denied my call.

⊕ ⊕ ⊕

I was eleven when I first saw the Arcana outside the induction arena. The electricity thrummed against my skin. A fierce need to be one of them, to march with pride and honor alongside them grew within me. I lunged for them: "I am here, my Arcana! Take me home!" I nearly flung myself into the procession. The Arcana heard me, their eyes slanted and piercing. Their voices boomed in unison, "Who said that?"

Mama pulled me out of sight, anger and fear swirling in her eyes. "If they take you, you'll be a slave. Alina, if they take you, they will use you up until you have nothing left." She kissed my hands, her lips lingering for just a moment longer on my scars. Tears streamed down her face. "Hide." She pushed me away so hard I fell against the pavement. By the time I looked up, Mama had run out into the street, screaming "Here I am! I am the one you are searching for."

That was the last day I saw Mama alive.

⊕ ⊕ ⊕

I shook my head. No, I stayed in the shadows, waiting. They would not find me today.

I flinched as I heard a twig behind me break. Before I could turn, a hand snaked its way around my waist, another over my mouth so I couldn't scream.

"I've been watching you for days, my sweet. Now you are alone, I can have my taste." A Hoarder. His breath felt hot and putrid against my cheek. I squirmed, bucking and wriggling, trying to get free, but then I felt a knife point on my neck.

A wet tongue slid up my cheek. I nearly gagged when I heard

the man's gravelly moan. "You taste good, darling. I think I will eat you up."

The Hoarder started hiking up my skirt, his rough, calloused hand on my thigh. I would be defiled in this very alley, shivering in shadows. Was this punishment for hiding from the Arcana? Was this really worth it? Twenty-two humans touched by the gods who could change the course of history and a sixteen-year-old girl about to be raped in a rotten alley was one of them. I felt a single tear slide down my cheek. Even if I screamed, no one would come. Our city was riddled with screams and tears—all courtesy of the King's Hoard.

I let the power inside me roar to life, the inner vibration making me dizzy, but I felt the tingling in my palms. I lifted my hand to the Hoarder's forearms and closed my eyes, searching. The man's soul seemed like black tar sticking to my hands. I wanted to flinch back, but I knew I had to be patient, whisper and nurture the goodness that might be suffocating in the blackness. I called to it, urging it to come out. *I am strength. I am the quiet whispering of your soul, your strength will bloom in my hand.* My Call echoed out into the shadows, even as my physical body felt the roughness of the man's hands fondling, his tongue darting out to taste my neck, my face. His fingers crawling their way up to my breasts. The fabric being ripped from me. I couldn't think about that now. I had to focus.

I called into the shadows coalescing around me. *I am the quiet whispering of your soul, your strength will bloom in my hand.* I stood in silence, waiting.

But there was nothing to reach for. This man's soul was nothing but rot and decay. There was no light in him left. No real strength.

My eyes flew open and my senses assaulted me.

I needed to fight.

He roughly turned my head towards his and his chapped, wet lips crushed against my own, just as he started unbuckling his pants. I bit him. I bit down until I tasted blood spurt in my mouth. He yelped, loosening his hold. I jammed my elbow up and back, straight for his nose. Swiveling around as he hunched over to catch his own blood, I kneed him in the groin and turned to run after spitting on his hunched form, and skidded to a stop. I tensed. I felt them before I saw them. A subtle electricity in the air, a pulse tapping against my skin.

Their Calls slammed into me. I wasn't prepared and my power, already thrumming on my fingertips, sang to them, betraying me. I swallowed hard as I saw the Arcana's red robes flutter into view.

It only took a few moments for the red robes to fill the narrow space The King's Arcana.

I squared my shoulders and faced them. I would not cower, run, or hide.

I also would not kneel as was law.

They stopped before me, silent. Hoods covered their faces. Their voices echoed in my mind in an eerie chorus. *Why have you been hiding, sister? Don't you want to bring glory to your King?* Tension crackled in the air.

My mind seethed, screaming. I wasn't sure if they could hear me, but in my mind I screamed so loud it shook the earth. *I am not a slave. There is no glory left on the throne. Just an old man and a black heart. Just a beast who has brought my city to its knees.* I gritted my teeth, waiting for the ornate sword sheathed at the Arcana's waist to slice off my head. I would prefer to be killed in this alley, than wear those red robes, than to wear the mark on my back.

Silence lingered, threatening.

Then one of the Arcana lowered his hood. He had a shock of black hair and pale, perfect skin, which looked so familiar. Where had I seen his face before? He moved so quickly I couldn't even jerk back. He grasped me by the hands, our palms touching. I gasped as his soul burst to life under my touch. Black earth under a bright sky. His call reverberated in my mind. *From these ashes, we will rise. I am the eve of the Rebirth. I am Death.*

I yanked myself away from him, stumbling to the ground. He was a man now, but I knew who he was...the timbre of his rolling words, the black hair falling into his eyes, those grey, stormy eyes. I swallowed hard. There he was, the messenger of my dreams. My solace in the night.

Death. He was Death.

His face of hard lines softened. Did he know me? Did he ever dream of me? I was surprised when his cheeks colored slightly and his jaw set as if he could hear my thoughts. His lips quirked up at one corner and he grinned at me. "Not a slave?"

His words cracked through my awe. I shuffled to my feet and stood to face them all, my features trained into a fearless expression. He *could* hear my thoughts. "Yes."

"Nothing but a black heart on the throne?"

I clenched my fists tight. *Just do it. Kill me and be done with it.* "Yes."

He still stared at me. "A black heart who has brought your city to its knees?"

Dying babies, wailing mothers, screaming daughters, starving men. People hiding in tunnels like rats only to be dragged out and raped or worked to death. This was my city. Broken. I was surprised when my voice quaked. "Yes."

Death stepped forward. "That is exactly what we wanted to hear."

The Arcana all removed their hoods and laid their hands on each other's shoulders, the final two resting their palms on Death's back. They looked to me and I blinked away my confusion at the expression of pure exhaustion and desperation. Death lifted his hands and in a sudden movement grasped my own, pulling me closer.

I gasped as the souls of twenty-one Arcana whispered their weaknesses to me as well as their hopes, their strengths, their...purpose.

I opened my eyes, quivering.

I knew what was coming.

And I was ready.

Death didn't let go of my hands as he turned to walk out of the alley. I didn't pull away.

⊕ ⊕ ⊕

The sand felt gritty between my fingertips as I knelt on the ground. It was the first sunny day in Zorilah in weeks, and it was blistering.

I had spent weeks with the Arcana—beaten by day for the king's amusement and trained at night.

"Feel the energy just beyond your reach. It will be muted, but it is there," Death said, *pressing my hands to the cement as I tried again to feel the souls in the next room. My eyes clenched shut. Fingertips grazed my cheeks. "Don't do that," he whispered.*

I opened my eyes. "Don't do what?"

"Force it."

The crowd nearly deafened me. I stared, squinting across the arena. Despite the chaos around me, I still heard when the lion roared—a sound so wretched and terrifying I nearly turned to run back to the huge stone doors. My fingers shook on the knife handle. I heard the clinking of the lion's chains. I still had a few more moments before they unleashed him. Still had a few moments to run.

I was chained to the chair, my arms clasped behind me. Judgment, a young man with flowing blonde hair, and Justice, his twin sister circled me like predators. Their faces a mask of indifference, but I knew what lurked underneath: despair. They had carried out the king's "justice" for so long, and they knew if the plan failed, they would be in this chamber for many more years handing out sentences to those who they knew were innocent. They asked me about the hiding places for the classless, my parents, my powers. I knew what their questions would be. I knew how to answer: with silence. My silence was met with their whips. Their expressions never changed, but at night when all was dark and the king slept and the Hoarders roamed, they would come to my chamber, embrace me and beg for my forgiveness. I never faulted them for the pain they caused me. I would bear it. During the beatings, however, Death stood at the side of the king, muscles jumping every time the whip cracked in the air.

He clenched his jaw when I finally met his gaze, the sun blotting out most of his face. I could tell he held his breath. I knew because he always did when he was nervous. It almost made me laugh. But I knew he would sense death here today. And while I knew he wouldn't say, I wondered if he sensed my own. The horn blew out a loud and long cry. I pivoted away from the Arcana's seats high up in the distance. It was time.

Death took a wet cloth and cleaned my back of the blood from the twin's whips. His fingers were gentle against my skin. "I wish there was another way."

I exhaled sharply. "We shouldn't wish for things we can't have. We need to work for the things we can." I sat up, holding my bloody shirt against my chest. "We can have our Zorilah back, Death..." All of the Arcana were called by their Mark, but with Death's fingertips still on my back and my face so close to his, it felt wrong to call him that. I had learned all of the Arcana had been taken from their families, all once had names and homes and people who loved them. I didn't know Death's name and in that moment, I wanted to. "What was your name?"

His sigh was so fragile and delicate in the dark. "I don't even remember. I was taken so young." He moved his fingertips over my scarred hand, then traced them up my arm, my neck, and to my cheek. "I am glad you still have a name, Alina." The lion charged. His huge body a mass of rippling muscle headed straight for me. I wanted to run. My mind screamed to run, but I didn't. I stayed still, waiting for the impact. I grabbed a handful of sand, and let my power well up inside me. I heard my heart pounding as the lion's paws thudded toward me. So close. So very close.

Paws and heartbeats.

Wait.

Paws and heartbeats.

Wait.

Paws and heartbeats.

Now! I jumped aside just as the lion nearly plowed into me. I grabbed onto his mane and pulled my body onto his back, clutching him tight. The crowd silenced for a moment. The lion twisted, trying to bite my side, to drag me off his back with his teeth. I heard more roars from the other side of the arena. More roars? I looked behind me and saw Hoarders unchain two more lions. Panicked, I jerked my gaze to the Arcana. Their mouths sagged open, surprise clear on their faces. But Death, his eyes were locked on mine. He started to stand. I knew he would try to stop this. I knew he would ruin everything.

I shook my head. *No.*

I closed my eyes and clutched the lion.

Everything has a soul; everything has strength that lives within them." The *Moon said so.* I reached for the animal's soul. The lion's jaws clamped down on my shoulder and I was flung off of him, skidding in the sand. My skin screamed in pain. I rolled onto my back as the three lions paced toward me. This was it. This was the moment. I closed my eyes. I placed my palms on the sand and reached.

The lions' souls reached back.

They surrounded me, and one stepped over me so I felt its heat and fur hovering above. The lion's roar shook my body. The people in the arena screamed and cheered. For once, they weren't the ones being beaten, being broken. I couldn't even muster anger toward them. I had hid in the shadows alongside them, quivering in the dark praying the Hoarders didn't find me, drag me out of my hole, use me up until I was a corpse, not even good enough to bury in the ground.

The lion roared again and his muzzle lowered to me, his teeth grazing my skin. I didn't try to run. I stayed submissive below him. I let go of the pitiful knife and placed my hands on his fur hide. I felt the ache of his hunger, the broken bones in his body, but deeper than all of that I felt his tired soul resting in my hands. Flashes of wide open spaces, sunlight, and running with the wind whipping through its mane were replaced by iron cages, rotten meat, and spear slashes.

I held all of their souls in my hands and whispered. *I am the quiet whispering of your soul. I feel your strength in my grasp. I feel your mercy.* I opened my eyes to see the lion's face above my own. *I can set you free. just need to live, I just need your mercy. I will set you free.* Their souls wildly bucked and trembled in my hands. They were confused, but they sensed my urgency, my plea, my promise. The crowd grew silent once more. I released my hands from the lion's hide and began edging my way out from beneath him. None of them moved as I shuffled to my feet, blood, sweat, and sand sticking to my back.

In the blazing sun, a girl stood in an arena bleeding with her whole city watching. As the girl stood, three lions bowed their heads. That girl was me. As the lions bowed, the crowd gasped. I turned to where the gold seats stood. The Arcana did not suppress their smiles. They stood and made their way to the edge of the seats to remove the barrier between the public and the king and his Hoard. My eyes scanned the people. They stood murmuring and confused. A girl mastered the lions, a girl had tamed beasts with a touch. They all looked so frail, so afraid, so weak, so broken. Fear cripples the soul until there is no strength or fight left. I just hoped I would have something to reach for. I knelt, touching my fingers to the sand.

"Strength isn't always about physical capabilities, it is about giving strength to the part of ourselves that need it most," Death said one night as we stared out of the chamber window into the dark city.

"And what do they need most? What do they need to fight?"

"Hope," he said. "We all need just a bit of hope to believe we are strong enough to fight and strong enough to win."

So that was what I gave them. A girl could face a lion and win. A people—as broken as these—could rise up and take back their city, and bring a king to his knees. Their souls—so many—were trembling bodies all around me, pressing down. But I didn't have to reach for them. They were already reaching for me.

"We. Are. A. Strong. People." My words were quiet and deliberate, but I knew their souls could hear. I opened my eyes and scanned the crowds. "We are a strong people," I shouted, raising my arms to the sky. I felt their souls careening towards the light, reaching up, up, up from weeds and dirt, fear and desperation. I felt their souls unfurling around me. I felt their strength like I did the sun.

I looked to their faces. They were the same people from only moments before: dirty, skinny, bruised, but there was a set to their features, a straightness in their spine. I pointed my gaze to the king and his Hoard. I felt the souls soaking up the light and latching onto my strength. In one slow, ominous motion, they all turned in unison towards the gold seats. The Arcana had cleared the path to the Black Souls. I shuddered before I could say the rest. I looked to Death. His soul was in my hands, too.

His voice echoed in my mind. *Today is a day of Death, Alina. But it isn't our day to die. Today is a day of Rebirth. Not mourning. Today we fight. Today, we make our world new. Today, the world is ours.* I held onto his words, and reached to all the souls swirling around me.

My voice was a war cry piercing the silence. "We are a strong people. And today, we will fight. Today, Zorilah is ours!"

Chaos erupted. The Arcana unsheathed their swords and charged. The lions roared and ran towards the Black Souls. The people were glorious warriors even in their tattered rags because their souls were strong and their spirits determined. I fell to my knees, a trickle of blood dripping from my nose. I shook from bearing the weight of so many souls, but as I looked to the chaos before me, as I saw the blood of the king and the Hoarders spill against the earth, I smiled.

I saw Death then. I knelt in the sand, watching as the dark promise of my dreams came true before my eyes: *from these ashes, we will rise.*

From these ashes, we will rise and be free.

Rochelle grew up wanting to be a novelist, but tucked away her stories when she entered high school. She graduated summa cum laude with a degree in Political Science and Communication when she was twenty years old. After years away from her writing, Rochelle picked up a pen and started fleshing out a character sketch that she outlined when she was twelve. That sketch was the start of the Ashes and Ice *story, her debut novel that was published in 2013. Her debut rocked bestseller charts only hours after its release. She plans on releasing its sequel in 2014. Rochelle lives in the DC metro area with her husband and daughter. By day, she works as a behavioral therapist and life coach. By night, she is a dreamer and is busy tapping out new stories on her keyboard. You can find her here:* **rochellemayacallen.com**

THE HERMIT

THE HERMIT

By Red Tash

AS I STROLLED THROUGH THE FLEA MARKET, THE MEMORY came unbidden: a gypsy tent awash with blood—deep reds and purples fading to brown before my eyes; the amber eye of the dragon, disembodied, palmed in the bloody hand of a child. The child looked up at me, a tiny girl with a hooked nose and silent tears streaming down her face. "My brother," she said, before choking on her sobs. "My brother."

I was too late to Autumnfell. Too late to save the boy from the sacrifice the birth of a dragon demands. The least I could do was save his sister. Her parents were easily glamoured into believing she had been consumed by the beast, and so that night, I helped her bundle her things into a shoulder pack and away we went, two vagabond seekers on the road to fortune.

Gypsies are a superstitious lot, and the fate of a true witch among them has never been kind. Zelda could have been burned at the stake if she angered the wrong man. Angering men seemed to be one of her talents.

"Hey, mister! How much for the old lamp?"

My reverie broken, I turned to find a greasy-haired wheeler-dealer with a paunch that told me he'd earned his keep over the years. He smelled like much-handled cash and warm peppermint, and his thick glasses magnified his eyes so much it hurt to look at him.

I held the lantern and let a bit of the Light spill out onto the man's booth. Beneath its glow, I saw forgeries, hidden gems, stolen goods, you name it. The true history of each of his wares was revealed under the lamp's beam, and he gasped before the sight of it. He took off his glasses, wiped the lenses hastily on his plain white t-shirt, and put them back on. "Well, I'll be damned," he said, before pointing up at the lamp. "Don't supposed you'd be willing to part with that, then," he whispered, picking up an old axe head the Light revealed as a relic of Abe Lincoln's.

"I cannot," I said. "But enjoy the profits of your knowledge, my son," I said, nodding at the axe head in his hand. "Could you point me toward the fortune teller's booth?"

A few steps away, a blinking neon sign advertised

YOUR FUTURE

flash

YOUR PAST

flash

YOUR LIFE

flash

YOUR DEATH

A brilliant blue palm blinked off and on beside it. Above, a yellow moon repurposed from a beer-branded bar sign was glamoured to display Zelda's knowing smile. The effect was uncanny, as though the hook-nosed gypsy moon watched passers-by, deciding their fates, waiting for them to come inside and pay to hear the news of their imminent fortunes.

It was uncanny, and it was true.

A thousand plastic orbs on a beaded curtain caught the Light and cascaded before my eyes. I waved them away, their veil of magic stronger than their cheap appearance promised, and entered the tent of one Madame Zelda, fortune teller.

Inside, a cozy waiting area greeted me, bedecked in mismatched, overstuffed furniture I believe is now called "shabby chic." Under the Light, I could tell Zelda had owned the pieces when they were, in fact, "brand new chic" and simply kept them until they reached their present states. Funny how people hold on to things, well past their time.

My lamp muted itself to match the dim lighting inside the tent. I saw a series of curtains leading to three different subsections of the tent. Every shade and pattern of burgundy and purple paisley was loosely sewn or stitched together. Hints of pink and gold were everywhere. A string of amber lights lined the edge of the room, at the ceiling.

The industrial fluorescents of the Trolling for Bargains flea market filtered in through the canopy, bathing everything in Madame Zelda's tent with a reddish glow. The light she had harnessed welcomed relaxation, contemplation, peace. It seemed business was good.

A pair of teenage girls with red, puffy eyes waited for the fortune-teller to call them beyond her curtain. The girls looked up at me when I entered, and then away, as if I weren't there. Suited me fine. My record with young women was abysmal.

There was no place to sit and neither of them moved to offer an old man a seat, so I leaned on my staff and waited. I was accustomed to being on my feet. I could wait a little longer to sit. I'd been avoiding Zelda for decades. I could wait a little longer for her.

"Zat's what you fink, daaaaahling," her familiar voice purred through the curtain.

The teens stopped their sniffling.

"'That's what you think?' Is she talking to us?" one of them asked the other.

A curtain moved and the heavily draped figure of an Eastern European woman with jet-black hair and huge, knowing eyes filled the space. Behind her, a muted television played Days of Our Lives, back-lighting the one and only Zelda. Despite her robes, she cut a surprisingly shapely hourglass in the doorway before loosing the curtain with lacquered nails as long as talons in shades of amber. Zelda's skin was flawless with the exception of the shade of foundation she'd chosen, but here in the red light of her indoor caravan tent, the effect was quite fetching. She glowed like an old gypsy Mona Lisa.

She glanced down at the lantern at my feet as she dismissed the teenagers. "No, Zelda no see you girls today, so sorry."

"But, we paid you already!" one of them gasped, before dissolving into tears.

"Zelda," I said. "Surely you can find it in your heart to help these young ladies. It does seem like an emergency." I spoke so quietly, the sobs of the teens would have washed out my voice to anyone else's ear. Not Zelda's, though. She could hear me across the miles if necessary. Such was the attachment of student to master.

Zelda narrowed her eyes and nodded. "Very well, but I see no good things for zees girls." She shrugged then pulled the curtain back to another room in the tent, indicating the girls should enter.

Zelda glared as I started after them. I lifted my lantern and shone it about the room. "You would prefer I waited out here and had a look around?"

Zelda stepped out of my way and allowed me into the small reading room.

The girls were already seated, one of them with her head down on the table. Her friend eyed me, asking Zelda "Is he going to watch?" The crying girl lifted her head.

By all rights, I could have taken over the conversation, but I waited for Zelda to answer. My authority in the situation was not important. I was curious to see how she'd handle this.

"Yes, um, my darlings, you are in for a treat today. Madame Zelda, she is old, yes? She is old and wise, but zis man...zis man was Zelda's teacher, girls. He is even wiser, and his gifts are...well, Zelda cannot begin to say. It is not every day that a seer of his abilities comes to the Trolling for Bargains flea market in Laurents County, Indiana." She pulled out her chair and sat, a look of triumph on her face.

"You are too kind. I really only want to observe." Smiling to the girls, I added, "Checking up on an old pupil, right?" I pulled out a chair and sat. We were quite the quartet around the little table.

They smiled, then one blurted out her question. "I want to know how long my Mom has to live." She almost didn't get the words out before the sobs began.

Zelda pulled out a deck of tarot cards from a shiny wooden box. She shuffled and cut the deck, then slowly flipped the first card so it faced her. From my vantage point, I could see it, but the girls could not. Death. I tapped the card as Zelda let it fall, and it transformed into another.

"Ah, my darling, you have drawn the de—ha ha—my darlings, zis is Temperance." She pointed to the wings on the angelic figure, and eyed me before continuing. "Zees mean your mother, she protected by guardian angel. Is Mommy sick, darling?"

The girl began to sob so deeply she could not speak. Her friend patted her around the shoulders before looking at Zelda pleadingly. "Is there anything else you can tell? Her mother has cancer. The doctors say it's not the good kind."

"No good cancers, darlings," Zelda murmured, as if discussing the weather, or what movies were playing. She shuffled and drew again. Death. This time, she lay the card down without flipping it.

"No, darling. I only see Mommy surrounded by peace and love." She reached out and patted the young girl's hand.

"I want to see the card," her friend said.

"No, you don't want to see any more cards," Zelda said, firmly.

The teen reached out to take the card and Zelda grabbed her by the wrist. Whispering, she warned the girl, "Never touch a witch's totem. Never. You understand?" The amulet that had lay fallow around her neck now crackled with fiery flame. The eye of the dragon swung heavily beneath Zelda's neck, just before her heart. The girl's hand turned white as Zelda calmly gripped her wrist like a tightening vise. "It is good thing your friend no watching you. You take her home, buy her ice cream, you watch zee chick flicks all night, okay? Tomorrow you make sure she spend lots of time with Mommy, as much time as possible, you understand?" She hissed it so angrily, the teen's face turned white. As white as her blood-deprived hand.

When the girls were gone, Zelda hopped right up. "You like a glass of mead, Friend?"

"Ah, like old times? Of course."

She brought me the goblet and I watched her face closely.

"What? You never big talker, Friend, but you come all zis way and zay nothing? Zelda not so soft, you know. Zelda take it."

I reached out for her deck and drew a card. Without looking, I knew it. Strength. As she stared at me I studied the face which had once been the model for the very card I held in my hand. "Time has changed you, Zelda, but soft isn't a word I've ever associated with you."

"You zink I should tell girl her dying mother has no hope? Share your wisdom, oh, wise one. Zelda not forget, you only one card above her in ladder. Beside, in zees many years, who to say we cards not change our aspects, eh? Are we not to grow? Or is zat only for human fools? Sometimes I think we cards biggest fools of all."

"If only I could have been permitted to be your proper teacher, Zelda. "After the lesson I'd learned at Monte Carlo, I'd never again denied a talented girl her teachings, no matter what the Merlins had to say on the matter. Still, my lessons to Zelda were behind closed doors, totally on the hush-hush, and she was never able to come out as a sorceress in training. After the Tarocco deck was published and our rogue wizard academy run out of Italy, we scattered. I was lucky to place her in a nunnery while the rebel son of the head Merlin fled to Britain with my apprentice and me.

I hadn't meant to abandon Zelda there, but when I'd come back to check on her, she was gone. She'd hidden herself well, too, taking up with the trolls and immigrating to America. Only in the past thirty years had I realized we both ended up in the same Indiana territory—me, an emissary of the new wizard order, working case files on a freelance basis, she as a...well, that was why I was here. What exactly was she doing?

"Hard for me to believe someone with Strength such as yours would be content telling five dollar fortunes to country rubes. Seems an awful waste of talent."

"Eh, what can I say? There are charms to country living, especially where no dragons, eh?" She sighed. "Even Zelda fall in love." She drew her lips tight after she said it, as if she regretted the slip.

"Zelda? In love?"

She sighed. "Yes, dahling, Zelda fall in love with little troll, dream of little gypsy-troll babies."

I couldn't help but smile. I sat the lamp on the table and the Light illuminated her face. Through the expired orange foundation, through the years of weathered skin, through the terse lips, I saw within her the same heart of the child who had refused to let her brother's sacrifice be in vain. As I watched, she produced a small polished wooden box, similar to the one which held her cards. She slid it across the table toward me.

"A gift for teacher," she said.

The Light showed me what was inside. The other eye of the dragon, the mate to the one around her neck. I opened the box and pulled it out, its pupil narrowing as it looked about the room.

"Zelda, you didn't," I said.

"I didn't kill it, no," she confessed. "Zelda only strong enough to blind dragon on her own, as a girl. Has probably died of old age by now, yes?"

"So that's where you went when I tried to reclaim you from the convent."

Her eyebrows arched. "You come back?"

"Go on and read my cards," I said. "Don't take my word for it."

"You no interfere with Zelda's reading zis time?"

"I no interfere."

"Smartass," she groaned. She flipped the first card. "Hermit. Biggie surprise. I do three card reading, okay?"

"Sure."

"Okay, zee Hermit means...well, is you, darling. Means you is painted into Tarocco deck forever, zat all of Europe knows you are rascal, are vagabond magic man. Means you no like other people—""Not true."

"No? You take up with someone new?"

I considered, for a moment, telling her about my new apprentice, Lucian; about my annual volunteerism with the League of Jolly Old Elves; that I had seen Merlin II and Merlin III recently at a wedding. The problem was, I wasn't sure if I could trust Zelda. I had never known if I could trust her. Even when she was my pupil, educating her sometimes felt like an exercise in keeping my friends close and enemies closer. I was never sure which one she was, so I always pulled her closer, just in case.

As I fingered the chain on the unblinking dragon's eye, I couldn't help but admire the person across the table, whether she was truly my friend or my foe. I might have been the teacher and she the student, but she was only a rung behind me in the Tarocco.

"Remember who you're talking to, Zelda. The Hermit is a loner. No, I haven't taken up with anyone."

She smiled, a sinister, knowing smile I never could discern. Was it sincere? Was it plotting? For all my wisdom, I could not see through her strength.

But it was this weakness keeping me distant. Not just from her, but from others. Sure, I had learned a lot, and I loved to teach. But the only way I could remain to live another day—to right another wrong—was to keep my cards close to my chest. As close as Zelda kept her dragon's eye.

She flipped another card. "Situation is...Hermit. Yes, yes, of course is Hermit, you are Hermit." She cut the cards again and drew, but did not flip. Hermit. "You mock Zelda."

"No, no, that's not my magic. I'm not doing that."

"Yes, Zelda is so sure of that! You avoid Zelda for five hundred years, then you show up and accept dragon's eye as gift and then insult Zelda in her own tent! The nerve! If you were anyone lesser I would cut that fool beard from your face!"

"Challenge is...

"Don't you 'challenge ees' me! I not read another card until you apologize." The dragon's eye around her neck flickered and seemed to vibrate subtly. I felt the one in my hand doing the same. I wasn't sure what the end result of this magic would be, but I feared it.

"Zelda, I do apologize, but I give you my word as a wizard, this disruption with the Tarocco is not of my doing. I want to see what happens next."

Zelda reached beneath the table and brought out a long cigarette holder, and a thin cigarette. She joined them, then leaned back to light her smoke on a candle. She took a luxurious drag then asked "Why? Why now?"

I spread my hands apart on the table linen, feeling the thin cloth beneath my papery skin. The printed paisley with violet and gold print on a red calico background fuzzed before me then remade itself in runes. For a moment, my eyes didn't know what I was seeing, until the ancient script clicked into place.

WHY YOU LEAVE

Zelda always had been a master at image manipulation. During the Enlightenment, she was adept at inserting her face into the paintings of many a master. She could send a message via minstrel or scroll, the messenger never quite understanding his role as conduit for her gift. I wondered if she were still up to that old magic today—if it extended to more than just runes on a tablecloth or a face on a beer sign. Truly, this woman was formidable. Should I pull her closer?

She snapped her fingers, and her television spoke in the next room. "Like sands through the hourglass," intoned the announcer, "so are the—"

"Why you abandon your pupil, teacher?"

I tapped the lantern and its brightness increased three fold. An orb burned like a miniature sun inside the cage. The dragon's eye on the table crawled slowly toward the box from whence it came. Zelda's eyes narrowed, but she continued to smoke, unmoved.

"Challenge is..." I said.

She rested the cigarette in a long, amber ashtray, and flipped the third card. Hermit.

"Is not funny, old one. Not funny." She stood. "I want you to go. Zelda no care why you came, she no care what you see. I no want to see you or anyone."

"Zelda, wait," I said. It was only then that I knew for sure why I had come. Frustration wasn't unfamiliar to me. I remembered my mistakes in Monte Carlo, my pride and arrogance, and the way I had set out on my own for far too long.

"Zelda, the Light shows me many things—some I want to see, and some I don't. It's a powerful tool, but it's not the only truth. Did you know that?" She refused eye contact for a moment, and I heard myself sigh. I took a deep breath, and continued, this time more softly. "I know you might not want to believe me, but I did come back for you. We would have slain the dragon together, my dear, but I fear you were already too strong and too bold to wait for an old man like me." I stood and moved the lantern to her side of the table. "My darling girl," I said, and she winced visibly. "You have a chance to walk a different path to wisdom than your arrogant old teacher did. This troll—he loves you?"

"I think so, yes," she whispered. Her face seemed as smooth and lineless as when she had been that little girl with the dragon's eye.

"Maybe loss and loneliness aren't the only paths to wisdom," I said. I pointed to the lamp. "My gift to you."

Zelda fell backward and nearly collapsed into her chair. The ashtray upended and her cigarette dropped to the floor. The area rug beneath it sizzled.

"Zee...Light of God?"

I stepped away from the table and headed through the curtain for the exit. "Let it light your way, my student."

"You no take your necklace?"

"You earned it, Zelda, I could never..."

She crossed the room and pressed the necklace into my hand, and her lips onto my face. She kissed me not like a needy child, but like a loving friend. For a moment, I knew I could pull her closer, but I chose instead to pat her sweet orange face and walk away.

Behind me, Zelda's television blared the start of a daytime game show. "Wheel! Of! Fortune!" the studio audience blared. Where the Wheel would take me next, I couldn't know. For the moment, I didn't want to know—I couldn't care. For that one golden moment, it was enough it had brought me here.

⊕ ⊕ ⊕

Red Tash is a journalist-turned-novelist of dark fantasy for readers of all ages. Monsters, wizards, trolls, fairies, and roller derby await you in her pantry of readerly delights. Tash is the author of the Amazon best-selling dark fantasies Troll Or Derby *and* This Brilliant Darkness; *and a columnist for both LouisvilleKY.com and InveterateMediaJunkies.com, where she does double-duty as a comic book reviewer. Tash's own work in comics is included in Scary-Art's* The Pit and the Compendium, Filthy Cake, *and is featured in Arcana Comics'* Steampunk Originals. *Prior to beginning her career in fiction, Tash wrote a nationally syndicated newspaper column on parenting and family life, among other publishing credits. A rabid social media junkie, Tash can be found on every conceivable corner of the internet, so just google her— she dares ya. Beyond writing, Tash has absolutely zero interest in anything, unless it is rehashing her glory days as rollergirl Tyra Durden of the Derby City Rollergirls & RollerCon's TeamMILF.*

You can find Red Tash at **RedTash.com**

WHEEL ⊕F F⊕RTUNE

VISTA BRIDGE

By MeiLin Miranda

THE FIRST SUICIDE ⊕FF THE VISTA BRIDGE AFTER JUANITA moved to Goose Hollow was a girl. The news said she was fifteen. Juanita didn't see her jump, but she saw police and medical examiners swarming the light rail service road where the girl landed.

The second time, a forty-seven-year-old man jumped. Juanita was waiting at the train stop nearby. She looked up, and there he stood at the railing. She felt the bad luck radiating from him even at that distance, and she wasn't surprised when he stepped over the side into the void. He landed on Jefferson Street in the middle of the morning commute. She called 911 so the cops could get there right away. No one should see that. She wished she hadn't.

Juanita had lived in Goose Hollow five months when the third, fourth and fifth jumped. The neighbors said it had always been bad, the Vista Bridge suicides, but this year was the worst. The city started scraping up funds for a barrier, but modifying beautiful, historic bridges took time. "It'll be months, maybe a year, before they finish the fence," said the man down the hall. "I'm organizing a volunteer suicide watch. Do you think that's something you'd want to do?"

County mental health trained Juanita to talk people down, and she took her place among the volunteers who walked the bridge. The first time she stopped a jumper, it was another teenaged girl. Juanita managed to touch the girl's hand, just long enough to turn her luck around. They sat holding hands on one of the concrete benches set into the bridge until the paramedics came. She listened to the girl's story: pregnancy, abandonment, and ostracism. "It's going to be okay," said Juanita, and it was. They stayed in touch. The girl's repentant parents took her back. She arranged an open adoption with an ecstatic couple, found a scholarship and started college.

The second time, a month later, Juanita offered a woman lingering near the edge a cup of coffee from her thermos. Startled, she took it; their fingers brushed, and again, it was enough. The woman went on to turn her failing business around and become a crisis counselor herself.

After she stopped the third jumper the next month, Juanita acquired a reputation.

This morning, Juanita watched alone; her partner was out sick. She didn't mind. Nothing would happen today. The odds were against it.

Juanita knew about odds. She'd worked for thirty years in a casino as a cocktail waitress before she retired. She had a reputation then, too. She'd been pretty—still was, if older—but the house didn't pay her extra for her looks.

"Table three, honey," the pit boss would murmur. "Guy in the plaid jacket."

"Do I have to?" she'd complained at first.

"Life isn't fair, Juanita, at least not here."

Juanita would walk over, tray held high, and touch Plaid Jacket's shoulder. "Can I get you a drink? They're on the house." She'd bring Plaid Jacket his rum and Coke, or just Coke if he wanted to stay sharp and keep his astonishing lucky streak going—and then he'd start losing. If Juanita liked Plaid Jacket—he'd tipped well, he'd been good to the other waitresses, or he'd just struck her as a well-meaning soul—she wouldn't touch him again. He'd walk away with about what he'd come in with, give or take. But if he didn't tip, or if he squeezed her ass, she'd bring him drink after drink, tapping his shoulder or brushing her hand against his each time, and he'd lose his shirt. No one knew why, least of all Juanita, but everyone in management knew she carried bad luck.

She never told them she could also be lucky. She didn't do it enough to raise suspicion, but often she'd see a loser, someone raw, inexperienced, over his head and radiating desperate bad luck—people's luck shone all around them. She'd touch his shoulder, bring him a drink and his luck would change enough to save him. Life wasn't fair, but it didn't need to be so harsh. Sometimes the losers quit while her touch lasted; sometimes they wouldn't. Juanita only touched the unlucky once, with one exception: a foolish woman she'd heard had come to earn enough money for a child's surgery. When the woman walked out with twice the winnings she needed, Juanita stopped her near the door. "Don't come back," she said, "don't ever come back, not here, not another casino. No gambling, ever. Your luck is played out. Got it?" The woman nodded and hurried away, still crying. Juanita never saw her again, and she wondered if there'd been a child. She never touched someone like that again.

Her own luck, she left alone. She worked hard, lived clean, and saved her money. She still got flats, had her heart broken, caught the flu, but things worked out, mostly.

Juanita talked to many people on the bridge, most just neighborhood walkers and sightseers there for the spectacular view. Of the rest who came to the Vista Bridge, some were mentally ill. More were unlucky. She couldn't help the crazy, but she could help the others.

Now, six months in, Juanita strolled along the bridge walkways in the early morning mist, her coffee thermos and some melamine cups in the bag slung at her hip. The cars hadn't started their daily trek down Jefferson Street far below, but the warning bells of the MAX trains as they pulled away from the Goose Hollow stop floated upward, their shrillness hushed in the morning air. When she looked toward the sunrise she could see the train tracks, the tall buildings downtown—you

couldn't call them skyscrapers—the luxury cars lined up on the car dealership rooftop on Jefferson Street, and trees trees trees. Somewhere in
the predawn clouds lurked Mount Hood. She loved this view, the little
city in the trees she'd adopted as hers when she'd left Las Vegas for good.

She came to the sign at the span's end reading, "We can help you
cross this bridge" with the suicide prevention number in bold. Below it,
another volunteer had taped a neon green hand-lettered sign: "Hi, you
matter! Can you talk for a second? Please?" around a big felt-tip marker
heart. Juanita turned back toward an identical set of signs at the other
end.

A woman stood near the concrete bench at the other end. Juanita
quickened her pace just enough so it wasn't noticeable; the woman might
merely be walking, and if she wasn't, Juanita running toward her might
spook her. The woman stayed where she was, hands braced on the railing, sometimes looking out at the trees and the almost-skyscrapers
and the luxury cars, and sometimes down at the train tracks and the
asphalt far beneath.

"Good morning," Juanita called. "How you doing?" The woman
turned her head, her gaze patient and expectant. "Can I get you a cup
of coffee? On the house." This didn't always work with the men, but
sometimes it made the women hesitate, at least long enough for Juanita
to get close enough for them to see and hear her more clearly. She tried
to get a read on the woman's luck, to no avail; it hid as if behind a door.
She couldn't read the woman's face, either. It constantly changed. Was
she old? Was she young? Juanita couldn't say.

The woman didn't move as she came closer. "Let's sit down and have
a cup, okay? We can talk things over," said Juanita. The woman drifted
to the bench between its two ornate lampposts and sat down. Juanita
breathed again; maybe she wasn't here to jump after all. Juanita kept her
movements deliberate and slow as she sank down next to the woman
and pulled out her thermos and a cup. Juanita believed "real" cups, not
paper cups, might make people less likely to jump. If they had a real
cup in their hands, somewhere inside they might be afraid to break it,
even though the melamine ones didn't break; she'd never thrown one

from the bridge, but that's what she'd heard. She handed the woman a steaming cup and a packet of sugar, making sure to touch her fingers.

The woman smiled and handed back the packet. "No sugar, thank you. Life is sweet enough, isn't it? Though I suppose it's bitter sometimes. It depends." Her voice bore a vague Mediterranean accent.

"Life isn't fair sometimes," agreed Juanita.

They sipped the hot coffee and looked toward the West Hills, the impending sunrise at their backs. A car passed, headed south across the bridge to the road rambling like a goat trail past the big houses of the city's well to do.

Juanita began to relax; this woman wasn't a jumper. "So can we talk a little? My name's Juanita. I'm a crisis counselor. If you're in trouble, I can help. What's your name?" The woman murmured something that sounded like Tuh-kay, and Juanita decided not to attempt it. "What brings you out this morning?"

The woman took her hand. "You do."

Juanita smiled and squeezed it back. "We're here because we care."

"Not 'we,'" said the woman, "you. You can't do this anymore, you know."

"I can't what?"

"Juanita, you have your finger on the wheel. I cannot be parceled out like this I am random."

Juanita turned away from the West Hills toward the woman, trying to gauge meaning from her expression, but it shifted from second to second. "I don't understand."

"Don't you? Think of a roulette wheel. What would your bosses do if...let's say if they knew you put your finger on the roulette wheel to make it stop where you wished it to from time to time, not where they wished it?"

"But I never did that. How do you know I worked in a casino?" Juanita tried to pull her hand from the other woman's grip, and stand, but her legs wouldn't work and her hand held fast. A car traveling northbound purred by; she briefly thought of hailing it, but what would she say?

"You never should have done it at all, you know, but those were small wheels. Cards—small things. That's all right or, at least, I can let it pass. These things you do now, these are greater things. This is the greater wheel. That's not all right. I can't let that pass."

Juanita's heart froze. "How did you find out? Did someone send you?"

"No, no. I come here for myself." The woman looked past her, and Juanita followed her gaze. The northbound car had stopped at the other end of the bridge, an expensive car like the ones on the dealership rooftop below. The driver got out and left the car running. Bad luck blackened the air around him, mingling with the exhaust. "You can't keep pouring luck like wine from cup to cup to cup," said the woman.

"You have to let me go, I have to stop him." Juanita struggled as the man walked to the railing near the far bench. She struggled as his hands flexed on the thick concrete railing. "You don't have to do this," she cried out. "I can help you, I care—"

He threw one leg over the railing, then the other, and was gone. He'd never even looked her way.

Juanita staggered a few steps toward the still-purring luxury car before she realized she could move. "Did you ever think why so many more people come here now you live nearby?" said the woman.

"You're saying I caused this? You're cruel enough to stop me from helping someone and then you have the nerve to say I caused this?" Juanita stared at the car, at the space where the man had been; sirens already wailed in the distance.

The woman walked up and took her shaking hands, turning her away from the empty car. "Not cause, so much. You just had your finger on the Wheel for too long. The number goes up, the number goes down, except when you interfere. I think perhaps it's time your finger can touch it no more. What do you think?"

Juanita stood stunned as if she'd had the wind knocked out of her. "Are you going to kill me?"

"No, no. I can't do that to you. But maybe you can/should/or will let me take this back from you. What do you think?"

"I don't even know how I got it," said Juanita. "Do you?" The woman shrugged. Juanita glanced down Jefferson Street toward the

MAX station; a small knot of commuters waited on the platform. The train would be late, but that's not why they huddled together facing the bridge. She looked back at the woman. "If you take this from me, will people stop coming up here?"

The woman shook her head. "I think people will come up here. They have since they could come up here. But maybe not so many. Or you could keep your finger on the Wheel and move away. But if you do, I think you'll keep doing this somewhere else. And I think I'll have to come again."

Juanita almost asked the woman who she was. "So what happens to me if you take it?"

"You go on as you have; you just don't get to change people's luck any more. I'll say this: you have honor. You never put your finger on the Wheel for yourself. Doing it for yourself, that's not fair, you know."

"Life isn't fair," said Juanita automatically.

"Ah," said the woman, patting Juanita's hands. "You understand."

MeiLin Miranda writes Victorianesque fantasy and science fiction from her 130-year-old house in Portland, Oregon. Her love of all things 19th century (except for the pesky parts like cholera, child labor, slavery and no rights for women) has consumed her since childhood, when she fell in a stack of Louisa May Alcott and never got up.

MeiLin has been a professional writer for most of the last 35 years, focusing on nonfiction until a cardiac arrest and near death experience in 2006 convinced her she'd better get moving if she meant to write fiction.

*You can find MeiLin at **meilinmiranda.com***

JUSTICE

JUSTICE

By Catie Rhodes

THE HARLEY'S ROAR DROWNED OUT ALL OTHER SOUNDS, and the rain drove into my face, stinging like needles. I ducked behind Wade Hill's massive back. That position treated me to yellow lines racing underneath my cowboy boots. My imagination supplied images of what the blazing asphalt could do to my skin. I forced my eyes back up just in time to see the eighteen-wheeler bearing down on us.

Not even slowing, it changed lanes and sped past. A gust of backdraft—wind and water—slammed into us, shoving us toward the gravelly shoulder where doom awaited. I sucked in my breath and tightened my knees around Wade's hips. He showed no reaction other than tightening his fists on the ridiculously high handlebars.

When the struggle ended, he half-turned and yelled over his shoulder, "You all right back there?"

"Yes," I screamed, getting a mouthful of rain. The yes was a lie.

I didn't like driving my old Chevy Nova in the rain. I loathed riding on this death machine in the midst of a late summer downpour.

"Good. Almost there."

That gave me no comfort. The mystery surrounding this journey had me on edge. I wanted to help Wade. In our short relationship, he'd been on hand every time I needed him. But this involved the Six Gun Revolutionaries, Wade's friends and sometime employers. I didn't see how much good could come of involving myself in their business. Sounded like a good way to get mashed flat.

Without warning, Wade whipped off the four-lane highway and down a blacktop side road. We traveled down that road until it dead-ended at a cattle guard and electronic gate. Wade punched in some numbers, and the gate slowly opened.

We rode down a concrete road into a grove of pines and stopped at another gate and cattle guard. This one had no keypad. Wade punched a button.

"Mojo Rider?" The voice was twangy cracker country. "You got her?"

"You see her on the security cam, don't you?" Wade's deep voice rumbled against my chest where our bodies touched. Remembering my boyfriend, a cop who'd have a conniption fit if he knew where I was, I scooted back. Dean would skin me alive if he ever found out I came out here. Then, he'd want to know everything I saw and heard. Only one solution existed: I could never tell him. Stupid and dishonest. That's me.

We rolled down a concrete driveway ending in a huge parking lot in front of a long, low, cinderblock building. The building didn't match the fancy concrete roadways, but the couple dozen motorcycles sitting out front explained them just fine. Whatever I'd expected on my first visit to the Six Gun Revolutionaries Motorcycle Club headquarters, this wasn't it.

Wade got off the motorcycle and helped me dismount. The big bike was made for a six-foot-six man, not a five-foot-nothing girl. My lips itched to ask Wade what I'd agreed to, why he said he needed my help as a friend, but the question stuck in my throat.

The battered black door of the clubhouse opened, and a grizzled, gray haired man stepped out and strode toward us, his braid slapping one tattooed arm. His gray eyes chilled me until I stood shivering in the warm summer rain. Shoving past me, he clapped Wade on the shoulder.

"Mr. Mojo Rider." The man's overly loud, rough voice reminded me of power tools with sharp edges. The two men did that thing where they sort of shake hands and sort of hug. Finally, he turned those horrible eyes back on me. "This is Peri Jean Mace?"

Wade nodded, put one hand on my back and said, "Peri, this is King Tolliver, President of the Six Guns and the person who invited you here today."

"Mr. Tolliver." I winced at the high, nervous pitch of my voice and held out my trembling hand. Tolliver snorted. He took my hand, gave it a limp pump, and dropped it. Tolliver met Wade's eyes, and something passed between the two men.

"You can trust her." Wade nodded. "I'll vouch for her."

My skin tightened, and I glanced at Wade, looking for a joke or a smile. He gave me neither.

"Get her inside." Tolliver turned and walked away.

Apprehension tightening my throat, I allowed Wade to lead me into the dark maw of the Six Gun Revolutionary clubhouse. The rumble of conversation stopped as two dozen eyes settled on us. The figures half-hidden in shadows and clouds of cigarette smoke were not the smiling lawyers and accountants who rolled into Gaslight City on their shiny Hogs with their new leather and their high-limit credit cards. These guys were the real deal.

Why the hell was I here again? Oh, yeah. I agreed to come because Wade once saved my grandmother's and my life. Helping him, if he said he needed it, was my duty as a friend. But being here brought back every rumor I ever heard about these guys. Outlaws, highwaymen, murderers, and, sometimes, philanthropists. One question stayed. What could they want with me?

King strutted to the room's center, holding four long-necked beer bottles. I didn't drink, but I figured this wasn't the time to announce that. Wade led me to the table, and I accepted the beer King Tolliver handed me. He motioned for us to sit like a nobleman bestowing favor. A man about Wade's age joined us, clapping Wade on the back as he sat. Wade smiled a real smile.

"Peri, this is Corman Tolliver, my best friend and King's oldest son. Me and Corman met in the sand."

"He means Iraq." Corman's straight white teeth and sun-damaged, heavily freckled skin gave him a rugged sexiness. His open shirt and perfectly combed goatee suggested he played it to the hilt. "Marines. Both of us."

King cleared his throat.

"Reason you're here today is my younger son, Isaac, his wife, and my grandson are missing. We'd like to use your gift to find them." King pushed his cell phone across the table. A picture of a shaggy haired man, a tattooed woman, and a grinning baby dominated the home screen.

"I'd love to help you." I paused for sincerity and to remind myself not to smile in relief. "But I can only see dead people."

"They been gone ten days." King didn't hesitate. "Isaac would-a called me by now."

What he didn't say hung in the silence. King thought his family dead, and he wanted answers. My grandmother, the only family I had, was dying of terminal cancer. I sympathized, but I still wanted to get away from this situation.

"Thing is, this doesn't work like those TV psychics. I can't just call a ghost to me, especially not someone I don't know." I glanced at Wade for help. He pressed his lips together. Oh boy.

"Peri, when I helped you last November, I was working for the Six Guns. Remember me telling you about that?" Wade's dark eyes held none of their usual mirth.

I swallowed hard and nodded. Dread settled over me, and I slumped in my chair.

"It's like this, Peri." Corman lit up a cigarette and gave me a grin that probably removed girls' pants all by itself. Too effing bad I wasn't buying. "Since Wade was working for us, we technically helped you out that night. And now we want you to help us. Understand?"

There was no acceptable answer but yes, so I said it. On cue, a guy with more body hair than a Pomeranian set a box of toys and clothes in front of me. The clunk it made on the table sounded like a gavel falling in a courtroom. Feeling eyes on me, I glanced up to see King watching. The light in his scary eyes danced. He loved this.

"One of them TV shows about psychic mediums said y'all can sometimes see the other side when you got the victims' belongings." King pulled a ruined pair of men's jeans from the box and tossed them into my lap.

I stared down at the ripped and stained material, fingering one of the holes.

"So where is he?" A hoarse voice called from the darkness.

"I've never done this before," I said. "Just give me a few seconds."

I expected to hear more catcalls, but the silence was worse. It slipped over my skin like a too-heavy coat, growing heavier with each second. I closed my eyes, trying to shake off the pressure, begging my mind to concentrate. And something spooky happened.

The room around me drifted away. The vision took me to a tree-lined roadside and into someone else's body. The jolt of unfamiliar thoughts, emotions, and someone else's aches and pains fueled my fear. My new and improved ability scared me every time it manifested itself in a different way. I concentrated on the sounds and smells, begging my mind to adjust so I could finish the task.

I willed my body to relax, counting down my inhales and exhales, and the vision took over my mind. Wind. Water running. Birds chirping. And the smell of something sharp and chemical. The man whose jeans I held and whose head I inhabited knelt on a bridge, looking into some clear water running over white rocks. I slipped into Isaac's mind, moaning as his emotions merged with mine.

Fear and worry. Mostly worry. A baby cried in the background. It was the source of the worry. Isaac feared what would happen to the baby, but he accepted his death. Legs surrounded him, hands held him against the concrete guardrail. Through the legs, I saw part of a long, green sign, the kind marking a creek or river. "eeping Woma"

Something bright exploded behind my eyes, and I jerked back into my body.

The room's silence was different now, worse. It was shocked.

"Wow. She looked like she was havin' some kinda fit." This from yet another voice.

King's head snapped up, and he pointed a finger into the crowed. "Shut up. Now." He turned his dead eyes on me, turning his rough voice into a soft croon. "What did you see, baby?"

I cringed at the pet name coming from this man and told him exactly what I saw, describing the words on the sign with as much care as possible.

"eeping Woma?" King squinted at me, unhappy with the little bit of nothing clue to his son's whereabouts.

"It was part of a word. I could see other letters, but the angle was wrong." I took out a cigarette, but my hands shook too bad to light it. King lit it for me, staring into my eyes. His eyes held almost as much emotion as a lizard's.

"Might know where that's at." The owner of the hoarse voice approached the table. The name on his vest was Trench Coat. I didn't want to think about how he got it.

"Oh yeah?" King acknolwedged Trench Coat with a disinterested nod.

"I grew up in Bandera. Used to be a place right outside the county line called Weeping Woman Creek. Nothing out there back then. We'd go to drink and party."

"This makes sense." Corman leaned across the table. "They were headed west, gonna take Justice to see Ashley's mom." He grabbed a faded, stained map off the table and traced a route with one freckled finger. "Her mom lives in Edwards County. Right here." He tapped the map. "See? They'd have gone that way."

"That's Holy Roller Country." Trench Coat probably hadn't seen his dick in years if his huge belly was any indication. "Think those sumbitches got 'em?"

That inspired a low rumble throughout the room.

"So where is Weeping Woman Creek?" Corman had more finesse

than his father, but his tone of voice indicated his patience was headed the way of the dinosaur.

"Right here." Trench Coat pointed one dirty finger at the map.

"My boy's dead?" King narrowed his eyes and pinned me with his arctic stare.

I closed my eyes. "Probably. They either hit him or shot him in the head. If you ain't heard from him in ten days…"

"We'll go there," Corman said. "Find Justice. Maybe Ashley. See what those fucking Holy Rollers had to do with this."

I sagged with relief, grateful to see this little job done and me no worse for the wear. I turned to Wade, expecting to see his grin, to see him standing, ready to take me out of here. Instead, he hunched over the table, holding his beer in both hands.

"She needs more clothes if we're riding that far. Dry ones."

I could have cried. Defeated, I sat at the table tracing the names carved into it while the men looked for clothes.

I found myself wearing a pair of assless leather pants over my jeans, a dry t-shirt scented with cheap men's cologne, and a beat up denim button down shirt. Wade found a woman's leather jacket and told me I'd want it after dark, especially if it rained.

"I don't understand why I have to go." I didn't want to ride motorcycles all the way to the Hill Country in the gray rain. Especially not with the Six Gun Revolutionaries. I wanted to be at my grandmother's house, exchanging pornographic text messages with my boring cop boyfriend. Guilt for running off with Wade ate at me. If something happened to me, what would my grandmother do?

"Because you ain't finished finding Isaac and his family yet. And you ain't figured out who's responsible." Wade stuffed the leather jacket into his fiberglass saddlebag. He looked up from his task and winced at the expression on my face. He put his hand on my arm. "I'm sorry about this. But there's nothing I can do that won't make things worse. And I couldn't blow them off. Please try to understand."

"How'd you get involved with them?" I leaned close to him and pitched my voice low. He sighed and crossed his arms over his chest.

"Met Corman in Iraq. Became friends. We saved each other's asses a few times. Got home, my girl had married another guy, and there wasn't much to ground me to civilian life. I got in trouble." He watched me. "Corman and King got me out of it. Understand?"

"Yeah." I knew about that kind of trouble.

Wade leaned in close. I noticed, for the first time, his black beard had threads of gray running through it.

"I'll make you a promise," he said in a near whisper, his breath tickling my face. "You will get out of this alive. Or we'll both be dead because they'll have to kill me first. You're the first real friend outside these dudes I've had in a long time, and I will take care of you."

There was nothing else to say. Wade threw his leg over his big two-wheeler. I climbed on behind him. Around us, more Six Gun Revolutionaries mounted their bikes. Several other members loaded a white paneled van nearly hidden at clubhouse's edge.

King and Corman walked to their bikes, positioned closest to the mouth of the concrete parking lot. Movements around us grew frenzied as the other men finished their preparations. The air stilled in anticipation.

King mounted his bike first and hit the starter. The engine turned over on the first try and killed the silence. Maybe one second passed before the air boomed with deafening mechanical thunder.

Wade turned to me, his face split by the widest of grins. Cupped in his palm was a set of orange earplugs. I took them gratefully and shoved them in my ears. They blunted the noise but did not erase it

The sound vibrated every inch of my body, all the way to the root of every hair follicle. In perfectly timed intervals, the Six Gun Revolutionaries took off in staggered pairs. By the time we got to the main highway, the noise and the utter intensity of it swallowed me. I was in the belly of the monster.

After three hours, my toes went numb. After five hours, my back ached, and I'd learned I could sleep with my forehead pressed between Wade's shoulders. His light pat on my knee woke me from a half doze in which I dreamed of a place that didn't vibrate or smell like gasoline, or hot tire rubber. He pointed at the Bandera county limits sign as we passed it.

We slowed, and I became aware of the roar of a motorcycle approaching fast. The guy who went to high school in Bandera flew past us, leaning over his handlebars, his wild hair flying behind him like a flag. He took the lead position and led us through the town's main street where tourists dressed in bright colors pointed and waved. The Six Guns grinned and waved back.

We found our way to the two-lane road in my vision and pulled to a stop in front of the sign reading "Weeping Woman Creek." The motorcycles shut off one here and one there until all were silent. Even in the silence, my ears rang.

Wade helped me off the motorcycle, and it was all I could do not to rock, imitating the constant motion of the last few hours. King and Corman came straight at me, both faces set in grim lines. Corman snatched my arm and dragged me to the bridge from my vision. I jerked out of his grip and went to the spot where Isaac, the man in my vision, had knelt. A rust colored stain peppered the white rocks in the creek bed. I gestured at it. Corman and King crowded next to me.

"Where is my brother, ghost girl?" Corman barked the words at me.

I ignored him and opened my second sight, something I'd been learning to do, and scanned the area. The white sand on the ground hurt my eyes in the late afternoon sun. I squinted into the shadows, praying I found King's missing family. And fast. King and Corman's veneer of nice could wear off any second, and I didn't want to be around when it did.

I didn't want to see a child's ghost, but I looked for a smaller figure thinking the spirit of a baby might be confused enough to hang around. The thought of a child hurt over Six Gun Revolutionary business sickened and angered me. But the thought of what the Six Guns might do if I didn't fulfill my end of our bargain worried me more. I believed Wade. He'd die fighting for me. But he would die. Then, I would, too. I had to make myself do this thing, like it or not.

A movement in the monochrome shadows caught my eye. The

apparition flickered and jerked, flitting at the edge of my field of vision. I motioned at King and Corman and headed toward the shadow, sliding down the rocky embankment in my hurry.

"Show us," I called out to Isaac's ghost, knowing he would take us to his earthly remains. Despite the heat, a cool otherworldliness burned at me, and I shivered in my damp clothes. Isaac's ghost appeared a few feet away, and I led my entourage along, dread at what I was about to see beating at me.

Poor Isaac. He looked no older than thirty, my age. Further proof I could meet an end like this, maybe today. Fifty more steps, and we stood before his corpse. Animals had been at him, but the fist-sized hole in his head was done by a man. The wind shifted, and the stench hit me. A low moan went up from the men around me, and I covered my face.

The hum of flies a few feet away drew my attention. Shouldn't they be here with Issac? I broke off from the pack and walked a few feet deeper into the woods, whispering a mantra of "please not the baby." What I saw struck me speechless.

I barely recognized Ashley from the photo on King's phone. Scavengers had picked away half the skin on her face and one eye. Her captors had tied her to a tree. The splash of blood on her inner thighs suggested they'd done quite a bit to her after tying her up. I backed away, holding my hands over my mouth, the horror of her last minutes playing in my mind

King approached me, stepping into my personal space. He yanked me against his chest, which was like hitting a brick wall. "Where's my grandson? Where's Justice?"

I shook my head, unable to speak. He was about to hurt me, and there was nothing I could do to stop him. A hand closed around my arm and jerked me away from King.

"Don't touch her. She ain't property of this club. She's helping us." Wade's calm voice carried only an edge of menace. That small rebuke made the men around us stiffen, some of them reaching into waistbands for weapons.

"Forget it, Daddy." Corman plucked something from the scrub grass near the body and stood, holding it up. A silver cross. "Holy Rollers. One of them must have lost it in the struggle. Bet they got Justice."

What struggle? In the vision, King's other son hadn't struggled at all. He'd been resigned to his fate, only worried about his wife and son. And how much of a struggle had poor Ashley put up? Finding that cross was awfully convenient, but I sure as hell wouldn't argue about it. The sooner I got out of this situation, the better.

"Sonsabitches. Bet they want money to get him back." King narrowed his eyes. "All right. Teeter and Mook is behind us in the van. Then, we're gonna get those fuckers."

I glanced at Wade, silently asking if we could leave. He gave me a slight nod. I edged toward him. About halfway there, my cell phone rang. All eyes turned to me, and I wished I could shrink into a little ball. I groaned and punched the ignore button. The phone immediately began ringing again.

"Answer it." I didn't even see who gave the order. With all those mean eyes boring into my skin, I just did it."Oh god, please don't take my baby." The woman's scream roughened voice raised the hair on the back of my neck. Helplessly, I hit the speakerphone button and held up the phone. "Don't do that. No, please, no. I never would've called you if I'd realized it was going to be like this."

King cut through the cluster of men, elbowing people out of his way and snatched the phone from me and held it close to his ear.

"Somebody shut her up." The male voice sound cold, calm, as if he listened to women beg every day. The sound of flesh striking flesh came over the speaker, and I swallowed hard, desperate to get away from this scene, these people. The call ended.

Conclusions and questions raced through my mind. Of course, Ashley couldn't have called me. She was dead right in front of us. I'd never had a ghost call my cell phone. It might have been funny had it not scared me so damn bad.

"She knew who killed Isaac," one of the men said.

"Sounds to me like she set it up," another voice said.

King and Corman exchanged a glance. Betrayal, especially from a woman, threw their authority into question. The air grew pregnant with tension. Wade gripped my arm and pulled me against him.

"I think I recognized that voice, and it ain't no Holy Roller." The young man speaking only had part of the Six Gun Revolutionaries emblem on the back of his jacket. His patch read "Prospect". I knew enough about this culture to understand he was new, trying to earn full membership.

Corman appeared next to the younger man. "Who is it Dolan?"

"I think it's Ashley's brother. I talk to him every month when I pick up..." He glanced at me and gulped. "Shipments in Austin."

King's gaze shot to me and then back at Dolan who nearly cowered. He'd given away something in front of an outsider. The little turd just put me in more danger from these thugs. Idiot. I wanted to kick the shrimpy little fool where it hurt.

"How sure are you?" Corman gripped Dolan's shoulder and spoke kindly, playing good cop to King's bad cop.

"Sure as I can be." Dolan swallowed hard, and a bead of sweat rolled down his forehead and dripped off his jawbone. "They got a place somewhere out here. Just don't know quite where it is."

"Toad went to school with Ashley," Corman said. "He's at work, but I can call him."

"Do that," King said and turned to me. "I heard you date a cop."

King held my eyes. In that second, I thought my fate was sealed. I knew something about shipments. I knew the Sixguns planned on making their own justice for Isaac's—and now probably Ashley's—murder. Begging wouldn't do any good. All I could do was act tough and hope it worked.

"You think I'd tell him about today?" I didn't have to fake my sarcastic snort. "He hates Wade already. This would be all he'd need to—"

"You don't need to say more." King held up his hand. You're loyal to Mojo Rider, and he says you're good, and I trust him with my life."

His locked onto mine, pinning me where I stood. My upper lip prickled as sweat broke out on it. King smiled, and his eyes drifted lazily over me, more to let me know he owned me for the day than out of attraction. "Unless you double cross me, you ain't got nothing to fear."

Corman, still on his call, turned a slow circle in the road, looking all around with a disbelieving expression on his face. A crack of gunfire echoed through the woods, and Corman dove off the road, stuffing his phone into his pocket. We all ducked behind the scant cover of the motorcycles. All of us, except for Wade. He slipped a sawed-off shotgun from one of the fiberglass saddlebags on his cycle. I cringed at the expression in his eyes. Amusement. Mischief. He put one finger to his lips and winked at me. Then, he slipped into the woods, walking in a half crouch.

I leaned against the motorcycle, wondering if he'd come back. Our young friendship gave me no indication of the odds. If he didn't come back, I'd be stuck with these men. I glanced around me at the dirty faces. Muscles clenched, I sank against the motorcycle and tried to think of what to do next. No plan magically presented itself to me. I wondered if a swan dive into Weeping Woman Creek would break my neck.

By the time I saw Wade dart through the deepening shadows, my shoulders were tight enough to throb. I pushed myself up and strode over to where he met King and Corman. They scowled at me, and I hunched my shoulders and crossed my arms over my chest but did not retreat. I caught the last of Corman's sentence.

"From what Toad says, their house is right through them woods."

"Then, they're the skinny-assed tweakers playing with guns." Wade's eyes sparkled. He was enjoying this. No matter how sorry he was to involve me, he loved the risk. "They don't even know we're here."

"So that's the murderers shooting?" Between the stress and the casual acceptance of the day's surreal events, I was fed up. Corman and King turned to sneer at me. I sneered right back. "Don't look at me that way. This is crazy. How can you act like this is normal?"

"It ain't so crazy." King put his hand on Corman's arm. "Ashley's been trying to get away from us. We told her to go, but she couldn't take Justice. She must've planned this trip so her brother and his tweaker friends could ambush them."

"Only thing, she didn't realize her tweaker brother done lost his grip on reality." Corman said. "Smokes most of what he cooks." He gave me a grin just like his father's. Fear chased away my righteous indignation, and I shrank back from him.

"I'm guessing he sold her to his friends. Carpet sharks'll do shit like that." King watched me through half-lidded eyes. "You know, get desperate and sell out their own. But, now, we gonna make things right and you gonna help."

"I overheard them talking." Wade told me. "They got Justice, and they're waiting for a baby broker to come pick up him and pay for him."

"So, Miss Peri, you going in to get my grandson." King said. "Nobody here knows you, and you can get Justice out of there safely."

"No," I said. "They have guns. They might decide to shoot me. Or tie me to a tree and rape me to death."

The cold-eyed monster who'd peeked out of King's face all day took over. He jabbed a finger into my chest, hard, and I resisted the urge to reach up and rub the sore spot.

"You will do this. Mojo here risked his life to save you and your granny's life last year. And you'll do this for me." He leaned into my face, so close his sour, cigarette-tinged breath nearly gagged me. "You hear me?"

I wanted to fight, to claw at his face, maybe even bite him. But any fight I started would end badly. One glance at Wade's face, full of dark, primitive anger, told me he was ready to fight for me if I wanted it. That sealed it. I was stuck.

"I'm going in with you," Wade said.

"What? No you're not." Corman narrowed his eyes at Wade. "Let her go alone."

"Oh, yes I am." Wade glared at Corman. "You're the one who wanted to bring her into this. I will do everything I can to keep her safe. And I'll beat you senseless if you try to stop me."

When the sky started to darken, we met the chaser van on a side road. Four club members, including Corman and King, crouched in the back amidst an arsenal. Wade rode shotgun, and Corman called out directions as I drove.

The indigo sky and blazing sunset hung over us. Was it the last beautiful thing I'd see? I didn't fear death or dying, but I'd never told my boyfriend "I love you" even though I did, and my grandmother didn't need the shock of me dying. If I left the earth this night, it would be with a heart full of regret over missed opportunities.

I found the turnoff easily enough and drove up to a turn-of-the-century rock house. A curtain twitched in the window, and nervous bile stung my throat. Showtime.

"All right," King said. "Y'all go on up, tell him you're there for the kid."

"Once he goes to get Justice, we'll exit the van," Corman said. "So be sure to leave the door partially open."

"Get the kid back to the van and wait for us," King said. "I'll signal if we want you to just go on and meet us back where we left the others. Understand?"

Wade and I both said we did and glanced at each other. The fear had left Wade's face. In its place was the same wild mischief I saw when we heard the gunshots on the road. I hoped he knew how to keep us from getting killed. Because I sure as hell didn't. I was so far out of my element, I might as well have been in a foreign country.

We got out of the van, both of us leaving our doors half open, and approached the house. The horrific situation had a dreamlike quality. As we crossed the plank porch, I reminded myself this was really happening. I knocked while Wade took a position where he couldn't be seen from the peephole.

A dude so skinny every rib plus his sternum was visible answered the door. He picked at a nasty scab on his chest and seemed to vibrate in place. When he realized I was female, his face slipped into a nasty leer. Wade stepped forward. Then, he turned sullen. "Whatchu want?"

"I'm here for the kid." I pulled the wad of cash King gave me from the pocket of my jeans and held it where the man could see it. His eyes widened, and he licked his lips. Damn, that was easy.

He needed some gank so he could think straight. He'd promise me anything to get it. I suppressed an eye roll. I had enough of this shit with my ex-husband to last a lifetime. My impatience took over.

"Get the kid," I said. He reached for the money, and I shock my head. A guy who'd let his sister be killed would sell his nephew as many times as he could.

The guy walked away without another word. Footsteps crunched on the ground behind us, and a warm body pressed against my back.

"What'd he say?" Corman's hot breath on my ear made me want to jerk away, but I didn't dare. The odor of gun oil on whatever he carried reminded me why I'd do as told.

"He's getting Justice." My heart thudded so hard I thought I'd pass out.

"Fucker," King snorted from somewhere behind me. "Double crossing bastard."

Anticipation spurred the adrenaline until I shook. Behind me, Corman inhaled deeply. I stood rooted to the spot, too freaked out to do anything else. After an eternity full of scary thoughts, the door swung open again. The guy stood before us holding a sleepy-eyed toddler. The kid's eyes widened at the sight of his grandfather and uncle, and he grinned and held out his arms, saying something I couldn't understand in baby talk.

"Take him." King shoved me toward the kid, and I did as he said, ignoring the angry shrieks and wiggling you'd expect from a scared kid being grabbed by a stranger.

Wade grabbed my arm and yanked me off the porch. Justice made a high-pitched sound I couldn't believe came from a human being. He kicked me so hard it was all I could do to hang on. I wondered if I really wanted kids after all.

Behind me, the tweaker babbled explanations, his words running together. I tried not to listen. The first gunshot echoed through the night air, and his body thudded to the floor. I forced myself to keep my eyes forward.

"Can you drive? I'm shaking too hard." I shifted Justice higher on my hip. His bucking had nearly dislodged him. All I could manage was getting one foot in front of the other as gunfire and screams played like the soundtrack of a made-for-TV war flick behind us.

"Yep. Just get in the passenger side." Wade's calm voice raked over my raw nerves, stinging like acid. I wanted him to freak out, too, but he wasn't going to. No telling what he saw or did in Iraq.

Sitting in the van, Justice's wails straining my eardrums, I had no choice but to look at the house. Flames now flickered behind the windows, and dark figures moved through the flames. Black smoke billowed out the open front door. Just as the flames grew so bright I thought King and Corman had fallen prey to their own mess, four silhouettes came from around the side of the house, carrying arm-loads of packages. Wade and I both stared straight ahead as they got into the van.

"Grampy! Did you hear the fireworks?" Justice scrambled back to his grandfather, his fit forgotten. Without his frightened wails, the roar of the fire didn't sound so bad.

"Go," Corman yelled as flames began to wink through the house's roof. Wade drove away, never speeding or showing nervousness, even when a fire truck sped toward us, its lights flashing.

The atmosphere at the meet-up point was one of victorious excitement. Sirens still wailed in the not so far distance. Nobody but me seemed to notice or care.

The club invited Wade and I to join them at an RV park owned by friends in Blanco County for a party. Wade thanked them but said he needed to get me back home to my boyfriend.

"That's right," Corman said. "You gonna tell Mr. Cop what you saw tonight?"

"What for?" Fatigue had eaten through my fear. I no longer cared what this outlaw did or said to me. I just wanted sleep. "I'd be in just as deep of shit as you guys."

Everybody in earshot howled as though I'd told the funniest joke in the world. Corman never cracked a smile.

"You just keep remembering that." He leveled his cold eyes at me, and chill bumps raced over my skin. King clapped Corman on the back hard enough to set him off balance.

"Get over yourself, boy. She's a friend of the club now…our pet freak, just like Mojo Rider there." King stepped forward and took my hand again. This time he kissed it, rolling his eyes up to mine and slipped me a pornographic wink. "You have a good ride home." To Wade, he said, "Thanks for making this right."

Pet freak? What did that mean? I glanced at Wade and took note of the way he cast his gaze down. Laughing, Corman and King walked away from us. Wade visibly relaxed, moving his hand away from his hip pocket. "Let's go home."

We locked eyes, and I knew I wouldn't ask about the freak remark. There was a time and a place for everything. It would come up eventually. I took one last look at the toddler sitting on someone's motorcycle. Dressed in a tiny leather jacket and cap, he laughed and clapped, completely comfortable in this environment.

I wondered what would become of the little boy named Justice. He had no choice but to grow up one of the Six Gun Revolutionaries. They'd teach him their customs and rituals, how they evened scores. One day, he'd be a king of this world, of these people. I doubted he'd handle things much differently than his uncle and grandfather.

"Do you think that kid got justice today?" I walked with Wade to his motorcycle. I put my hand on his shoulder and swung my leg over the bike.

"I think justice is different things to different people," Wade said. "Sometimes all you can say is you lived to meet another dawn."

This day taught me more about Wade than a million conversations could have. Despite the discomfort and danger of this lifestyle, I understood the draw.

It was right there in front of me. The road stretching out before us promised endless possibility. It held invitations of adventure and romance, the perfume of oil, gasoline, and leather its own kind of aphrodisiac. Out here with the wind in my face and the thrum of power between my legs, justice was defined by the moment. Worries about incarceration and death mattered in another world. And that's why I let the subject drop and closed my eyes and let the road roll underneath the tires.

⊕ ⊕ ⊕

Catie Rhodes grew up in the piney woods of East Texas where there wasn't much to do other than daydream and make up stories. From that dark and shadowy world come both her Peri Jean Mace Paranormal Mysteries and her horror short stories.

Catie is that kid your mother warned you about. She lies. She cusses. She never washes her hands after petting the dog. And she still wears checkered Vans.

She lives with her husband and little dog in the overcrowded and overly noisy Houston, Texas suburbs.

*Find out more about her at **catierhodes.com**.*

THE HANGED MAN

PATH OF SACRIFICE

By Matthew Bryan

SUBDUED LIGHT GLINTED OFF THE SHORT BLACK HORNS rising from the forehead of the demon. He sat, almost lost in the tall-backed, overstuffed arm chair, waiting. Calm, even features gave no evidence of the turmoil roiling behind his green-slitted eyes. He barely twitched at the quiet knock on his chamber door.

He glanced toward the unwanted intrusion then looked over the room. Everything was as it should be, no evidence of any forbidden contraband visible. *Who could be at my door this late?* He rose slowly, careful to not make a sound as he slipped into a crouch toward the locked and barred door. He listened for a moment, wishing he had put surveillance cameras in the hall when he had done the rest of his chambers. It was a minor regret on a long list and far from the greatest, so with a shrug he straightened up and opened the door.

"Quick," the figure said, slipping past Mkai.

He quickly looked up and down the corridor before quietly closing the door, locking and barring it again out of habit. He turned to his late night visitor, allowing a tired smile to form on his lips.

"What is it Fsol?" he said, "And why are you creeping around?"

"You wouldn't believe what I just found out. I came straight here, as quickly as I could." Fsol said, dropping onto the couch. "You'll understand why when I tell you what I learned."

"That sounds ominous. Have you been snooping around where you shouldn't again?" Mkai said, resuming his seat. "You know it has become far more dangerous now with our new queen."

"Old habits and all that. I think you'll agree that it was worth it," Fsol said, leaning forward. "I found out why Kalia has ordered us to Earth. Why the urgency to corrupt and convert as many humans as we can."

He licked his lips, the forked tip appearing for a flash before disappearing behind jagged fangs. Sweat beaded on scaled skin as Fsol fidgeted in his seat before sliding to the edge to lean even closer to Mkai.

"She is planning war. War with Heaven. She is determined to succeed where Samael failed."

Mkai's heart thudded hard in his chest as he fell back in his chair.

"War with Heaven? Is she insane?" he said, instinct keeping his voice low as he spoke words of treason. "Samael didn't even war directly and look at the result. Even those, like us, who didn't side directly with him were thrown from His Grace. What does she hope to accomplish?"

"That is what sent me running here old friend." Fsol said, excitement stealing over his face. "She has a plan, and I think it might work."

Samael had a plan as well.

"What's her plan? How does she expect to succeed where Samael failed so drastically?"

"The souls. She will build an army of the Damned and with them, invade Heaven. She will tear down the Gates of Heaven and bring us unto His Light, with the souls of His favorites to lead the way."

Silence crept across the room as Mkai worked through the news. It was audacious, but Mkai felt in his bones this plan of Kalia's would indeed succeed. *At least in getting us into His presence, but what's to stop*

Him from simply destroying us? It was a sobering thought. *His favorites may very well lead us into Heaven, but could also lead us to oblivion.*

"I can see how it may work" he said, choosing his words carefully, "But I don't think it will be as easy as that."

"There is more to her plan but I didn't catch it," Fsol said. "They moved out of range."

"They? Who was with her?" Mkai asked. "Where were they?"

"Her throne room. I found an old abandoned passage and it led to a tiny room above her throne. That's where I heard everything And who else but Kalia's shadow, Lilith."

"You know what they would have done to you if you were caught?" Mkai shook his head. "One day your habits will get you killed."

"But not today, brother." Fsol grinned and sat back. "So, what do you think?"

Mkai thought for a moment, mind whirling with possibilities. He looked at his friend, wondering how much to gamble.

"I think you need to show me this passage. Our entire existence could be at risk and I, for one, am not willing to trust Kalia has our best interests at heart." He knew he risked charges of treason with such a statement, even one made to his oldest friend."Of course. Let's go." Fsol stood. "It's a rather cleverly hidden passage and, if we're careful, no one will ever catch us."

I hope not. This could be more important than Fsol knows. Mkai followed him through the door, flipping a switch to turn on his hidden cameras.

⊕ ⊕ ⊕

An hour later found Mkai back in his favorite chair. Fsol had shown him the passage and the chamber at its end, the only light streaming from the throne room below. A quick glance had shown it was empty, not a surprise this late. They agreed to take turns watching to try to discover more of Kalia's plans and had separated. Mkai returned to his room, mind churning over the risks Kalia was taking.

Once settled in his chair, he couldn't stop his mind from falling, spiraling down dark and painful memories. With a resigned sigh, he stood and made his way to the empty hearth. Mkai had never lit it, mainly because the temperature in Hell was already hot enough. But mostly because he was heartsick of fire. Outside his chambers, fires burned everywhere he turned. The smell of sulfur and the crackling roar of flames assaulted his senses. Silence reigned and he found his need for quiet growing stronger every day. It had been too long since he had been back to Earth.

He reached out, pushing and twisting certain stones until, with a click, the mantle front dropped, swinging free on its hinge. He gazed at the few items hidden so carefully. Possession of them under Samael's rule didn't mean much. Perhaps a short time banished, not really a punishment to Mkai. But under Kalia's harsh new laws, owning contraband meant severe punishment. Loss of a limb, torture and death were all possible. Regardless of the jeopardy, he knew he could never get rid of them.

He picked up a child's soot-covered doll, the beautifully carved face chipped, paint worn to a faint memory. His heart cramped in his chest and he had to clench his jaws to stop the sob of grief from escaping. Mkai fought a losing battle against the memories handling the doll always brought. Part of God's punishment. Banishment from His Light wasn't enough. Nor was He satisfied with the twisted and marred forms He forced upon those who dared question Him.

No. His greatest punishment was the *gift* of perfect memory. Every moment of his existence was etched into Mkai's mind, just waiting for him to turn his attention to it. Thus it was handling the doll brought the exact memory of burnt flesh to his nostrils, the cries of terror and pain assaulting his ears. He dropped to his knees, body wracked with silent grief.

Three hundred years gone and her memory still tore at him. The tiny waif had captured his heart from the very moment he saw her in the park and, without realizing it, he had broken his first rule of dealing with humans. Distance. It was the only thing that kept him sane. With an existence spanning eons, the short life spans of the humans he watched flickered like candles in a night's breeze. Distance was all that kept their loss from scarring too deeply.

But not that day. There was no way to guard his heart against the innocence of the child's questions. Four short days later, it all disappeared in a gout of fire and smoke as the girl and her entire family were killed, murdered in a ploy by Mkai's bitter rival, Ortag.

He arrived at the park to meet the child. When he couldn't find her, Mkai set off to the rundown building her family shared with several others. It wasn't long before he caught the stench of burning and made out the column of smoke slowly building in the distance. Heart plummeting, he ran the rest of the way. Bolting around the corner, the terrifying scene before him dropped him to his knees. Three houses were engulfed in flames, screams of terror and pain audible over the roar of the inferno. He knew it was his imagination, always trouble for him, but even now, centuries later, he swore he heard her clear voice calling out his name.

Mkai stood there for hours while the fire burned, the humans scuttling around attempting to stop the fire from spreading. Almost the entire block was lost, but all he cared about was that one single house. It was obvious to one so accustomed to fire and its methods her house had been the center. Walking through the ruins later, it was also obvious it was no accident.

The doll was all he was able to salvage from the ruin. In the midst of the burnt out wreckage, he had sworn vengeance on who he knew was responsible. Ortag. Rivals even before the fall, their hatred only grew stronger through the long years since. They rarely struck directly at one another, but that day Mkai let his anger loose. Ortag paid for his actions with the loss of an eye before Samael had decreed against death challenges.

Mkai shook himself free of the memories and stood once more. He carefully placed the doll back in its spot, smoothing its dress before closing up the hidden drawer again. He laid his hand on the mantle and silently sent up a prayer to the child and her family before turning to his bedroom. His dreams that night were tormented by screams and fire and him running, always running, but never getting anywhere.

⊕ ⊕ ⊕

Mkai woke hours later, eyes gritty and body sore from the restless sleep. He forced himself to dress, throwing lukewarm water on his face before slipping out of his rooms. He barely remembered to turn on his security as he left on his way to the hidden chamber. It was his turn and he was hoping to find out more about Kalia's plans.

He retraced his steps from the night before and slipped into the hidden passage without running into anyone. The quiet echo of his footsteps kept him company as he walked down the twists and turns until stepping into the small chamber, dimly lit from below. He made his way to the small crack in the base of the wall and carefully laid down, peeking into the room below.

Mkai smiled grimly at his luck. Kalia stood at a small table, almost directly below him, the demon Lilith beside her. Their beauty struck him for a moment and he again marveled that such twisted evil could be hidden beneath such a facade. He shook the thoughts loose and focused on the two below.

"Mistress, how can you be sure?" Lilith said, her velvet tones a caress to Mkai's ears.

"I have sources beyond you. Trust me when I say it's true." Kalia answered pouring water into a glass, frost crawling across its side. "He is on earth and he must be found. The only other piece of information I could learn was he is in Los Angeles."

"I accept it is as you say, but how can we be expected to find a single man when that is all we know? We do not know his age, his race, what he looks like, not even his name."

"It is a daunting task, I am aware," Kalia said harshly. "But it will be done. He will be found."

Mkai saw Lilith stand up straighter, the jut of her full breasts drying his mouth. Lilith had that effect on every male, demon and human alike. He didn't blame the humans for their obsession with her.

"Yes, Mistress, word has been sent out to look for a male in his midtwenties and he will be found, but it may take time." Mkai saw her pause and lick her full lips before continuing. "But I do not understand why he is so important."

"Because of who he is, more than for his gifts. We must find him and you, with your own gifts, will convert him to our cause. Then he will lead our army unto his Father's gate and Heaven will be ours."

Mkai's heart almost stopped when he realized what he was hearing. God had sent His Son once more to earth and, somehow, Kalia knew. For a moment, he wondered where she got this information, but the intensity in her voice left no doubt it was true. He shivered at the thought. God's Son leading her armies to heaven could indeed win her the war.

Kalia and Lilith were still speaking but Mkai tuned them out, mind whirling. He stood, careful to not make a sound and slipped down the corridor heading back to his chambers. He had a lot to think about and decisions to make and not a lot of time.

He hurried down the passage, barely taking a moment to ensure that there was no one around before ducking out into the hall. Mkai made his way to his rooms, mind full of possibilities.

Once locked securely inside, he dropped into his chair, heart heavy in his chest He was faced with a choice, again. Millennia ago he had been forced to make the same decision. He had made the wrong one then, even if not consciously. Did he have the courage to do what was right this time? Hours later, his hopeless quest for an answer was interrupted by a quiet knock. He couldn't summon even a small smile when the door swung open to reveal Fsol.

"We need to talk."

Mkai thought about the coincidence of Fsol appearing now. But this time it was Mkai with news to share.

"There was nothing going on in the throne room so I thought I'd come and see if you had heard anything."

"Sit my friend. I did indeed hear something. As large, if not larger, than the news you first brought me." Mkai took a seat across from his friend. A jab in the back made him realize he had been so preoccupied that he hadn't even put his weapons away. He shook himself mentally and leaned forward, beckoning Fsol closer.

"I heard the rest of her plan. And I think she is indeed insane."

"Why? What did I miss?" Fsol said , seriousness stealing away the small grin ever present.

"There is a search going on as we speak. A search for one man." Mkai paused and took a deep breath before exhaling slowly. "They are search- ing for the Son of God who has been sent to offer salvation to mankind once more. They intend to have Lilith seduce and corrupt Him and in doing so, convert Him to their cause. And he will lead them into Heaven."

The rush of words seemed to have a physical impact on Fsol, pushing him back into the couch. His eyes went wide and unblinking from shock. Mkai let his friend absorb what he'd said for a moment before continuing, only then realizing that there was no choice for him. There never was.

"He is in Los Angeles and they are hunting him. I intend to go there, this very night, and I will find As'hame of the As'rai protecting the city and I will tell him everything. And," he paused, amazed at how calm he felt, "I will ask him to let me join him."

His quiet statement of defiance struck his friend hard and Mkai watched as Fsol stood and started pacing before the empty hearth.

"How can you do such a thing?" Fsol finally asked stopping and sit- ting once more. "This could work! We could win Heaven! Why would you risk it all? The As'rai destroy us when they can, why do you think this As'hame will be any different?"

Mkai shrugged. "He may not be, but I think, of them all, he will give me space to speak. Once he hears all I know, I think he will accept me. If not, he may destroy me. It matters not, my friend. I have had my fill of this existence. I'm tired. So very tired. As long as he listens to me and acts to prevent this from happening, I don't care if he kills me. As long as he listens."

"But why?"

Mkai gestured. "Aren't you tired of all of this?"

"How can you be so short sighted? We could win Heaven! And you would ruin our chances?" Fsol said, anger lacing his voice.

"Because I chose wrong last time, as did you. We have a chance to make up for it this time. Come with me, my friend." Mkai implored, "Come with me and help me save the world."

"No!" Fsol cried, "I can't see any reason to risk all we could win for the barest hope."

Heart breaking, Mkai watched his oldest friend, the closest to a true brother he had ever had, begin pacing in front of the empty hearth. He was getting more worked up with each step and it was then Mkai realized one of them would not leave this room. He sighed to himself and slowly stood to face his friend.

"I understand your fear Fsol, but honestly how can this life be more horrible? Ever since she took over things have been worse than ever. I know you're not happy with some of the things that have been happening. Can you imagine for a moment what it would be like if she accomplished her goal?" Mkai said, leaning on the back of the couch, three short steps from his friend.

"Do you think God would allow her to take over Heaven? He might not destroy the humans but there is nothing stopping Him from simply obliterating us with a thought. Invading Heaven would accomplish nothing." Mkai said, need rasping in his voice.

"I don't ask you to believe, though I wish I could convince you." Mkai paused stepping closer, "But I do ask that you not stop me. I won't force you to do something against what you believe. Please extend the same courtesy to me."

Fsol stopped his pacing and looked at Mkai, anguish apparent on his scaled face. He met Mkai's eyes momentarily before dropping his gaze to the floor. Mkai could see the conflict tearing at his friend and hope stirred in his chest. It fizzled, twisted up and died as he realized he had no real choice. This was too big, too important to risk, even for Fsol. He steeled himself and took the final step, holding his right arm out to his friend.

"If you can't, brother, at least give me some time to get away, a chance to follow my own path."

Mkai watched, breath stuck in his chest, as Fsol stared at him. He sighed with relief when Fsol's shoulders slumped in defeat and he nodded.

"For you, Mkai, for all that we had together I will wait." Fsol said quietly. "I can give you two hours to get clear before I have to report this to Kalia. That should give you a solid head start."

"Thank you," Mkai said and embraced his friend, "The world thanks you for this chance."

A tear broke free and slid slowly down Mkai's scaled cheek as the dagger he had pulled from behind his belt slid between his friend's ribs. Fsol stiffened with a gasp and he clutched at Mkai. He stumbled on knees suddenly gone weak and Mkai caught him before he could fall. He carefully eased Fsol back onto the couch, the dagger hilt standing up tall, a slight quiver in it as the skewered heart tried to keep beating.

"I am sorry, brother. More than you can ever understand. But this is bigger than you and me, more important than either of us. She cannot win. It would mean the end to everything. And I couldn't risk it. Be at peace, and if there exists anything for us after death, wait for me. I doubt I will be long."

Tears fell freely as he watched Fsol's eyes dim. With a final rattle, he let go and death claimed him. Mkai arranged him on the couch, refusing to look at his dagger. With two gentle fingers, he closed Fsol's lids and rising, quickly gathered together a couple things. Opening the mantle he gently took out the small doll.

"You will be avenged. After so long." Mkai kissed the doll softly and placed it back into the mantle and closed it with a click.

⊕ ⊕ ⊕

Two days later found him standing in the shadows of an alley. His journey had been uneventful until now and his nerves were stretched thin waiting. He watched As'hame, the angel he had come for, as he worked through a gang of human thugs. They had come to prey upon a defenseless woman and the As'rai showed them why it was such a bad idea. Mkai tried to calm his beating heart. He prayed he'd be allowed to speak and couldn't help but chuckle at the thought of a demon praying. The angel sent the last of the thugs running and Mkai judged it was time to speak.

"You enjoyed that a little much, don't you think?"

⊕   ⊕   ⊕

Matthew has been obsessed with reading (and writing) since he could walk. Coming home on the first day of kindergarten mad because he couldn't read was just the first sign. It has just steadily got worse and the fascination with creating worlds with words finally exploded. This spring will see his first book, In Heaven's Shadow, *in print. Edited by the fantastic Annetta Ribken, he is quite excited to share it with the world.*

He lives in the Great White North...no not as far as Edmonton — in Calgary, Alberta Canada. Born and raised (notice the avoidance of the phrase grew up...) in a small town the move to the big city was a bit of a shock. He's traveled around a bit and that has helped broaden his experience. All of which comes out in his writing.

*You can find Matthew here: **authorsnotes.ca***

DEATH

TRANSFORMATION

By Timothy Bryant Smith

"ROSE?"

Rose stirred in her sleep.

"Rose, sweetie, I need you to wake up."

She cracked one eye open to see her mother leaning over her.

"Com'n, Rosie…you have to get up."

Rose peeked her eyes open a little wider this time. Something wasn't right. Usually, when her mother woke her up, the first rays of sunlight were already beaming down on her face, illuminating the walls of her bedroom in the light of daybreak. It was still dark… and wasn't it Saturday? No school today, she remembered, why was Momma waking her up so early in the morning? She muttered something under her breath and turned over in her bed in protest.

"Rose. Now. Momma needs you to get up and get dressed right now."

She didn't sound angry, but she wasn't kidding around either.

Momma's voice sounded weird, too; gravelly and hoarse…stern but somehow sad. Rose wasn't sure if she was in trouble or not.

"What, Momma?" Rose muttered, "What's going on?"

A drop of liquid splashed down on Rose's forehead as her mother stroked her hair. Rose opened her eyes all the way to see her mother's face. Even in the dark, with just the hall light shining through the bedroom door, Rose saw something was wrong. Her mother's eyes were puffy, her nose red and raw, her cheeks flushed, and she was fully dressed in her jeans and favorite Grateful Dead t-shirt.

"It's your Pee Paw," Rose's mom whispered. "We're going to go see your Pee Paw."

They spent the next few minutes getting Rose out of bed and into some clothes. Rose's mom packed her toothbrush, a few changes of clothes, and even grabbed her favorite comic, "V for Vendetta", to put into the book bag she toted every day back and forth to her fourth grade class.

Rose knew it was going to be a long trip if they were going to see Pee Paw. He lived in Tennessee and it was an "all-day-long trip" in the van before they got to where he lived. Rose didn't mind the time it took, though. She loved to see her grandfather during summer vacations and there were always plenty of cool things Pee Paw would have planned for her when they'd visit.

Two summers ago, he'd taken Rose hunting for a week in the woods with nothing more than what they could carry in their backpacks. He'd taught her how to read a map with a compass, how to make a campfire with a flint, and how to boil water from the streams to cook with and to drink. He also taught her the constellations in the night sky while they ate.

Last summer, they tracked a buck in the woods for nearly two days before they found him munching peacefully on some wet, green grass in a small lea. When Rose unslung her rifle to take the shot, her Pee Paw quietly motioned to her to put her gun away. For the next hour Rose watched, crouched in a thicket, as her grandfather slowly closed the distance between himself and the buck—about thirty yards—from upwind, in broad daylight, not making so much as a sound. And when he'd gotten close enough, he smacked the deer on its butt with his hand.

The buck, instantly terrified, jumped straight into the air, kicking wildly about, and bolted away into the woods, never to be seen again. Pee Paw just laughed and laughed as he walked back to where Rose lay in the woods with her rifle.

"Why didn't you shoot it, Pee Paw?" Rose asked him, astonished by what she'd just seen. "Why'd we track him for so long if we weren't gonna shoot it?"

Rose's grandfather looked sternly, but spoke to her in his gentle way.

"Listen to me, Rose. Any fool can kill something. It takes no skill to kill," Pee Paw's stern gaze dissolved quickly into the familiar smile Rose knew and loved. "I never said we'd hunt the deer to kill it. We hunted the deer to remind it of how much its life means. To remind it to be vigilant, to be aware; to live, fight, make babies, and survive. Yes, we could have killed it, but by sparing its life that deer now owes us a debt." He then smiled slyly. "And one day, that deer now knows, we might come to collect."

⊕ ⊕ ⊕

Rose slept most of the way in the back seat of the van. When she awoke, she saw the sun low in the sky. She counted the road signs for Knoxville becoming more frequent, and knew they were getting close. Normally when they went to see Pee Paw they would cross the big bridge over the Tennessee River. But this time Rose noticed her father turned a different way when they reached the city. Eventually, her dad pulled into the parking lot of a big building with lots of windows.

"Aren't we going to Pee Paw's cabin?" Rose asked.

Rose's mother turned around in her seat, drew a deep breath, and looked at her daughter. "Pee Paw is inside the hospital, Rosie. There's something I need to tell you, ok?"

"What is it, Momma?"

"Pee Paw's heart has been very sick and last night it stopped working."

"Is he gonna be ok?" Are we still going to go camping?" Rose asked.

"I don't think so, sweetie. Pee Paw's heart has been sick for a long time and the doctors told us it was time to say goodbye."

"Say goodbye?" Rose repeated back to her, not fully understanding what her Momma was saying.

Rose's mom drew in a deep breath. She tried to let it out slowly before answering, but Rosie saw the stoic face she'd kept plastered on her face all day start to break down.

"Yes, Rosie," Momma half-sputtered. Her lips drew tight, her chin started to wrinkle, and tears streamed down her face. "He is going to pass very soon. So we have to be strong, ok? We have to not be scared and tell Pee Paw how much we love him."

⊕ ⊕ ⊕

As they walked into the hospital, Rose and her dad each held one of her Momma's hands. Rose's mom warned her that Pee Paw wasn't going to look very good and there would be a lot of machines and tubes. She said it would make it hard to see him like he used to be…and it was important to try not to ask too many questions.

They rode in the elevator to the 13th floor. As the doors slid apart, Rose saw a big desk with nurses and TV monitors. Her nose wrinkled at the odor of Mr. Clean and band-aids. She saw her Uncle Bishop and his girl-friend, along with her Aunt Faith, talking to one of the nurses behind the desk. Rose's mom and dad hugged everyone and more tears and conversations followed, conversations Rose didn't understand. She didn't care, really. She just wanted to see her Pee Paw.

A white-haired doctor spoke with the adults as they walked down the hall to room 13-22, using words like "resuscitate", and "heroic measures". Rose waited patiently with her hand in Momma's, and remembered not to ask any questions.

The florescent light tubes in the hall ran the length of the ceiling in pairs. Rose noticed a couple of bulbs had burnt-out or flickered on one side or the other. It reminded her of the last night she'd stayed with Pee Paw the previous summer at his cabin in the woods.

⊕ ⊕ ⊕

She and her grandfather settled into a nightly ritual of sitting on the porch, Pee Paw with a Pabst Blue Ribbon in one hand, a funny smelling cigarette in the other. Rose sipped off the cache of Diet Dr. Pepper Pee Paw procured for her and relentlessly masticated on a piece of venison jerky he made in his smokehouse out back. They sat in silence for the most part that last evening, listening to the sounds of the Tennessee summer night. The pale blue bug zapper occasionally arced off, announcing the introduction of yet another moth to its sudden and electrified end.

"Why do the moths fly into the light, Pee Paw?" Rose asked. "Don't they know they'll die?"

"Because the light calls to them," her grandfather answered.

"Aren't they afraid to die?" Rose said, "Don't they want to live?"

"There's a big difference between being afraid to die and no longer wanting to live, Rosie. A moth isn't born a moth, you know. It's born a worm." Pee Paw drew deeply off his funny smelling cigarette, held his breath for a moment, then blew the smoke out into the Tennessee night air before continuing. "It hatches from an egg attached to a leaf, high in the trees where the light of the sun keeps it warm, way up in the sky. When the worm hatches, it falls far away from the light and onto the earth where it lives its life as a sticky, helpless thing."

"So it has to become a moth to fly back to the light?" Rose said.

"Yes, but it has a journey to make first before it can return."

"I don't understand," Rose said through a mighty yawn. Her legs still burned from the trail hike they took earlier that day, but she loved these talks with Pee Paw.

"After the worm falls from the light, it spends its life in the cold wet mud looking for food and trying protect itself. It has a sad and lonely life. It only knows hunger and helplessness," Pee Paw flicked the nub of his rolled cigarette off the end of his porch and grabbed his beer. "Its life in the mud is hard, full of suffering and danger. Most worms end up as food for other animals, so worms spend their time digging deeper and deeper into the mud, into the cold and darkness, hoping to escape these dangerous things. But the worm can only dig so deep before it grows tired and weak, so when it is done running from what it fears, it stops and becomes still."

"Like it freezes?"

"More like it surrenders, but yeah."

"What happens?" Rose yawned again. Rose saw her Pee Paw smiling at her in the dark. She loved hearing his stories, but she was so tired. The harder she fought to stay awake with him, the sleepier she seemed to get.

"When the worm finally surrenders to what it fears, and becomes still in the cold and darkness, it can feel the warmth of the sun heating it from above. That warmth calls out to the worm and draws it back towards the warmth and light."

Rose listened to her Pee Paw's voice as he spoke; steady and calm—low but with a consistent strangely sad cadence. His eyes searched out into the darkness of the woods as the words continued to flow from his mouth. It seemed to Rose as if her Pee Paw was not explaining, but remembering.

"Very few worms make it back to the surface, but those who make it do so knowing they must strive for the light rather than survive in the darkness."

"What happens, Pee Paw?" Rose whispered as the sound of her Pee Paw's voice lulled her closer to sleep.

"It must climb the great tree from which it fell, Rosie. The tree that will take it closer to the embrace of the Sun. When it reaches the top, the worm offers itself to the light."

"How?" Rose's eyes drooped...

"It wraps itself in a cocoon and hangs upside down from a single, silken thread where it waits."

"Waits for what, Pee Paw?"

"It does not know..." his voice trailed off into the night air along with smoke he exhaled from his lungs.

Rose never heard the rest of the story of the worm's journey and its transformation into the moth. She awoke the next morning in a warm bed, and felt sad when her mom and dad picked her up the next morning. She hugged her Pee Paw goodbye, as she always did, and promised to call him when she got home. Which, like every good grand-child, she never did.

⊕ ⊕ ⊕

Walking hand in hand with her mother and father down the flores-cent-lit hallway of the hospital, she wondered what she was about to see, and felt scared. Very, very scared.

As the door to room 13-22 opened, she saw a tiny room. Two beds, one by a window with the last of the day's sunlight shining through onto the wall above it, and the other next to a small bathroom door. She saw someone's feet sticking out from underneath a blanket on the bed by the window and heard all sorts of machines making strange noises—chirps and whistles, buzzers and blips. Rose decided it would be best if she stayed hidden behind her mother's and father's legs until some-one told her what to do and where to stand.

"Daddy?" Her mother leaned over the bed of the person with the exposed, white, bone-like feet. Rose could not see her Pee Paw, as the rest of his body was hidden from Rose's view by her mother's body and a large machine with numbers that blinked like her alarm clock at home.

"Daddy? We made it. We're here," said Rosie's Momma.

Rose heard a mumbled response from her grandfather, but she couldn't understand what he said.

"Yes. We all came, we're all here."

Another muffled response from the bed.

"Yes, Rose too," her mother said. "Would you like to see her?"

Rose's mom turned and motioned to her daddy. He slid a chair next to the bed, and helped Rose stand in it.

At first, she didn't recognize the man she saw. This was definitely not her Pee Paw. This man was an old man, with a gaunt, pale face and dark rings under his sunken eyes. Plastic tubes protruded from his arms. His skin looked white as a skeleton. A tiny plastic mask on over his nose and mouth fogged up as he labored to breath.

"There's my little Rose," he said. "I've been waiting for you, sweetie."

"Pee Paw?" she said. He looked so sad and thin. His voice crackled and sounded hollow from behind the strange mask. "What happened?"

Her grandfather looked at Rose's mother. "Why don't the rest of you give me a few minutes to talk to my granddaughter, ok?"

Slowly, the adults left the room until no one remained but Rose and her grandfather. As the door closed behind them, Rose felt her chest and throat start to constrict as she looked at her grandfather. The reality of what was happening to him finally hit her. In one sudden rush of emotion, tears started to well up in her eyes and drip down her cheeks.

Pee Paw attempted to sit upright. As he did, he grimaced in pain and exhaustion, as if every bit of strength he had left was put into the effort. This was not the man she once saw smack a buck on its butt after sneaking up on it. He was dying, and she only just now realized that it was a matter of when and not "if".

"I love you, Pee Paw," she sobbed as the lump in her throat began to make it impossible to talk. "I love you so much."

"I love you to, Rose," he lifted his bony hand from beneath the covers and wiped the tears off her cheek as his own tears trickled down his.

"Rose...I need you to help me, ok? Will you do something for me?"

She nodded her head wondering what she could possibly do to help this man she loved so much.

"The light is calling to me, Rose. Do you remember? Do you remember the worm? Will you help me get ready?"

"Yes, Pee Paw," she wept. "Tell me how to help."

"I need you to make my cocoon for me."

Rose's Pee Paw instructed her how to tuck the blankets on the bed tightly around his body. She wrapped his thin feet so they would not poke out. She slid her hands up underneath his frail legs and hips, making sure he was swaddled as tight as could be.

"Hug me one last time before you cocoon my arms, Rose," he whispered weakly, his breathing erratic and harsh.

She embraced her grandfather, holding him close for a long moment. Carefully she tucked his arms underneath the blankets, pulling them taut over his shoulders and neck so only the tubes poked out from underneath.

"Is it time, Pee Paw?" she asked. "Is it time to grow wings and fly back to the light?"

"I don't know, Rosie. I hope so. Worms don't ever know what they're going to become when they surrender to the light, they just know they'll become something greater than what they were."

He paused for a few seconds, and again his eyes trailed off, just as they did the last time they spoke; as if he were no longer explaining, but remembering. When his gaze came back to focus, Rose saw a joy and love she knew she would always remember.

"But know this, Rose. Whatever I become, no matter how amazing my wings might be, or what great visions I see as I fly high into the sky, what I'm about to become will never be as beautiful as you are to me right now."

And with that, Rose watched her Pee Paw close his eyes as the last few rays of sunlight coming in through the window dropped off his face.

⊕ ⊕ ⊕

Timothy Smith lives in North Carolina where he and his wife split their time between running their restaurant, indulging in creative projects, and spending time with their two dogs. A life-long student of symbolism and creative expression, Timothy has always enjoyed exploring the eclectic myths and archetypal characters of various religions and their respective cultures throughout history. Inspired in his youth by the insights of Jung, Campbell, and other authors who defined the field of comparative mythologies and their impact on culture and the human condition, Timothy has studied and practiced various systems of divination since his childhood. This is Timothy's first contribution to an anthology, but hopefully not his last.

TEMPERANCE

REPLY ALL

By Anne Chaconas

Date: Friday 13 June, 9:45am
From: Williams, Temperance
To: Arcana Enterprises <Distribution List>
Subject: Leaving early today

Please be advised that Mr. Mammon is leaving at noon today to attend a tennis tournament, and will be unavailable until Monday. All urgent matters should be brought to his attention no later than 11am.
Thank you,

Temperance Williams
Executive Assistant to Stan Mammon, VP - Arcana Enterprises

Date: Friday 13 June, 9:47am
From: Kaiser, Victoria
To: Mammon, Stanley
Subject: RE: Leaving early today

Oh, is that what we're calling it now? A "tennis tournament?"

Date: Friday 13 June, 9:50am
From: Mammon, Stanley
To: Kaiser, Victoria
Subject: RE: Leaving early today

If you want, I can ask Temperance to send out an email clarifying my weekend activities. What would you like me to have her say?

Date: Friday 13 June, 9:51am
From: Kaiser, Victoria
To: Mammon, Stanley
Subject: RE: Leaving early today

Have her say you'll be riding me roughly in the back of an El Dorado.

Date: Friday 13 June, 9:52am
From: Mammon, Stanley
To: Kaiser, Victoria
Subject: RE: Leaving early today

Ooh. Kinky.

Date: Friday 13 June, 9:53am
From: Forza, Geraldine
To: Williams, Temperance; Arcana Enterprises <Distribution List>

Subject: RE: Leaving early today

FYI, Mrs. Kaiser will also be leaving early today, around 1pm. All matters needing her attention should be brought to me no later than noon. Thanks!

Geri Forza
Executive Assistant to Victoria Kaiser, Marketing Director - Arcana Enterprises

---

Date: Friday 13 June, 9:55am
From: Williams, Temperance
To: Forza, Geraldine; Justia, Marie
Subject: RE: Leaving early today

Boy, it must be nice to be rich and single, huh? This is fifth time in two weeks that Mammon's cut out early. Tennis tournament today, wine tasting last week, conference in Vegas two weekends ago. I can't remember where he went the other two times.

Date: Friday 13 June, 9:56am
From: Forza, Geraldine
To: Williams, Temperance; Justia, Marie
Subject: RE: Leaving early today

The rich and married do it just as often. Vikki's been leaving early every other day, it seems. I guess it pays to be married to the boss.

Date: Friday 13 June, 9:57am
From: Kaiser, Victoria
To: Mammon, Stanley
Subject: RE: Leaving early today

Not as kinky as we were on Tuesday.

Date: Friday 13 June, 9:58am
From: Mammon, Stanley
To: Kaiser, Victoria
Subject: RE: Leaving early today

My nethers still tingle.
Love you in that skirt today. If it was any tighter, I'd be able to see the outline of your panties.

Date: Friday 13 June, 9:59am
From: Kaiser, Victoria
To: Mammon, Stanley
Subject: RE: Leaving early today

You're assuming I'm wearing any.

Date: Friday 13 June, 10:01am
From: Justia, Marie
To: Forza, Geraldine; Williams, Temperance
Subject: RE: Leaving early today

Where does she even go? It can't be work-related; she's got all her little minions that she sends to conferences. And it can't be personal; the boss hardly ever takes off early, he works most weekends (I would know, he keeps me here working with him), and you know he'd never let her go anywhere alone. Honestly, I don't even know why she has a job here. I never see her do a damn thing. It's completely unfair. What's she even doing right now, Geri?

Date: Friday 13 June, 10:02am

From: Forza, Geraldine
To: Williams, Temperance; Justia, Marie
Subject: RE: Leaving early today

She's sitting at her computer, typing something and giggling.

Date: Friday 13 June, 10:02am
From: Williams, Temperance
To: Forza, Geraldine; Justia, Marie
Subject: RE: Leaving early today

Sounds like she's hard at work.

Date: Friday 13 June, 10:03am
From: Justia, Marie
To: Forza, Geraldine; Williams, Temperance
Subject: RE: Leaving early today

I saw her in Atlantic City when I went last weekend, at the blackjack tables. Losing the Kaiser fortune, no doubt. Can't imagine she's particularly good at cards. Don't you need to be smart to do well at card games? I didn't say hello to her, OBVIOUSLY. I don't think she saw me…or she pretended not to recognize me.

Date: Friday 13 June. 10:05am
From: Forza, Geraldine
To: Williams, Temperance; Justia, Marie
Subject: RE: Leaving early today

Wait…last weekend she wasn't in Atlantic City. She told me she would be at their Hamptons house. Her mother was visiting or something.

Date: Friday 13 June, 10:06am
From: Justia, Marie
To: Williams, Temperance; Forza, Geraldine
Subject: RE: Leaving early today

It was definitely her. I'd recognize that blonde dye job anywhere.

Date: Friday 13 June, 10:07am
From: Williams, Temperance
To: Forza, Geraldine; Justia, Marie
Subject: RE: Leaving early today

Maybe she was originally going to go to the Hamptons and then took a detour. God knows she takes the private jet wherever she wants. TOUGH LIFE SHE LEADS.

Date: Friday 13 June, 10:10am
From: Kaiser, Victoria
To: Mammon, Stanley
Subject: RE: Leaving early today

Rendered you speechless, I see. Is the thought of my naked ass too much for you? It certainly wasn't too much for you when you had me bent over in the copy room yesterday.

Date: Friday 13 June, 10:12am
From: Mammon, Stanley
To: Kaiser, Victoria
Subject: RE: Leaving early today

Not speechless. Merely temporarily detained. Your husband was just in my office, wanting to go over his presentation notes for that conference he's attending this weekend.

Date: Friday 13 June, 10:13am
From: Kaiser, Victoria
To: Mammon, Stanley
Subject: RE: Leaving early today

Don't talk to me about that asshole. I can't wait for him to leave for the weekend.
What time are you coming over?

Date: Friday 13 June, 10:14am
From: Mammon, Stanley
To: Kaiser, Victoria
Subject: RE: Leaving early today

7pm. Will you be alone by that time?

Date: Friday 13 June, 10:15am
From: Williams, Temperance
To: Forza, Geraldine; Justia, Marie
Subject: RE: Leaving early today

You know who WAS in Atlantic City last weekend? Mammon. I was just looking at my calendar to see where he'd been going off to the past two weeks, and that's where I have him staying last Saturday and Sunday. The Borgata in Atlantic City.

Date: Friday 13 June, 10:16am
From: Justia, Marie
To: Forza, Geraldine; Williams, Temperance
Subject: RE: Leaving early today

That's where I saw Vikki. The Borgata. Which is interesting, because I just checked the boss' calendar, and he wasn't in Atlantic City last weekend. He was in San Diego, meeting with investors.

Date: Friday 13 June, 10:17am
From: Forza, Geraldine
To: Williams, Temperance; Justia, Marie
Subject: RE: Leaving early today

So he DOES let her go places alone. Or maybe they went to San Diego together and then made a pit stop in Atlantic City on the way back?

Date: Friday 13 June, 10:18am
From: Justia, Marie
To: Forza, Geraldine; Williams, Temperance
Subject: RE: Leaving early today

I saw her on Saturday morning.

Date: Friday 13 June, 10:19am
From: Williams, Temperance
To: Forza, Geraldine; Justia, Marie
Subject: RE: Leaving early today

Maybe they met up with Mammon there.

Date: Friday 13 June, 10:20am
From: Forza, Geraldine
To: Williams, Temperance; Justia, Marie
Subject: RE: Leaving early today

Maybe SHE met up with Mammon there.

Date: Friday 13 June, 10:21am
From: Williams, Temperance
To: Forza, Geraldine; Justia, Marie
Subject: RE: Leaving early today

No. You think? I mean, they're friends outside of work. Well, Mammon and Kaiser are. Vikki just does whatever Kaiser does. Or tells her to do.

Date: Friday 13 June, 10:22am
From: Forza, Geraldine
To: Williams, Temperance; Justia, Marie
Subject: RE: Leaving early today

I saw Vikki and Mammon having dinner at Le Bombardier last Wednesday. Sans Kaiser. Didn't think anything of it at the time, but...

Date: Friday 13 June, 10:23am
From: Williams, Temperance
To: Forza, Geraldine; Justia, Marie
Subject: RE: Leaving early today

That can't be right. Last Wednesday evening Mammon was at a wine tasting. I remember because he was waiting to hear back about the Vermont deal and he told me where he was going to be in case I needed to get a hold of him. Marie, where was Kaiser last Wednesday?

Date: Friday 13 June, 10:24am
From: Justia, Marie
To: Forza, Geraldine; Williams, Temperance
Subject: RE: Leaving early today

Kaiser was out of town last Wednesday. Wednesday and Thursday. At merger discussions. In New York.

Date: Friday 13 June, 10:25am
From: Williams, Temperance
To: Forza, Geraldine; Justia, Marie
Subject: RE: Leaving early today

So Kaiser was out of town. Mammon lied about where he was. And Vikki was having dinner at a fancy French restaurant with the guy who lied about where he was while her husband was out of town. MAMMON AND VIKKI ARE SO DOING IT.

Date: Friday 13 June, 10:26am
From: Forza, Geraldine
To: Williams, Temperance; Justia, Marie
Subject: RE: Leaving early today

OMG.

Date: Friday 13 June, 10:26am
From: Justia, Marie
To: Forza, Geraldine; Williams, Temperance
Subject: RE: Leaving early today

NO.

Date: Friday 13 June, 10:27am
From: Williams, Temperance
To: Forza, Geraldine; Justia, Marie
Subject: RE: Leaving early today

YES.

Date: Friday 13 June, 10:30am
From: Kaiser, Victoria
To: Mammon, Stanley
Subject: RE: Leaving early today

Yes. Alan's flight leaves at 6pm. I'll be alone by 7pm. And naked.

Date: Friday 13 June, 10:31am
From: Mammon, Stanley
To: Kaiser, Victoria
Subject: RE: Leaving early today

I can't wait to make you purr like a kitten again. A NAUGHTY kitten.

Date: Friday 13 June, 10:32am
From: Kaiser, Alan
To: Forza, Geraldine; Williams, Temperance; Arcana Enterprises <Distribution List>
Subject: RE: Leaving early today

Be advised, I'll be leaving at 3pm today. I'll be reachable via cell phone and email.
Thank you,

Alan Kaiser
CEO – Arcana Enterprises

Date: Friday 13 June, 10:33am
From: Williams, Temperance

To: Kaiser, Alan; Forza, Geraldine; Arcana Enterprises <Distribution List>

Subject: RE: Leaving early today

Oooh, look who else is leaving early! Perhaps a little Mammon sandwich on a Kaiser roll is in order? Vikki's already got hands-on experience, she can show her husband how to tickle the Mammon pickle.

Date: Friday 13 June, 10:35am

From: Forza, Geraldine

To: Williams, Temperance; Justia, Marie

Subject: RE: Leaving early today

TEMPERANCE YOU JUST REPLIED TO THE WHOLE OFFICE

Date: Friday 13 June, 10:35am

From: Williams, Temperance

To: Forza, Geraldine; Justia, Marie

Subject: RE: Leaving early today

OMFG I REPLIED TO THE WRONG EMAIL

Date: Friday 13 June, 10:35am

From: Justia, Marie

To: Forza, Geraldine; Williams, Temperance

Subject: RE: Leaving early today

OMG TEMPERANCE

Date: Friday 13 June, 10:35am

From: Williams, Temperance

To: Forza, Geraldine; Justia, Marie

Subject: RE: Leaving early today

I AM SO FUCKED

Date: Friday 13 June. 10:37am
From: Justia. Marie
To: Forza, Geraldine: Williams, Temperance
Subject: RE: Leaving early today

Kaiser just ran into Vikki's office.

Date: Friday 13 June, 10:38am
From: Williams, Temperance
To: Forza, Geraldine; Justia, Marie
Subject: RE: Leaving early today

OMG. AND???

Date: Friday 13 June, 10:38am
From: Justia, Marie
To: Forza, Geraldine; Williams, Temperance
Subject: RE: Leaving early today

And nothing. I can't hear anything. Geri, can you hear/see anything?

Date: Friday 13 June, 10:38am
From: Forza, Geraldine
To: Justia, Marie; Williams, Temperance
Subject: RE: Leaving early today

No, nothing. Totally quiet. He's just staring at her computer. She's staring at him.

Date: Friday 13 June, 10:38am
From: Forza, Geraldine
To: Justia, Marie; Williams, Temperance
Subject: RE: Leaving early today
Oh wait. He's yelling now. Something about kittens???

Date: Friday 13 June, 10:38am
From: Forza, Geralding
To: Justia, Marie; Williams, Temperance
Subject: RE: Leaving early today

Kittens? WTF??

Date: Friday 13 June, 10:40am
From: Williams, Temperance
To: Forza, Geraldine; Justia, Marie
Subject: RE: Leaving early today

OMG I can hear him now.

Date: Friday 13 June, 10:41am
From: Forza, Geraldine
To: Justia, Marie; Williams, Temperance
Subject: RE: Leaving early today

He's yelling. He's saying he's going to kill Mammon. Temperance, I think he's going to Mammon's office. HIDE.

Date: Friday 13 June, 10:41am
From: Mammon, Stanley
To: Williams, Temperance
Subject: RE: Leaving early today

Temperance, please come to my office IMMEDIATELY.

Date: Friday 13 June, 10:41am
From: Williams, Temperance
To: Justia, Marie; Forza, Geraldine
Subject: RE: Leaving early today

OMG

Date: Friday 13 June, 10:41am
From: Forza, Geraldine
To: Justia, Marie; Williams, Temperance
Subject: RE: Leaving early today

TEMPERANCE HIDE

Date: Friday 13 June, 10:41am
From: Williams, Temperance
To: Forza, Geraldine
Subject: Out of office

Thank you for your email. I am currently out of the office. I will respond to your email as soon as I return.
Sincerely,

Temperance Williams
Executive Assistant to Stan Mammon, VP - Arcana Enterprises

Date: Friday 13 June, 10:41am
From: Justia, Marie
To: Forza, Geraldine; Williams, Temperance
Subject: RE: Leaving early today

TEMPERANCE ARE YOU OKAY???

Date: Friday 13 June, 10:41am
From: Williams, Temperance
To: Justia, Marie
Subject: Out of office

Thank you for your email. I am currently out of the office. I will respond to your email as soon as I return.
Sincerely,

Temperance Williams
Executive Assistant to Stan Mammon, VP - Arcana Enterprises

Date: Friday 13 June, 10:41am
From: Mammon, Stanley
To: Williams, Temperance
Subject: RE: Leaving early today

Temperance. NOW.

Date: Friday 13 June, 10:41am
From: Williams, Temperance
To: Mammon, Stanley
Subject: Out of office

Thank you for your email. I am currently out of the office. I will respond to your email as soon as I return.
Sincerely,

Temperance Williams
Executive Assistant to Stan Mammon, VP - Arcana Enterprises

Date: Friday 13 June, 10:42am
From: Justia, Marie
To: Forza, Geraldine
Subject: RE: Leaving early today

It looks like Temperance has left the building.

⊕ ⊕ ⊕

Anne Chaconas was born in Guatemala City, Guatemala, and made it her mission from around the time she was three years old to move to the United States (where, she told anyone who would listen, all the music was in English, which automatically meant life was better—flawless toddler logic, people). She fulfilled her mission at eighteen when she moved to Connecticut to attend a small private university in New Haven. There she bounced from major to major, finally landing on Literature (and guaranteeing herself absolutely no job prospects upon gradua-tion but absolutely exceptional cocktail party conversational skills).

After realizing people down South were much nicer (and the food was much more fried), she moved there in 2007. She currently lives in North Carolina with her husband, two kids, four cats, two dogs, and entirely too many books. She is a work-at-home mom, and spends her days making things in the Crock-Pot, chang-ing shockingly awful diapers, getting sunburned at the park, and working on her prose and for her marketing clients during those 45 minutes when the kids' naps overlap and those fleeting hours after they go to bed.

Anne writes many things, but has found her true love in humorous non-fic-tion and parenting essays. She is currently working on two books, Embrace Your Weird *(a how-to guide on how to be happy from someone not academically qualified to write such a guide) and* A Stork Flew Over The Cuckoo's Nest *(a collection of essays, limericks, and assorted musings on pregnancy, childbirth, parenthood, and other unnatural acts).*

She also swears. A lot.

*You can stalk her online at **about.me/annechaconas**.*

THE DEVIL

HOARDER

By Patti Larsen

JANE HOVERED NEAR THE RICKETY WOODEN YARD SALE table, discomfort clear in every line of her body. The thumb and index finger of her right hand absently reached for the gold band no longer gracing her left ring finger, though the indent of twenty years of marriage remained.

Annie bumped her shoulder from behind, a little smile on her face. "You look like someone's torturing you," Jane's younger sister said, tossing her blonde bob, mascara laden lashes winking. Jane hated how great Annie looked, fit and happy. Diamonds of happy matrimony glinted from her hand, a slap in Jane's face.

It just wasn't fair. Why did her life have to fall apart? But she forced a little smile and shoved her shoulders down from the tense mountains they made on either side of her ears.

"Sorry," she said, even as she hated the automatic reaction of apology left over from years of trying to make Bob happy and never succeeding. "I haven't been to one of these before."

Annie swung her designer bag over her shoulder and grabbed Jane's arm, pulling her closer, fake nails digging into the soft flesh of her arm even through her jacket.

"A little retail therapy," Annie said, lip-gloss shining in the sunlight of the bright June morning. Jane shifted sideways, out of the path of a pushy older woman who pawed through the offerings on the table, "never hurt anyone."

Retail therapy used to be Jane's favorite when two incomes kept her comfortable, if not happy. But now Bob was gone, the cheating Angela with him—what were best friends for?—Jane hadn't been able to afford much in the way of new clothes or nick-knacks for the house until she'd gotten her very unstable feet under her at last.

The woman behind the table smiled at her, rumpled and weary, the strained, almost bitter undertone making Jane retreat a little even as her eyes settled on the sweet statuette perched near the cash box. A lovely mermaid smiled at her, iridescent shell sparkling in the sun. The painted maid's hair glowed richly red, eyes clear blue, darling smile showing perfect white teeth as her flawless human body blended into the carefully painted scales of her fishy green tail. Jane's hand went unconsciously to her own hair, once that gorgeous shade, now faded to brown and threaded with gray. Her limber, attractive young body was long gone, too. One of the reasons Bob left her, he said.

Jane's eyes burned with tears as Annie, unknowing, uncaring, left her there staring at the statuette. The sudden need to flee, to hide in the small house she'd barely been able to afford on her own and never come out driving her back from the table.

Until the old woman pushed her again. Something inside Jane snapped in that moment as the woman's grubby paw reached out to take the statuette. To touch Jane's precious memory. In a move nothing like her normal passive and quiet nature, Jane shouldered the old woman aside and grasped the mermaid in her hand, holding it out, shaking slightly, to the woman behind the table.

"How much?"

⊕ ⊕ ⊕

Annie's lack of enthusiasm over the statue, which she deemed 'quaint', did nothing to deter Jane. She'd found a side of herself previously unknown, an aggressive side okay with getting what she wanted. The surge of joy and excitement buying the mermaid brought her was as powerful as the rush of a heroin injection.

Jane ensconced the statuette next to her bed, where she could look at it before she slept and where it would be the first thing she woke to each morning. A reminder of the new Jane. As she fell into sleep that first night, she was positive the statuette smiled just for her.

Life became the passion of the purchase. Jane's job working as an insurance technician allowed her to do so from home, and afforded her enough money to indulge in her current favorite past time—yard saling. Anticipation of each weekend's goodies was only partly satiated by the exploration of thrift and dollar stores she discovered after timidly Googling the topic.

Annie wrinkled her nose immediately the next time she came to visit at the pile of goodies Jane eagerly showed her, perched on the spare bed.

"What do you want all this junk for?" Just seeing Annie handle her precious discoveries with her filthy, clammy hands made Jane's newfound temper boil.

Their visit didn't last long.

An introvert by nature, it was easy for Jane to fall into a happy routine over the next six months: working all morning with a quick trip to the thrift shop over lunch before finishing her day. It became harder and harder to keep her time in the stores down to the half hour she'd booked herself, turning quickly into two and sometimes three hour marathons she paid for by working well into the night. But to Jane, it was worth it.

When she realized she could no longer sleep in her own bed because it was full of things she just had to have, Jane paused. A flicker of concern passed through her mind, but only a flicker. The moment her eyes settled on the mermaid, doubt faded and her happiness came back.

Jane scooped up the little statuette and carried it to the living room, setting it on the end table beside her recliner. She often dozed in the chair for a few moments after supper looking over classified and yard sale adverts, so it seemed logical to make it her full-time sleeping place.

Especially if it meant she had more room for her stuff.

The first time she heard the statuette whispering, Jane thought it was the television. But no, that soft, sweet voice, the words she couldn't quite make out, they came from the mermaid. Crazy? Maybe. But Jane wasn't willing to admit it. Not when hearing the statuette's lovely murmuring gave her such peace. It was so much easier to fall asleep to the sound and she welcomed it.

Even better the first time she answered it. Opened her eyes in the deep of the night to that glittering blue gaze. "You're so beautiful," Jane said, stroking the mermaid's perfect hair, the ceramic warm to the touch. "I wish I looked like you."

It was easy then to tell the aquatic maid everything, to let go of all of her hopes and fears and dreams and old pains, to weep at last for the loss of her marriage and the pathetic hopelessness of Jane's existence.

"Until I found you." She kissed the mermaid's little head and hugged her close.

And the mermaid whispered happily back.

Annie wasn't welcome any longer. Not after the disgusted look on her face, the snide comments about how hard it was to walk down the hall. Her realization Jane slept in her chair. Jane put a stop to her visits right then and there, using some of her newfound passion to muscle her normally dominating sister out the front door.

It was with great satisfaction Jane slammed it in Annie's shocked face.

The statuette approved, the whispering congratulatory. Jane beamed in joy as she pulled herself over the piles of wrapping paper, blankets, a toy house, scrapbooking supplies and tupperware dishes, into the kitchen for a celebratory snack.

Jane rifled through the plastic bags full of new groceries she'd set on top of the old, deciding on a chocolate bar, nose wrinkling slightly at the scent of rotting food, quickly gone from her mind as she returned to her chair and held the statuette while her mouth tingled, full of yummy sweetness.

Work fell to the wayside. How could she focus on other people's problems when she had the statuette to talk to? Bills piled up, her phone cut off, internet. There, she couldn't work anymore anyway. She just managed to keep the lights on by applying for social assistance, meals in her stomach from the food bank. The part of her cringing in shame over using such services wasn't nearly as loud as the thrill she felt buying more things.

Jane ignored the ringing of the doorbell, never answering, knowing it was Annie or one of the nosy neighbors who complained all the time about the stuff piling up in the front yard. They needed to mind their own business. Until she heard a man's voice telling her it was the police knocking. Jane blinked into the sunlight, scowling at the two young officers.

"We've had calls," the first said, while the other looked over her shoulder into the house. His face judged her, raised her anger while his partner went on. "From the neighbors."

About the smell, he said. And the condition of her property. Jane turned and, for a brief heartbeat, everything stopped for her. She saw the mess. But not for long enough. Not with the mermaid tucked carefully against her chest in one protective hand.

Jane made empty promises to the officers, about cleanups and garbage bins, before closing and locking the door on them. Returning to her chair and the statuette.

Always the statuette.

Jane was sleeping when someone broke the door down. She pushed her way through the piles near the entry and found Annie, backed by a crew in masks and gloves.

"We're here to clean this up," Annie said, hand over her nose, horror on her face. "Jane, you have to or the city will make you move."

No, no. Never. The phone was in her hands, 9-1-1 called, the police summoned.

Trespassers. Defilers. The cops came, Annie fought, Annie pleaded.

Annie left.

Just how Jane wanted it.

As Jane turned in triumph, shimmied her way back to her chair, her arm bumped the wobbling stack of magazines she'd placed on top of the old books she piled on the six bags of curtains she rescued from destruction. The mermaid fell from her grip while Jane reached for her, terror seizing her heart, the statuette bouncing over the heaped-up garbage, coming to land against the bones of a small animal.

She had a...dog? Jane's mind snapped open. No, no dog. A raccoon, it looked like. Jane tipped her head back, looked up. A gaping hole in her ceiling disgorged insulation from the blackness. When had that happened? She staggered back, eyes going wider and wider as she stumbled away from the horror before her.

And saw. For the first time. All of it. Smelled, tasted the rot in the air, the heavy pall of waste and decay. Looked down at herself, her unwashed body, the stringy length of her hair falling over a filthy sweatshirt she'd never seen before. Fell to her knees and sobbed into her hands, barely able to stand the stench of herself as the piles and heaps and stacks closed in around her.

Jane stumbled to her feet, heading for the door, reaching for the distant knob, Annie's name on her lips.

Stop.

The whisper. A voice now. Jane paused, heart pounding in her chest.

Don't.

"I can't live like this." Her hands shook, mind reeling as she understood she'd been talking to a statuette, she'd most likely gone insane and, instantly, blamed Bob automatically before the voice spoke again.

More.

Jane's mouth gaped open, the reek of her own breath making her dizzy as she ran her tongue over teeth fuzzy with plaque and worse things.

"No more." She hugged herself. "I'm done."

More.

Jane took a step toward the statuette the smiling face of the mermaid now somehow changed, bitter, angry. Morphing into evil. Jane crouched to touch it.

Yes.

She fell back, panting, grasping desperately about her as the voice, clear now, demanding, pulled her in to madness. Jane felt some fabric, jerked free a rotting t-shirt, wrapped it around her hand and lifted the statue. The draw of the siren's call through the flimsy material wasn't reaching her anymore.

Her awakened horror was stronger.

"Enough." Jane turned toward the door again, heading down the hall. "Enough." As she climbed over piles, panting, tears now trickling down her face, her true strength finally won, and she screamed at the statuette, "ENOUGH!"

The door was so close. Outside beckoned. Fresh air, a new life. Leaving this behind...Jane found herself smiling through her tears. Yes, she'd lost it for a while. But she could start again.

And this time would be different.

No. No. No. The statue almost burned in her hand, the heat reaching her through the worn fabric. Jane clutched it close, stumbled over a collection of Barbie dolls missing parts and hair and fell hard in a crumpled heap of garbage. Something broke under her knee, wetness staining her pants, the reek of rotting citrus filling her nostrils. Jane reached out with her free hand for support as she struggled to rise.

Felt the pile beside her shift.

Slide.

Fall.

She purchased the six bowling balls only two days before, stacking them on top of the old bookshelf she filled with baby clothes and the comic-book collection she meant to catalog. The shelf was weaker than she thought, gave way as her grasping fingers used it to steady her.

And it all came tumbling down.Jane landed on her belly, the first ball crushing the small of her back and severing her spinal cord just before the pain came. The second, an instant after the first, took out her right arm, at the elbow, bone powdering under the twenty pounds of falling resin. But Jane barely registered it.

Not when the third struck her in the back of the head.

Darkness closing in, Jane's eyes locked on the mermaid, sitting pretty and perfect, upright, looking down at her.

Smiling again.

Annie broke through the front door a week later. A kind young officer comforted her as the firemen pulled the body out of the front hall, after first unloading a dumpster full of garbage in order to reach Jane's decaying body.

"It's my fault," she sobbed on his blue shoulder. "I should have tried harder."

Annie had to force herself to enter the house after the funeral, but it needed to be done and there was no one else. She rescued the sweet mermaid statuette from the floor before one of the crew could trample it, stuffing it in a bag. Jane loved that statuette. It was the least Annie could do to save it.

The cleansing of the house took four full days, leaving behind a home that would never smell fresh again. Still, the For Sale sign swung at the end of the driveway the day Annie had the yard sale. Most of what Jane brought into the house was garbage, but some of it could be salvaged and Annie wasn't beyond making a little money on the whole thing, considering how much Jane's death and debt already cost her.

A young woman with a sad expression stood back, hands clutching her purse. Annie watched her with the shrewd attention of a true saleswoman, noticing where the woman focused. The mermaid statuette sat, shining and lovely, front and center and the buyer couldn't seem to keep her eyes off it.

"Only ten dollars." Annie said.

The woman smiled, hesitated. "Will you take five?"

"Seven." Annie slid the mermaid into a plastic bag, but the woman shook her head and stepped forward, hands sliding around it as she lifted it and met Annie's eyes.

"Sold."

The mermaid smiled.

⊕ ⊕ ⊕

Patti Larsen is an award-winning young adult writer with a passion for the paranormal. Now with multiple series in happy publication, she lives on beautiful Prince Edward Island, Canada, with her very patient husband and five massive cats.

Find Patti at about.me/pattilarsen.

THE TOWER

AFTER THE FALL

By Jordan L. Hawk

THE MEDALS TUMBLED FROM MY HAND INTO THE TRASH-
can, glinting with silver, bronze, and gold on their way down. One by
one, they hit the bottom with a loud clang, to nestle amidst shards of
broken glass and frame, and crumpled paper.

There. The last of it. Gone.

Maybe now the nightmares would end.

The doorbell rang, its cheery tone jarring. I turned from the trash-
can in what had been a home office, but was now just another room to
collect dust and unwanted memories. Too fast: my leg trembled, and
only my cane kept me from hitting the floor.

I hesitated at the door. What would happen if I pretended I wasn't
there?

And I wasn't, not really. W.D. McConnel died months ago. Nothing
remained but a ghost, still clinging to flesh.

They'd ship me back to psych, though. Where doctors would prod and pry, nurses watching to make sure I swallowed the mountain of pills. They'd ask questions and try to slide their feelers into my brain, just like Hayden had—

I opened the door.

A man stood on the other side, his hand raised to knock. Honey-brown hair, drawn back in a ponytail, a long nose. Eyes blue as the sea off the Arabian Peninsula, clear and calm.

Gorgeous.

"Raphael Jones, with AJ Home Care Services," he said, tapping the little badge clipped to his t-shirt. A canister vacuum hung on his back, and he wore a belt with dusters and spray bottles clipped to it. "They told you I was coming?"

"Yes." Had his bosses given him my name, or just my address? I watched his face, but as far as I could tell, he thought I was just another soldier. Someone who'd protected others, but now couldn't even take care of himself.

That was bad enough.

"May I come in?" he asked.

"Sorry." I stepped back, leaning on the cane. "I'm Darin," I added, and held out my right hand from the force of long habit. It twitched spasmodically, and I hastily let it drop again.

"Call me Raph," he replied. His glance at my hand acknowledged the twitching, but his gaze didn't linger. I couldn't decide if that was better or worse than pretending he hadn't seen at all.

What was he thinking? What was I supposed to do? Make small talk? Get out of his way so he could get the job done?

I would have known, once upon a time, his emotions as easy to hear as a radio broadcast.

Gone now. All gone, just like the medals.

Embarrassed, I turned to hobble back into the living room. "I'll just let you get to work," I mumbled.

"Sure, but if you have a minute, I'd like to make sure the work order is right. Sometimes the lines get crossed, so I always like to check."

"Oh." I stopped and looked back at him. "I see."

His smile warmed his features and made me ache in places I thought had died along with everything else. "The work order says minor maintenance and janitorial duties: dusting, vacuuming, emptying the trash, and cleaning the bathroom. Is that right?"

I fixed my gaze on his sneakers. Acid chewed a hole in my gut and my face burned. I wanted to tell him no, it was all a mistake. Leave, get out. I don't need you. I can empty my own fucking trash.

My hand spasmed, and the right side of my face twitched.

"That's right," I said.

"Great." His smile looked sincere, but I was sure if I could just hear his thoughts, it would be a different story. Pity, maybe. Or a healthy man's contempt for a broken one. "I'll get started, then."

I retreated to the living room and sat in the recliner where I spent most of every day. The curtains were drawn tight, but I heard the tap of rain against the glass of the windows. I didn't bother turning on the light, and the TV remote had an inch of dust on it.

Sound told the story of Raph's progress through the apartment: the tread of his shoes, the clank of trashcans, the whirr of the vacuum cleaner. My nerves twitched at every sound, insisting there couldn't really be someone else here, because I couldn't sense the tapestry of thought and emotion, which made up a living being.

I closed my eyes and tightened my hand on the cane, fingernails scraping the wood, like a man clinging to a ledge. Like I'd clung to Hayden's hands when he heaved me up from the ground, just before he—

"Holy shit!"

The exclamation jerked me half out of the chair, old reflexes screaming. Raph stuck his head in the door, a bright grin on his face. "Sorry," he said. "I'm supposed to stay professional, but I just saw your Parking Lot Mastodon CDs. And the poster!"

"Signed by the whole band," I said. That had been a night. The lead singer had given me a "special performance" back at their hotel. "You're a fan?"

"Hell, yeah!" Raph leaned against the doorframe, his eyes alight. "So what did you think about the Ice Age album?"

⊕ ⊕ ⊕

"I don't know why we have to do this," I said. "Can't you just call me on the phone?"

Anita Wannamaker stood in my living room, observing everything with a critical eye: the closed drapes, the dusty TV, the picked-at remains of a crappy frozen dinner. My "case handler," they called her. It sounded better than "person who has to make sure you haven't hung yourself from the shower curtain."

"When was the last time you left the apartment?" she asked, ignoring my question.

I shrugged, cane tapping as I limped after her. "I go out."

"Other than to physical therapy?"

My face spasmed. It had been bad today, maybe because I'd dreaded her arrival all week. "People stare."

"People are jerks," she said succinctly. "I don't give a damn about them. I'm asking about you. Sitting alone in your apartment without human contact isn't healthy."

What the hell did she expect me to do? Act like nothing had happened? Act like I still had some kind of future? Like my brain hadn't burned out, like I hadn't come down in a shower of glass and blood—

"I have plenty of contact," I said. "Raph comes by twice a week." And I dreamed about him more often than that.

"Raph?"

Damn it. "The home care guy."

She arched a single, skeptical brow at me. "And you have long conversations, I take it?"

I couldn't turn away fast enough to hide the heat in my face. Because we did have long conversations. About music, at first. Then sports. Our hometowns. The foods we liked to eat. Nothing serious, nothing that really meant anything.

"Interesting," Anita said, folding her arms over her chest as she studied me.

"He's just running up the clock."

"These services get paid by the job, not the hour."

My stupid heart lurched, a second of euphoria, like when you jump off something high and get that instant of free-fall, before gravity takes over.

Before the crunch of breaking bone when you hit the ground.

"Oh," I said.

Anita sighed. "Get out of the apartment. I mean it, William. Don't make me file a bad report on you."

"What are they going to do? I was honorably discharged."

"No one ever really leaves Psy Squad," she said, and headed for the door.

"So, um…"

Raph shut off the vacuum and turned to face me, an expectant smile on his face. God, he was gorgeous. A year ago, I would have known instantly if he was interested.

Ha. As if.

"Yes?" he prompted, when I didn't say anything more.

This was stupid. "You probably know the Parking Lot Mastodons are playing at the amphitheater Friday."

"Yes," he said. Was there something hopeful in his voice? Or was I reading too much into it?

"Well, um, I've got tickets, and I was wondering if you…I mean, you probably already have tickets, and plans, and—"

"Darin?"

"Yes?"

He leaned a hip against my disused desk, his smile taking on a dimension that might have been flirtatious, or might have been my imagination, because how the hell could I tell? "I'd love to go with you."

Oh. Oh, hell. I hadn't thought about what to do if he said yes. "Great," I managed.

"Dinner first? At the Indian place near the university?"

He remembered I liked Indian food? "Okay," I forced past the constriction in my throat, which was mostly panic but maybe something else as well.

His smile broadened. "I'll pick you up around seven, then."

⊕ ⊕ ⊕

We pulled up in front of the amphitheater. Thanks to me, we could park in the handicapped accessible areas, rather than having to walk a half-mile from the nearest empty lot. "Here we are," Raph said, putting the car in park.

"Yeah," I said. And I found myself smiling. The right side of my face spasmed, but he wouldn't be able to see it from the driver's side.

People had stared during dinner, but I thought at least half of them were too busy ogling him to even notice me. Maybe all of them.

We'd laughed over the meal, and he'd fed me bites of his navratan korma. He was even sweeter and funnier away from the apartment. God, it felt like a date, a real date.

Like I was a real person, and not just the shadow of a dead man.

It wasn't too bad in the parking lot, with people still drifting in, or hanging out waiting for friends. Not too bad in the line, either, until we got to the security guard wanding everyone.

"You on something?" he asked, scowling at my twitching face.

"N-no." Heat suffused my cheeks; people were definitely staring at me now. Raph, who had made it through already, stopped to listen, which made it even worse. I didn't want to remind him.

"Oh yeah?" The guard's glare turned contemptuous. "Then why is your hand shaking? Too long since your last fix?"

"Back off." It took me a minute to recognize the angry snarl as Raph's.

"Hey! You want to be thrown out with him?" The guarded demanded.

"It's okay," I mumbled at the ground. Shame suffused me; I'd never backed down from a fight in my life, and now here I was taking shit from some overpaid rent-a-cop. "I'll wait in the car."

"Like hell." Raph's eyes flashed fire as he glared at the guard. "Do you know who this is? This is Major William Darin McConnel. You know, one of the guys who helped take down Hayden? The terrorist? So show some fucking respect."

The breath in my lungs turned to glass.

The guard's eyes widened, and he looked past the twitch and recognized the face of a ghost. "Oh shit! I'm so sorry, sir, I..."

He said more, but I couldn't hear anything over echoes of Raph's voice. Each word fell like a shard of broken glass, fracturing tinier and tinier as it hit the floor. Major. William. Darin. McConnel.

He'd known. He'd always known.

I was an idiot.

I turned and ran, as best I could with the cane, but no one can outrun the truth.

"Darin!" Raph shouted from behind me, but there was no Darin. There was nothing, just an empty shell, a space where William McConnel had been. And I hoped, I really thought—

What? That the dead would come back to life? That I would?

I limped blindly past the car, past everything, people stepping hastily aside as the madman came through, as if I might drag them down with me. The landscaped grass stretched before me, down a slope, and I tried to flee, but my leg betrayed me,

and

I

fell.

I fell down the stairs in a shower of glass and blood.

I fell down the slope, my cane tumbling free from my hand.

And I hit the ground.

I thought I'd died that day, when Hayden burned out my talent and threw me aside like a piece of trash. But I hadn't, not really. Despite the pain, despite everything, I'd been in free-fall all this time.

"Darin!" Raph dropped to his knees beside me, and I struggled to shove him away. "Sweetheart, what's wrong? Tell me?"

"You knew. You never said—I didn't think—"

His arms, strong and warm, wrapped around me. "I don't understand. Of course I recognized your name. You're a hero."

I choked on a laugh, because it was all a lie. Icarus's wings had melted, even though the sun had burned down to something dark and cold. "I'm not him," I whispered. "Or I was, but he's dead, and there's nothing left but this. This wreck."

Raph's scent, of coconut aftershave and warm skin, enveloped me as he leaned closer. "You stopped a terrorist. You saved lives."

I shook my head, my body a gaping wound, pumping out darkness. "I should have waited for backup. But I thought I could handle him. A lone telepath...how could he have any chance against me? So I charged in, and he...and he..."

"Burned you out," Raph said quietly.

Hot fingers in my brain, accompanied by laughter. I'd tried to fight back, used everything I had, and if the whole squad had been there, he wouldn't have had a chance.

But they weren't, so I was the one who had no chance, vessels rupturing in my brain as he overloaded the psychic centers. Then, when I lay bleeding from my eyes and nose and ears, unable to stand, he picked me up and threw me through the glass dividing the penthouse from the stairs to the lower level. I'd lost consciousness halfway down. I had really never hit the ground until now.

"Yes," I said. The stark truth. "And now there's nothing left."

"You're wrong."

"Without Psy Squad, without my abilities, what do I have?"

Raph's fingers touched my jaw, gently turning me to face him. "Your sense of humor?" he suggested. "Your passion for music? Your concern for others? Maybe I asked for the assignment because I wanted to meet William McConnel, hero, but I'm here tonight because I want to spend time with Darin."

He leaned in and very carefully, very gently, kissed me.

A part of me didn't want to believe it could be true. I wanted to shove him away, and go back to my apartment where the drapes were always shut, because that was familiar. I could deal with it, with just waiting for death to get around to stopping by for a visit.

Instead, I kissed him back.

"You still have so much to offer," he whispered against my lips, once the kiss ended. "And if you can't see it right now, can you at least trust me enough to believe I do?"

I swallowed thickly. I felt drained, as if I'd been fighting gravity for months, and finally given in to rest on the solid earth. "I'll try."

"Thank you." Raph hesitated then dug in his pocket, pulling out something shiny. One of the medals I'd thrown away.

"I saved them from the trash, just in case you changed your mind," he said, ducking his head with a blush. "I hope you don't mind."

"No." I could always tell him to toss them later. But maybe I wouldn't. Maybe someday I could look at them again and see them as a part of my past, not a death knell to my future.

The sound of music rose from the amphitheater, accompanied by the muffled roar of the crowd. Raph gently traced my jaw with his fingers. "Maybe the concert was a little much to start with," he said.

"You're probably right." I summoned up a smile, and found to my surprise it didn't feel half as awkward as I'd expected. "Why don't we start off smaller? Your place?"

Raph's fingers twined gently with the shaky fingers of my right hand. "I'd love that."

⊕ ⊕ ⊕

Jordan L. Hawk grew up in the wilds of North Carolina, where she was raised on stories of haints and mountain magic by her bootlegging granny. After using a silver knife in the light of a full moon to summon her true love, she turned her talents to spinning tales. She weaves together couples who need to fall in love, then throws in some evil sorcerers and undead just to make sure they want it bad enough. In Jordan's world, love might conquer all, but it just as easily could end up in the grave.

THE STAR

L'Etoile Flamboyant

By Samantha Henderson

LAST NIGHT I DREAMED ABOUT THE PAINTED CHILDREN: the Dragon Leviathan, the Boy Made of Horses, and the girl, L'Etoile Flamboyant. In the dream, I sat at the edge of the cliff beside the ruins, not far from where I lie now, but I was straight and whole again, the tiger reclining beside me like an outsized housecat. The water at the foot of the cliff glistened in the starlight, and the Children were in a boat, little wider than a rowboat, looking up at me. The girl stretched out her arms, and I shifted as if to rise. The tiger gave me a lazy nudge. *Not yet*, it said, silently. *We are still at the business of dying.*

⊕ ⊕ ⊕

It doesn't matter where I came from and what I was before, when there were cities with power that came from vast engines, water came with a turn of the wrist, there were telephones and television and flying a mile above the ground was taken for granted. In the chaos that came with the ending of that world my body was broken more than once, and I lost my family and our beautiful house filled with beautiful things, like crystal glasses to serve chilled wine and machines that sang.

Or perhaps I was always crippled, an indigent. Perhaps the woman, my girl, my boy, or the things I remembered having are some of the many stories people create after a world is destroyed and remade. Truth becomes a house built from splintered lumber, and it's better to tread carefully around the bad joins and makeshift foundation lest the whole blessed structure comes tumbling down. That is why, as part of the grace we share in this violent world, no one asks a lot of questions. No one disturbs the fragile foundation of another's truth.

I joined Hobart's Carnival because one of his mares got loose. I found her in the waste behind Goddard's market, where I was cleaning blood from the stalls for my bread. I got a piece of rope around her neck, and found her thrushy foot. I had it soaking when Hobart found me—I'd learned about curing horses from when Goddard's was a post-stop, before they gave up and sold the animals for meat—and he offered me bed and board to stay a week until it was cured. Better food than Goddard's, so I agreed.

Hobart didn't like me much, but even after the beast was fixed he kept me on—in part because I'm good with horses, but there are many more able-bodied that can keep a hoof sound and stop the mares from bickering. When the Carnival started to move and it was time to strike the tents I saw him eye me with my back so twisted I couldn't scurry up the poles and bring the sailcloth down. I saw him think *useless trow*, for everyone with Hobart's, fortuneteller and fairy dancers included, did double duty and knew not to shirk their share of labor, down to fighting if it was needed. I would have been dumped in the next backwater we played, had it not been for the tiger.

Hobart had found or bought or stolen, in the back alleys of the world-that-was, a tremendous, slinky, striped beast that twisted in its cage like the tawny embodiment of the jungle itself. Hobart's was a good show, with horses that danced and curtseyed enough to please any girl, and acrobats that played their dangerous games overhead with a cheerfulness that seemed to welcome death. But most people have seen clever horses and know a boy who can do a trick or too. Few people, even in the world-that-was, have seen a tiger up close enough to understand the orange-black immensity of it, its slow burning gaze, the ivory architecture of its jaws as it yawns its contempt. A tiger is a threat, a delightful creep of fear along the spine, and a promise as well. People will come from their farms in the valleys, their lairs in the cliffs and pay hard-won coin to see a tigerHobart had been able to control the beast so far, to make it leap from its cage and sit like a housecat, to roar on cue and offer its paw. But he knew that dark rumble from the creature's side as it contemplated the first and second row meant one day soon it would shrug off his will and make a red harvest of the tent.

When I stood in the aisles and let the tiger see me, that rumble stopped and the cat became quiescent, calm, and bowed its grisly head under Hobart's touch. When I reached into its cage and patted its flank after feeding—Hobart let nobody but himself feed the creature its meat— it grumbled and settled down into sleep. It was a strange kind of love. Whether because my crippled spine made me suitable prey, or whether I smelled of the sins of a past I couldn't remember, I saw in the tiger's regard a restrained hunger, a willingness to wait until the right moment to snap my ill-healed bone, to sink its teeth into my belly. The tiger took pleasure in that suspended time between the decision to kill me and the actual act, and I was content to live upon its whim.

The tiger—and I, to keep it from killing the rubes—were necessities now that Khasar had left the Carnival. They called Khasar a soul-eater, what used to be called a hypnotist, but he wasn't a sideshow trickster that made you recite the alphabet backwards and bark like a dog. And they told me he didn't work the day shows at Hobart's Carnival, the time when hard-faced children laughed at the clowns juggling handkerchiefs and young girls fell in love with the dancing horses. During the day, the snake handler hefted a milky albino python over her head, and acrobats spun fluid down the ropes from the summit of the big top, and the air was tinged with the smell of burning sugar and cut grass.

But we must make our way in a hard world any way we can, so Hobart's had a night circus, where the snake handler did something quite different with the python, and the fairy dancers wore paint and nothing else, and the smell of sugar turned to musk. Children didn't come to the night circus, but their fathers did, and their uncles and brothers and a few of the bolder women. The night circus was when Khasar flourished. He would ask for three volunteers—never more or less—and sit them in straight-back bentwood chairs, facing the audience. With a word he would cast them into unnatural sleep, with another wake them, empty eyed. At his bidding, they would rise and climb the air, step by step on the aether. Twenty feet up they paced restlessly over the audience's heads, until he called them down again, and made flame sprout from their fingers, and made them weep blood.

At night in the dust and amber light of the tent, it would be a simple matter for a skilled illusionist to find a way to make people walk on the air. Thin ropes, which, in their mesmerized state, they were convinced they could walk, or maybe thick sheets of glass judiciously placed. This is what they told themselves in the morning, back to wresting a living from a shattered land with no magic to it. Those he made paddle the empty air overhead never remembered what happened. But during those musky nights when Khasar commanded the tent, the snake handler told me that there was not a wight there, no, not even the carny folk, who did not believe that he could take the soul out of a man and replace it with something inhuman. Fallen angels, the fortuneteller whispered. The animals who have died in the service of the carnival, the snake handler said.

I only knew what they told me because a few nights before I found Hobart's wandering mare limping through Goddard's garbage, something had gone wrong with Khasar's act. The rubes sat, listened, opened vacant eyes, climbed the air as before. But although the hypnotist snapped his fingers and spoke the words to bring them back, they stayed—so they said—possessed, and climbed the upper air of their own dwellings in a manner most disconcerting. It was a rare, green place the Carnival had landed, so there were many people, and they were not half-starved and fearful. By the time their relatives were back to have an accounting, their blood-weeping kin in tow, Khasar had disappeared into the night, and Hobart thought it sane to do likewise, even into the gritty dry places where garbage-heaps like Goddard's were the best shelter.

We were headed for another green place now, a city half-drowned in the sea, they told me, where the trade was rough but profitable. On the way, wherever we saw clusters of houses and not too many desperate-looking men, we stopped and made a little show, not bothering to unfurl the big tent. They came to see the fortuneteller, the horses, and the tiger yawning in its cage. I suspect some of them were as entertained by seeing healthy horseflesh as anything else, because I kept the mares and the lone, put-upon gelding as glossy and sound as they had ever been.

It was after one of these half-shows, when we were packing for an early departure, that Khasar returned with the Painted Children. I hadn't known him before, so the uneasy feeling when a man, tall and well built with black hair as glossy as my horses, came to the hitching-fence and asked to see Hobart was a surprise. He had a spiky moustache full of wax and a will of its own, which should have made him absurd, but his eyes, flat and shiny as a snake's, put an end to all impulse to find him funny. He had three small figures with him, shrouded and still, and as he was led away to see the carnival master by one of the fairy dancers (who stifled a squeak and trembled when she saw him) I saw that each was joined to each, and then to Khasar's wrist, by a thin gold chain, almost invisible in the morning light. *Soul-eater*, I thought, as I finished wrapping the horses' legs for the journey.

No one knew what bargain Khasar struck with the carnival master, and no one asked where Khasar found his children. No one much liked asking the hypnotist anything. He didn't perform or exhibit his finds while we traveled, and all three of the children rode on the back of one horse, a normally lazy mare who acted as if they weighed nothing, but who also sometimes paused and tilted her head towards her back, an un-equine look of puzzlement on her face.

I wondered whether they were children at all. They were child-small, of course, two boys and a girl with heads a little too big for their height and wide, clear, set-apart eyes. Glance at them quickly and there'd be no doubt; you'd take them for children, as a matter of course. But study them at a distance, or speak to one, however briefly, and you'd wonder. There was a way they had of moving, too fast between one stance and the next, as if they stuttered on the air, and any word they said was as if they sculpted it in their mouths before they said it. I remembered, or thought I remembered, a story from the world-that-was, of green-skinned children that were not children who came to a small village and died without revealing where they had come from, and everyone was left with an indefinable sense of mystery and wrongness.

Maybe it was simply hard to imagine anyone putting ink and needle, in such detail, so extensively, to a child's tender skin—for we could see, through the thin shrouds worn by Khasar's small retinue, patterns blossoming over every visible square inch of them. It could not be that he had inked them himself—this was the work of months and years, not to mention the time it would take to heal. He must have bought them, but who in this world would have the time to make over human children into such creatures? The carnies whispered, at the campfires when Hobart and Khasar were nowhere in sight, that they were a kind of fallen angel, the embodiment of the broken souls Khasar put into the bodies of his subject-victims, the ones who walked on air and wept blood. They said that the time he was away he'd hunted out the three who hadn't come back to themselves, and rendered their bodies into these painted forms. Nonsense, I thought, because why weren't we all done-and-dead when the hearty folk who lived in that last green place hunted Khasar down, him and anyone who sheltered him?

We came to the place where the sea had fingered into the basin where a city sat, leaving enclaves that glowed at night along the shore. We found the place Hobart remembered from the last great circle the Carnival followed, above the still, brown waters of the old city, a flat place with a three-domed building at the edge of a cliff. A distant echo of my old self whispered observatory, and through one of the broken domes I could see the remains of a telescope. The able-bodied raised the big top beside the ruins, where an obelisk still stretched toward the sky, the figures incised into the sides long since defaced. Brown hills rose behind us, carved with ancient trails, and the fragments of an old sign that stuck up out of the ground like broken teeth.

We rested a day, while people came from the enclaves to see what we were about, marveling at the jugglers and the tiger. When it was time for the show, we learned that Khasar, once again, would have nothing to do with the day circus, and that he kept the Painted Children (avoiding that cruel word, Tattooed) for the nighttime.

I saw them waiting with Khasar while the snake charmer writhed and the acrobats twisted naked, and though the soul-eater flashed me a gutting-knife glare, I went to stand with them. He still had them chained with a thin gold line that shouldn't have held a kitten, and they peeked at me through their shrouds.

Khasar mopped a fat drop of sweat from his temple, but showed no other sign of nervousness. When Hobart, playing ringmaster, promised the crowd a wonder of the world and when those in the audience who had heard of Khasar murmured in anticipation, he unlooped the chain from one of the boys, thrust the lose end in my hand, and muttered at me to keep them there.

Khasar walked to the center of the ring, where the arclights could swivel and pin him under their glare. The boy followed him like an acolyte. He eyed the front row occupants one by one, as if considering cows at market, judging just how long he could keep them waiting, wondering what he would do, what the small figure beside him was for.

"Gentlemen," he intoned, just before they got restless. He let a small smile curl under his moustache and eyed the women scattered here and there in the stands. "And…Ladies."

I saw some of them shiver as if he'd made phantom fingers dance across the backs of their necks.

"It is my pleasure to share with you something so rare, so precious, that I feel confident in telling you that you are an exclusive group, some of the very few who have the opportunity to see such."

In the background, Hobart took a deep breath and blew it out. I could smell sweat and sawdust. I turned to one of the children, the girl. She was looking at me intently, almost at my eye level because of my broken back.

"Don't be afraid," I told her. It was absurd. All small things should be afraid at the night circus.

She tilted her head as if she didn't understand me. The thin chain bit into my fingers. I winced as she placed the tips of her fingers on my wrist.

"The first to be revealed, the Leviathan!"

Khasar tugged away the boy's covering. There was silence at first, as the people tried to understand why they should marvel at that most ordinary of things, a child. What did it matter that he was ink marked?

Khasar whispered the next, his voice vibrating in every crevice of the tent.

"Leviathan, Serpent of the World!"

The boy—if it was a boy—stood, head bowed in the spotlight, naked but for the patterns on his flesh. His nakedness didn't register, however, because he seemed entirely clothed in the figure that began in green-and-gold glory at his ankle and wound thickly around him: knee to thigh to waist to shoulder. The coils shone with the burnished weight of hundreds upon hundreds of scales, and it was breathtaking to consider that they must have each been drawn and not grown. The snaky creature lay heavy over the boy's shoulder, and the head rested on his chest—a monstrous head with golden eyes and tendrils coiling from jaw and temple, teeth overlapping the lower lip, a hint of smoke about the nostrils.

A susurration grew from the crowd as they understood the artistry, the brutality of the thing. At the sound, the boy raised his head and looked at them with flat despair. I felt the girl's hand creep into mine, and behind me, past the flaps of the tent kept open for ventilation, the tiger's vigilant eye hot on my back. The hiss of the crowd settled to the floor of the tent and spread like night fog, just over the threshold of hearing, independent of them.

Khasar knew his audience now, and didn't give them time to recover. He threw open his hand towards me and the children in the aisle, not even looking at us, and like an automaton I obeyed, unlooping the chain from the second boy's wrist. He walked towards Khasar with a tremulous grace, and I understood that the hypnotist held them in a thrall that made a gold chain an iron cuff, and escape unthinkable. The hiss continued in the still, over-warm air.

I felt the heat of the tiger's gaze on me and then a cool pause as it blinked, indifferent to Khasar's powers. *You know what to do*, it thought, a lazy purr in my head. *And I will not kill you until it happens.*

With a flourish, the soul-eater whipped away the shroud. "The Horse-Boy," he declaimed, and if it wasn't as grand a name as Leviathan no one noticed.

Two horses before, two horses behind—ink-black, bay, leaf-brown, and palomino. His body was quartered with them; each took the entirety of one flat pectoral or shoulder blade, extended down a nipped-in waist and hipbone or buttock. Their legs were his legs. They were caught mid-gallop, and as he shifted his weight under the hungry eyes of the audience they quivered and twisted, and if the hiss continued in one corner of the tent, from another came the urgent drumbeat of hooves. They ran out of him, not as if he was a canvas or a tattooed boy, but as if he was a vast prairie. The crowd leaned close, and I saw in them a primal longing to mount and ride. The gift of a horse is to be not one place but another, something I felt through my fingers when I groomed the carnival horses.

With the audience still enthralled by the dragon and the horses, Khasar turned his burning eyes to the girl and her hand clenched on mine. Still, we were both powerless: I removed the chain and she walked out to him. The boys moved apart while the girl stood before Khasar an entire, breath-holding minute. This time he said nothing. He only nodded, and she lifted her arms, the shroud falling away and pooling, discarded, on the trampled grass.

The entirety of her body was inked the blue of a sky at the edge of twilight, contrasting with the pale yellow mass of the star incised in the center of her back. It looked like she was a vessel carved so that an internal flame blazed outwards. The rays of the star were elongated, and edged in black, extending high between her shoulder blades, across her ribs, and down almost to her buttocks. The rest of her was spotted with smaller, gilded stars of eight points that seemed to float above her skin.

"The Star," he whispered, and let the word hang a moment. "L'Etoile Flamboyant, the Burning Flame, the Light that Illuminates. Imagined and sought for in the world-that-was, here only for you, Gentlemen and Ladies."

Cutting through the wonder, a gasp. Khasar had broken the bargain implicit between entertainer and entertained, ignored the tender, implicit bargain between the con man and the rube. No one at the carnival mentioned, ever, the world-that-was. Knowing this, he made a sign and the lamps cut out. In the sudden twilight, the Star glowed, pulsing, a fragile heart brutally exposed.

Khasar's last words dropped, stones in the gut of a river. "Never will you see anything so rare."

A snap of fabric, and the Star vanished; the light came on, making everyone blink, and Khasar and the children were gone. I pitied the acrobats who tumbled and contorted afterwards, trying to make that dazzled, moon-struck crowd smile. Before, when Khasar's act was finished, the audience was pleasantly fearful and craved the sex-tinged refresher the acrobats could provide. Tonight they had gone inside themselves and nothing could coax them out, and the performers had the bewildered air of a whore trying to pleasure a dead man. After, Hobart declared Khasar and the Painted Children would be the last act, assuming anyone came back.

It was even odds whether we would fill every space the next night, or be run out. Perhaps if we battened on the green of a single township, they would have none of us. But here, with settlements scattered around the edges of a new and alien sea, high on the hills beside ruins, we've become some sort of hybrid of circus and temple, and Khasar's Painted Children the vessels of a dreadful and compelling sacrament.

⊕ ⊕ ⊕

A path wound down the cliff, and at its base a trickle of pure water poured into the brackish sea. I led the horses down, two by two twice a day to water them, so they didn't foul the sweet water higher up. Hobart's had camped beside the drowned city about a week, and I was leading two mares to drink and bathe a bruised fetlock when I spied a small shadow between them. I didn't know which of them had slipped from Khasar's golden chain, and I hunched my twisted back further so I wouldn't see. As the horses sucked water I heard one of them whicker, and a small splash, and I did look then, to see a small dark figure arrowing, swift towards the center of the sea.

I halted up the path and wondered which it was, and how Khasar would balance his act between Star and Dragon, Dragon and Horse, Horse and Star. On the green in the center of the triangle of tent, obelisk, and three-domed ruin, the soul-eater stood snarling at Hobart, the two remaining children head-bowed beside him. I just registered that they were the Star—Le'Etoile, he called her—and the Horse-Boy when there was a great roar and a shadow that struck at the same time. Something writhed as it rose behind the ruins, coil upon green-gold coil, and a head twice the size of my tiger's cage.

The mares screamed and reared, and it took all I had to tug one down. The other pulled away and ran for the brown hills and the broken teeth there. We never saw her again. I could hear the other horses screaming, and prayed that their tethers held and that they didn't break themselves apart against the ropes.

Suspended in the sky and twisting upon itself like an eel in water was Leviathan, Serpent of the World. It had no wings but flew nonetheless, as if the air was a thick medium it had mastered. Its head was half mouth, its mouth was half fangs, each like an ivory dagger, and its flame-gold eyes glared at Khasar. Swift as a sparrow it lunged at him, the ferocious maw wide. Hobart jump-stumbled to the side, sprawling on the grass.

Swifter than a sparrow, Khasar drew a knife and grasped the Star's thin arm, pulling her to him and the point of the knife to her throat in one fluid motion. The point dipped into the skin beneath her jaw, and

I imagined I saw—at too great a distance to see—a welling drop of blood that was not red. He never took his eyes off the Dragon.

The beast stopped, mouth open, spanning the soul-eater from head to waist. A neat snap and Khasar would be cut in two—just a pair of legs and an abbreviated waist, spouting scarlet—but the girl would vanish down her brother's throat. The Dragon drew back, just a fraction, impossibly suspended and the heat of its eyes blazing just as furiously.

Water, I thought. The water had hatched this creature as if the boy was a mere egg, the tattoo a shadow of what was inside.

The Star said something—softly, but we were all dead silent and frozen, even the mare in my grip. We'd never heard any of them speak, and it mattered little now we did, for it didn't even sound like a human speech—more like the popping of a broken branch, or the sizzle of a stone falling from the sky to earth.

The Dragon's mouth snapped shut and the head tilted toward her. She made that sound again. Khasar didn't move, except to tighten his grip on her arm. She didn't look at him.

The Dragon recoiled, segment by segment until it hovered again over the ruined observatory. Its golden glare bathed all of us, one by one, as if it considered a hostage it could take in its turn. But we knew Khasar loved none. Love is a rare thing these days; we use each other to live, to grasp us in midair like the catcher in the trapeze act. I am loved only by the tiger.

If the Dragon devoured any of us, Khasar and Hobart would not even shrug. With a low growl that rattled the earth, the Dragon shot away like an arrow. In passing, the tip of its tail flicked a dome, crumbling it like sugar.

The Night Circus was cancelled that evening, while Khasar regrouped. By some miracle, we lost no more horses, although Hobart, angry at the loss of the evening's takings, cuffed me hard for losing the mare and my ear trickled into the hay all that night.

⊕ ⊕ ⊕

I don't know how the Dragon escaped, but I saw Khasar leading his two remaining children in their shrouds to the tent, saw the Star stop suddenly, like a sleepwalker awaking, saw her dart forward and tug the gold chain away from the boy. Khasar whirled about but was slower with a grasping hand than with a knife, and the Horse Boy danced away, found sure footing, and ran.

At first I thought he was running to me, but then I realized the cliff was open at my back and he would pass me by on the way to that oblivion. Khasar uttered a word I didn't know, except I knew it was terrible, and gave chase, leaving the girl standing alone. In my mind's eye I soared over the scene, as the Dragon might, seeing the boy, a tiny dot, Khasar, a bigger dot streaking after, and many other dots, at the edge of comprehension, beginning to converge on the boy.

His legs pistoned like any other horse, faster and faster, and even after he went over the lip of the cliff they stuttered in the air, carrying him even further. The air gave beneath him and he fell, even as the horses burst forth from his body, even as the Dragon burst forth from the other boy's body, deep in the sea. Peering over the precipice, I could see how it should have been as hooves, flaring nostrils, thrashing manes hatched from his chest, his back—as he landed they would've galloped off in all four directions, lost like my poor mare yesterday.

But the fall was too short, perhaps—no time to emerge fully. Or, like real horses, the fall was too much. The rest of the carnival were at the clifftop, and when he hit the ground everyone drew in breath, a quick hiss, to ward off the pain of an expected blow. I could almost see the earth bend beneath him like a rubber sheet. I clapped my hands over my ears as the horses, four of them, bay, brown, black and golden, half-hatched from his body, writhed and screamed.

Khasar watched, turned, and marched back to the Star, who made no attempt to run herself. He stood before her a long time, and when he moved his right hand there was a noise from the rest of the carnival, a small movement forward. Even carnie folk, at the edge of extinction, have their limits , and he stopped, for once uncertain.

He must have done something, though, because that night as he led her, solo, to the tent she wore a mask of pulped and gilded paper. Long spines of stripped feathers grew from it, a shimmering blob of feather left at each tip, and gave her the look of an exotic insect. Through the eyeholes, a black shiny glitter made her look less human, more like a bird. But also, if you knew where to look, skin bruised purple-black, so it looked like her face was painted. I didn't see the show but I heard the rubes leaving, and swearing that L'Etoile Flamboyant had risen in the air, to the apex of the tent, and showered down gold.

I was squatting by the tiger's cage, thick in its cat musk, when Khasar and the Star left the tent. There was a barrel-fire, for warmth and light, in the center of the green, and I saw Khasar slide between the girl and the orange glow. I have my own stupidity to blame for not seeing it sooner. I thought Khasar kept the Children away from the campfires so no one would see them close in the firelight, but it was the girl he was keeping from fire—the open flame of the bonfire, the contained metal heat of the warming bins. Her bruised eyes beneath the thick paper of her masked darted, openly longing, craving the flames. No, not the flame. The glowing coal beneath.

I moved as fast I ever did before, in the world-that-was, and knocked the barrel over. Flame and embers spilled along the ground like gold coins, and burning wraiths flared through the air. Startled for once, Khasar dodged one, and lost track of the girl, who bent to grasp a glow-ing coal that tumbled to her feet.

The outside of the coal was ash-black, and the living heart of it glowed where her fingers smudged the ash away. She lifted it to her lips and bit. Split apart, the coal blazed yellow at the core, red on the outside, and I waited for her scream as her lips burned and her tongue shriveled.

Water for the Dragon, Air and Earth for the poor Horse, and Fire for the Star. It was like Khasar, in his arrogance, to try to tame the elements.

He reached for her but she blazed forth, her mask and shroud gone in an instant. He recoiled, arms over his face, as she became too bright to look on, and the shadows she cast on the ground were so black they were voids, and one could trip inside and fall forever. The earth could never contain such light, and she rose, higher and higher, the deadly shadows shifting beneath her. Higher past the obelisk, the top of the tent, higher than the Dragon had squatted in the air, higher and higher until the sky blazed with a new star, brighter than the moon.

⊕ ⊕ ⊕

The carny folk knew their best chance lay with Hobart, so no one stopped Khasar when he came at me to break me the final time. I made a play at pushing him away, at protecting my head, but once he beat me to my knees, I knew it was no use. The blows came again and again, until I could smell nothing but my own blood. When he stopped, I lay in a red-blaze blindness, hearing the tents come down, equipment being packed away, the horses laden. It's easy enough, after all, to find some-one to take care of the horses. Outside my swollen eyelids, I could feel the heat of starlight, so bright the carnival could break camp and travel.

It was quiet after they left. All I could hear was the stream trick-ling to the salty sea, and something that might be the hiss of L'Etoile Flamboyant. But presently there was a padding of four feet, and a cat's rank smell, and the warmth of the tiger beside me.

⊕ ⊕ ⊕

I know when the sun rises and the Star fades the tiger will kill me, and there is a melancholy pleasure in the idea of the end of the waiting and the consummation. I hope afterwards the beast will not be lonely, and will find someone else to love.

I lie content, with my blood congealing on the ground, the tiger doz-ing beside me while the new star blazes overhead.

⊕ ⊕ ⊕

Samantha Henderson lives in Covina, California by way of England, South Africa, Illinois and Oregon. Her short fiction and poetry have been published in Realms of Fantasy, Strange Horizons, Goblin Fruit *and* Weird Tales, *and reprinted in* The Year's Best Fantasy and Science Fiction, Steampunk II: Steampunk Reloaded, Steampunk Revolutions *and the* Mammoth Book of Steampunk. *She is the co-winner of the 2010 Rhysling Award for speculative poetry, and is the author of the Forgotten Realms novel* Dawnbringer. *For more information, check out her website at* **samanthahenderson.com.**

THE M⊕⊕N

THE M⊕⊕N

By J.H. Sked

SHE WENT T⊕ SEE JESS AFTER THE D⊕CT⊕R BR⊕KE THE
news. She'd known it was back before the tests, before the call from
the surgery. She'd been here before, had done the chemo and the drugs
and endured the operation to cut the monster out. She'd had Arthur
then, and the kids were still in school. She'd had no choice but to fight.

"I can arrange chemotherapy sessions to start from next week."
The doctor said, peering at his notes.

"I don't want chemo," she told him.

"Anna—"

"I'm nearly seventy," she said. "Just how much extra time would
this buy me?"

He'd said nothing, just blinked at her miserably.

"How long?" She asked, gently, because she felt a sudden flash of
pity. Being a white knight was useless when your shield was rejected.

"Three months, maybe," he said.

Jess lived in a neat cottage just off the main street, with several cats and a rabbit, Mr. Thistles, who ruled all of them with an iron paw.

Anna rapped smartly on the door and opened it.

"Tea's on the table," Jess called. "I hope you brought biscuits, woman!"

Anna grinned and slipped the packet of ginger snaps out of her purse.

The beaded curtain tinkled softly as Jess stepped through it, still in the gaudy robe she wore for clients.

"Nobody wants a fortune told by someone wearing a track suit and sneakers," she'd once told Anna mournfully.

She stopped just past the doorway and tilted her head at her friend. For a second, Anna caught a glimpse of the girl who'd swapped lunches with her during recess so many years ago.

"Oh, damn it all." Jess said, and Anna burst into tears.

⊕ ⊕ ⊕

"I can't heal this," Jess told her.

"I know," Anna said. Although Jess was a good healer, and a strong one, she'd said the same thing years ago, when Anna had her first bout with the monster.

"I can take some of the pain, when it starts getting bad."

"Thank you," Anna said, and felt a huge amount of relief. The pain was what she most feared.

"You'll come then, when it gets bad?"

"I'll come," she said, and patted Jess on the hand. The skin felt soft and fragile.

⊕ ⊕ ⊕

She went to Jess the first time for the pain as summer turned, flirting with autumn in a rush of gold and bronze.

Jess worked over her for nearly an hour, and they had tea afterwards. Anna brought raspberry creams and they giggled like schoolgirls at Mr. Thistles herding the cats from room to room.

She visited again just before Halloween, now well past the time her doctor had expected to read her funeral notice. This time, Jess worked for close to two hours, and there were bourbon creams with tea but little laughter; both of them simply too exhausted for mirth.

In mid-November, Jess came to her. Anna stopped her after an hour.

"It's helped, I promise. But killing yourself won't stop this."

Jess sighed and sat down. "The morphine's not touching it at all now, is it?"

Anna shook her head. "I think I'm nearly done, Jess," she said quietly. She nodded at the elderly tortie washing a paw on the window. "The kids wanted to take Mitzi back to London, but I couldn't bear to give her up. Will you take her in, when the time comes?"

"I'll take her, pet. Don't worry about Mitzi, she'll fit in with my bunch just fine." She patted Anna's hand. "I have something for you."

Anna perked up. She'd almost drowsed off while Jess hovered over her, but she could feel the warmth left from the healing drain away, chased out by the thing wrapped around her organs.

"Better than morphine?" She smiled, and Jess nodded.

"Oh, I think so."

Jess hauled her handbag off the floor and drew out a slim box.

It looked like an old-fashioned cigarette case, with a steel-blue pearlescent finish and silver trim.

A tap of the silver button on the side and the lid swung silently up.

"Oh!" Anna exclaimed, and her eyes widened.

"What? What happened?"

"Didn't you smell it? The most incredible perfume, Jess." Her pupils were huge. "It was wonderful."

Jess looked at her and smiled. The pain-lines bracketing Anna's mouth had relaxed a little.

"What is it?" Anna peered into the case.

It was lined with midnight blue velvet. She saw odd little flashes of light nestled in the material. Anna squinted a little, but couldn't make out the stones. Some sort of crystal or diamanté, she guessed. There was a pattern to those bright little pinpoints, but she was too tired to figure it out.

There was a single Tarot card nestled in the velvet on one side of the case. Wafer-thin, it gleamed against the velvet. The whites shimmered opalescent, the yellows and oranges gold and copper and bronze. An amethyst scorpion crawled out of sapphire waves. The grass flickered emerald.

The card name was written in jet at the bottom.

"The Moon," Anna said. "Jess, this is beautiful. Can I—may I touch it?"

"It's yours," Jess said.

Anna reached into the case with shaking fingers and lifted out the card.

It was a little smaller than the usual Tarot cards Jess used, and fit quite nicely along the length of Anna's hand.

It lay there sparkling for a few seconds, and then something like a sigh filled the room. The card cracked into three sections and Anna squawked in dismay.

"It's okay, pet," Jess said quickly. "Put the top two sections back in the case, and I'll tell you how to use it."

Anna rested the pieces back on the velvet. One of her fingers brushed against a winking diamond, and turned numb with cold. She stuck the tip in her mouth and raised her eyebrows at her old friend.

"You can use the first piece whenever you like," Jess said. "It will give you three weeks, pain-free. Time enough to do something you've always wanted, but put off until later."

Anna looked at it. This piece held the scorpion, and the waves lapping against the edge of emerald grass.

"How?" She asked.

"You have to eat it."

"Will you stay with me?" She could have sworn the scorpion waved a shiny claw at her.

Jess gripped her fingers. "Always. But listen, Anna, because once you take the first piece you have to take the others when the time comes. It's the price of using this."

"You told me once that large magic always came with a price," Anna mused.

"Sometimes the price is worth it," Jess said.

"What will the other pieces do?"

"The middle part will give you three days," Jess said. "The last one will give you three hours, but there won't be any pain afterward."

"You mean it will kill me."

"Yes."

They sat for a while in silence.

"Three weeks with no pain?" Anna said eventually.

"Yes," Jess answered.

"When do I have to take the other two?"

"That's your choice," Jess said. "But once you take the first, you won't pass until all of them are done."

"Pass!" Anna snorted. "What a silly word that is. It's not like I'm writing a test, is it? I'm hardly likely to fail. Call it what it is, Jess."

"Die, then," Jess whispered. "You won't die until you've taken all three pieces. That's also part of the price."

At Anna's sharp look, she sighed. "Death isn't always a bad thing, Anna."

"I know," Anna said, thinking about the little pile of morphine tablets gathering in the bottle. She'd started collecting them a few days ago when they stopped working as well; skipping the scheduled dose unless the pain was so bad she had to take one. "I know."

She reached for the first piece, gleaming on the table between them.

"I always wanted to see Greece," she murmured shyly. "Will you come with me?"

"I'd love to," Jess told her, and Anna placed the scorpion in its sapphire bed into her mouth.

The taste exploded over her tongue. Honey and wine and sunlight. Anna felt a single sharp prick—the scorpion, planting its sting in her tongue—and then it vanished in the warmth spinning through her body. It rushed through her veins, travelled to her hands, to the feet she'd thought would never be warm again, to her womb and liver and heart and groin. Anna cried out, once, head thrown back and heart pounding, and when she could think again, she found Jess gaping at her.

"Oh, my. That's been a while," Anna said. She was blushing furiously.

"Did you just—"

"I most definitely did." Anna drew in a deep breath. "Is that going to happen every time?"

"No idea," Jess steepled her fingers together and looked at Anna over them. "I didn't know it would happen this time. How are you feeling?"

"Book the tickets, Jess," she said. "We're visiting the Parthenon."

⊕ ⊕ ⊕

They saw the Parthenon, and so many ancient temples they blurred into one. They drank wine and ate hugely at the little tavernas they stumbled over, and daringly dipped into the bright blue sea sparkling under the Grecian sun.

In mid-December, Anna found herself contemplating the little blue tray again. The effect of the card didn't taper away; it stopped. She'd taken the first piece with that glorious sweetness at four in the afternoon, and exactly three weeks later at four the pain slammed back into her.

Jess had warned her. They'd been back from their holiday for two days, and she was sitting at the kitchen table waiting for it, expecting it; and still it bent her over double, trying not to scream. For a few seconds her vision pin-wheeled and she had a momentary hope of passing out. Then pain filled the world, and she clutched at the tabletop, not realizing until much later that she'd peeled back two of the fingernails on her left hand.

When she could finally move again, she reached out with trembling fingers and took the pills waiting for her on the table. Her seat was damp; at some point during the monster re-announcing its presence in her body she'd wet herself.

Anna sat and waited for the morphine to work, looking at the sun-kissed skin on her hands and crying quietly.

⊕ ⊕ ⊕

She didn't use the next piece immediately. She found keeping the lid open at night meant she slept easier—the nights she let the perfume into her room meant nights she only woke up once to take her morphine.

⊕ ⊕ ⊕

In December she booked a train ticket to London. Jess booked a taxi and got her onto the train, and she sat very still in her seat for the two hours it took to reach Euston station. The train was quiet, but she waited for the passengers around her to collect their bags and step out of the carriage before she opened the case.

The middle piece held two four-legged creatures. Anna thought they were a dog and a fox. The figures radiated bronze and copper against emerald grass, a shiny jet path winding between them. The fox glanced up at her and winked. The dog panted, chased its tail, then paused and stared at her.

"Hmmph!" Anna said. She was careful not to touch the velvet inner of the case this time as she lifted the sliver out.

She hesitated, holding it cradled in the palm of her hand, and both of the animals sat down on their haunches and waited.

"Thank you," she whispered, and popped it into her mouth without checking for a response. She didn't want to feel guilty for eating them, but she did. They'd guarded her sleep for weeks; it felt like discarding old friends.

The wafer dissolved in her mouth. At first it was sweet, but it quickly turned bitter and sharp. Anna grimaced and swallowed hard. She felt something lick the inside of her cheek, felt the soft pad of tiny paws over her tongue. Her throat distended briefly as something feeling like a foxtail brushed against it.

She swallowed again, with the bitterness of a thousand tears resting in her mouth, and the warmth she'd been praying for flooded through her body.

Anna sighed and closed the case.

⊕ ⊕ ⊕

She spent Christmas with the children, and ate too much stuffing. She played with the baby, now just starting to walk, and slept without pain in her daughter's spare room. Every so often, she'd feel something furred rub against her from the inside, and the taste of tears gathered on the back of her tongue.

She took the morphine pills on the train twenty-one minutes before the pain was due back just as they left London. An extra two hours with her family against possible public humiliation was worth the risk. It paid off; she was cresting the morphine wave when the beast roared to life, and she'd made very sure to use the bathroom before she got on the train. Although, when the time came she must have made some small noise, because the girl across from her looked up from her magazine.

At her stop, Anna shuffled slowly off the platform and made her way to the parking lot where Jess waited with the idling taxi.

Jess took her home and made them both a cup of tea. Anna sipped and told her about taking the wafer, and how the baby had wrapped the dog in tinsel on Christmas morning.

"Anna," Jess said. "Come stay with me." She leant forward and grasped Anna's hands. "I don't like you being by yourself now.""I can't be under your feet all day, Jess. And your clients—"

"Bugger the clients!" Jess snapped. "I don't get any bookings from now until almost February anyway, you know that. Let me help you."

"You have," Anna whispered. "You already have, pet."

"Have I? Have I really?" Jess let go of Anna and buried her face in her hands. "Part of me thinks I haven't helped you at all. I'm watching you fade and bloom and fade again, and it's killing me to watch it."

"I'm sorry," Anna said helplessly.

"No." Jess lowered her hands. "No. You must think I'm the most selfish creature, Anna. Don't be sorry. But let me help you for this last bit, please. I'll beg if you want me to."

Anna snorted at her. "You couldn't beg if your life depended on it, woman." She reached out and touched Jess on the arm. She could feel her warmth, emanating through the soft cardigan. Her *life*.

"I'll come. Tomorrow," she added, looking around the little kitchen she'd spent so many years in. "I need tonight here."

Anna drifted slowly from room to room with Mitzi padding along behind her. Here the bedroom, where she'd lain with Arthur for forty years, and the awful time just after his passing, when she'd cried herself to sleep for months wearing his shirts. Here the children's room, now just another spare bedroom with a white and yellow comforter and a print of Paris on the wall. Here the bathroom, with its cracking, ancient bathtub and the toilet tucked modestly into a corner. Arthur had put the plumbing in himself. The lounge was dark and tiny. She barely used it in winter; the kitchen was large, bright, and easier to keep warm.

She sat at the table with Mitzi perched awkwardly on the seat beside her, and had a cup of tea.

"It can't be that hard, surely," she told the cat. "People do it every day."

Mitzi yawned, showing sharp little white teeth.

"I think I'm nearly ready." Arthur would be waiting for her, and the little one she'd slipped at seven months. She remembered the tiny little fingers and soft skin, before they took him to the Angels Yard behind the old hospital. The church wouldn't bury an unbaptized child, and she'd never stepped into a house of worship since.

Mitzi would be taken care of, and she'd signed the house over to Jess. She was ready, and past ready to be free of the monster.

She'd wait though, for the New Year. No use spoiling everyone's Christmas.

⊕ ⊕ ⊕

Two days into the New Year, Jess caught her crawling to the bathroom. There was nothing left on her frame; Jess picked her up and carried her to the toilet, then back to bed.

Anna asked for her pills and Jess sat silently beside her and together they waited for the morning.

"She talks to me," Anna said, as they watched the stars fade. "The moon."

Both of them glanced at the slim case beside the bed.

"What does she say?" Jess asked softly.

"She tells me it won't hurt. That I will dance, if I wish it, in silver light. She says..." Anna licked her lips and Jess handed her the water glass. "She says I am loved."

"You are," Jess said. "You are."

Mitzi curled up at the foot of Anna's bed that night and didn't wake up.

They held a little funeral in the back, and buried her near the roses. It was unusually warm for the season, and Jess managed to scrape a little hole for the old cat to rest in.

Anna didn't speak for the rest of the day.

That evening she came slowly into the lounge, holding the case.

"Are you sure?" Jess asked.

Anna nodded. She'd taken nearly a handful of pills and they hadn't done a thing. She was sure.

It tasted of sunlight, of roses, of friendship and a warm smile.

"Dance with me, Jess."

She was light and young and free, and they danced around the old couch and armchair.

Anna broke away and twirled. She looked at Jess and smiled.

"Love." She said, once, clearly. Her voice filled the room.

"Love," Jess agreed, and watched the clock hands turn behind her friend.

⊕   ⊕   ⊕

The author of Wolfsong, Blood Moon Dance, *and the* Blue Moon Detective *series, J H Sked was born in South Africa and moved to London, England in 2003. She currently shares a flat with a long-suffering housemate, several hundred books, and a kindle, and has an on-going war with pigeons and most forms of technology.*

*You can follow her misadventures at her blog **jhsked.blogspot.com** or chat with her on twitter **@jhsked**.*

THE SUN

THE STRANGE CASE OF SAL AND THE SOLAR ELIXIR

By Tristan J. Tarwater

SAL PULLED HER H⊕⊕D BACK, L⊕⊕KING ⊕VER THE CRATPED chaos of the caravan's interior. The medicine man had advertised "Astronomical Remedies, Cure-Alls and Liquid Solutions" on the side of his cart and in his grandiose speech given under the shade of the oak tree in the town square. Her ma warned her against venturing too close to the man and his cart at night. Her pa laughed to himself while the tall, dark man with braided hair and a top hat spoke of the miraculous quaffs lying beyond the curtained entrance to his cart.

But she had been crying in the copse when his orange cart had rolled past, praying to the Red Father to bring her something, anything to get out of marrying Lem. Sal heard the clink, clink, clank of the large metal bells he had tied to his cart. The sight of the white horse and the orange cart threaded through the line of trees like stitching and Sal watched and followed behind the cart, joining her family in the town square.

Medicine men weren't to be trusted, Ma had told her. Her father said, "Any man with no family and of able body should be fighting in the Frontier War. Give husbands and fathers the chance to love on their families and plant their fields."

But Sal watched the man speak, holding a bottle of something in a color she hadn't ever seen before, promising vivacity, uninhibited loquaciousness, and other words Sal didn't understand but could tell were good things, things to desire in oneself.

"I'm here to see what you've got," Sal said, feeling nervous and quite certain it was the correct way to feel.

The medicine man looked up from the small stove, his face shining with sweat. Sal wondered at all the shelves, boxes and bottles crammed on shelves in what seemed like a meticulous manner throughout. "What's your name, woman?" he asked. He stood up, seeming taller in the small room.

"Sal," she answered without stammering. That was enough. She knew better than to give strangermen her full name and this was one of the strangest she had come across in her life. But he'd come to their town and had something she wanted, at least Sal hoped.

"Sal," he said, and his voiced whistled. "What do you want?"

Her mouth fell open but no words came out. What did she want? She wanted a lot of things. She wanted to get out of Green Ravine. She wanted to not have to wash clothes in the creek only to have the wind blow them into the dirt. She wanted her brother back from the Frontier War, where the plains met the forest, dark and wet and cold and full of sharp arrows and swords and guns. She wanted Lem to not want her. She wanted to walk past the field of sunflowers full of seeds and see the great nations. Miz with its spires and vast navy. Qamer with its chains and silks. To burn her apron and visit the temples of deities both alive and dead.

"You said in your pitch you have things people don't know they want or need," Sal said. She heard the horse snort outside, as if laughing at her. "I's hoping you could tell me."

"A pitch, eh?" he asked. He smiled, looking over his items, holding his hands out towards them. "Well, Sal, I am no psychic," he said. The way the medicine man said it made Sal think someone else was a psychic. She looked around, foolishly, no one in the room but the two of them. "You will have to help me."

"I'll do what I have to," Sal said. She wished she hadn't, once she had said it. Now the man made a sound like a snort, laughing at her. "I mean to say, you can count on me. I'll tell you what you need to help me."

"You sound so desperate and so bold," the medicine man said. He held one finger up, letting it pass over the boxes and bottles like an antennae, trying to pick up something. The bottles seemed to flicker with light as his finger moved over them and Sal took another step closer, to make sure she wasn't seeing things. "I hardly think you need my help," he murmured.

"Things ain't always what they seem," Sal muttered back. She watched as he stopped short and turned around, crossing to the other side of the caravan and opening a cabinet that looked too big for the small space but there nonetheless. The medicine man produced a key from a chain around his neck and he opened the cabinet. Something fell out. He said something that sounded like a curse under his breath. Papers rustled and things that sounded lighter than paper rustled.

He pulled out a box, square in shape. It was made of some kind of dark wood, the top carved with circles within circles. He placed it on the table and undid the clasp keeping it closed and raised the lid.

Sal sucked in her breath. As he drew back the lid, light shone from inside. Within the box were the same circles, like tracks, and vials of glowing, colored liquid embedded in the dark material of the base. The odor of something burning and metallic filled the air and Sal drew closer. If she squinted hard enough, she could swear the tiny vials were moving slowly in their tracks. Did the box have some kind of mechanism in the bottom? What was this?

The center of the box held the biggest vial. It glowed, yellow-white. The medicine man picked it up gingerly, holding it in his hand like a baby bird he didn't want to crush.

"You can have this," he said. "For a price."

"What do you want?" Sal asked, looking at the round vial. She wanted to reach out and touch it now but it looked so hot, she wondered how the medicine man held it.

"Bring me something," he said slowly. "The start of which is so insignificant, the result of which is so far removed from its beginnings, it seems like...a miracle."

Sal frowned slightly. The light from the vial illuminated the medicine man's features, clean shaven and sharper in the dark caravan. "How long do I have to get it?" she asked, thinking about the white horse outside and the habits of traveling medicine men.

"I'll leave by sun up," he said. He flashed a smile at her, a smile like a crescent moon lying on its side. "Bring it and the elixir is yours." He placed it back in the wooden box and Sal watched the trail it seemed to leave in the air, watched its light glow and then fade, shut out once the wooden box was snapped closed. "Sun up," the man said.

"I've got it," Sal said. She could imagine the way the vial would feel in her hand, warm. Not warm, hot. Almost too hot but hold it she would, uncap it and drink it down. And then she'd be rid of this town, these people. She'd see the things she wanted to see. "You won't be disappointed."

"If you say so," the man said with the same type of smile. Sal felt like she should hurry. The sun had been down for some time and she had snuck out of the house without her mama or Pa. Without saying anything more she turned and left.

What was it the man had said? Something with a small start which had grown big. A miracle. She stared up at the sky and saw the stars. In school, she had learned they were made of gas. A scientist of Miz had discovered it and though the Church opposed her findings and warned people against it initially, the evidence had been sound and the possibilities it opened intrigued many throughout the scientific community. Sal wasn't a scientist. She was a nineteen-year-old woman, trying to avoid being stuck in this town.

The only lights glowing in the town at this hour were the ones in the saloon. It wasn't a big saloon, not like the one in Templetown, where they went on the high holidays. But it was big enough for those who wanted a drink, a game, or a place to relax after working on their farms and fields or in the mill. Sal didn't usually go. She liked drinks but her Ma made a decent ale at home and Lem usually hung around the saloon. She'd work her cloak to hide her face but it was too warm this night to keep it for long. With a sigh and a push of the swinging doors, Sal entered the drinking establishment.

Sal squinted against the bright light, seeing the full chairs and tables. A band played music, a guitar, violin and hand drum, the singer's voice pretty over the conversation of the townsfolk. A few people looked at Sal as she entered but she just nodded and made her way to the bar, sitting down at the counter.

"What'll it be, Sal?" the bartender asked. Kila was nice, Sal thought. Warm, never gossiped like her daughters, didn't water down her drinks. The robust woman smiled, putting a glass in front of her before Sal could answer.

"Four Corners," Sal said. Kila smiled and raised her ruddy brows. Sal had brought money on the off chance the medicine man charged money. Why had she thought that? Sal sighed as Kila poured the elements of the drink into the glass, the fizz of the soda water making a quiet rushing sound she barely heard over the noise of the bar.

Sal dropped the coins onto the counter and thought. The start of things. Her drink was made of four ingredients, though it seemed like three. Soda water, salt and the special brew Kila made in her kitchen, which was herbal but sweet. Four ingredients to make one drink. Soda was water and gas. Salt was a stone. Alcohol was made from grains. Sal knew that. She stared up at the rows of bottles on the shelves. Grains or vegetables or fruits.

Wheat came from seeds. Most plants did. The sunflowers in the oil fields grew from seeds, black and shaped like tears. A single sunflower could produce over a hundred seeds. Sal took a sip of her drink. It was room temperature but made her mouth feel cold. There must have been mint in it.

Sunflowers made seeds for oil. Wheat made flour for bread, grains for food. Did the medicine man want her to bring him a sunflower? She doubted it. Seed to sunflower. She took another sip of her drink and wondered if the bars in Miz really had ice year round, shaved ice on the streets with syrups to go over them. Sal had had snow sweetened with milk and honey but it must taste different on a hot day, when sweat dripped down one's brow.

Sal didn't think a bottle of alcohol was the answer either, so she finished her drink in silence and then turned to go, waving a solemn goodbye to Kila before she made her way out.

A warm breeze brushed past her, quiet, the clear sky deep and full of stars. Sal looked up at them as she walked, trying to think of what the man could be asking for. A miracle. What types of things were miraculous? Magic was miraculous but no one used magic in the Ravine. All users of Magic lived in the cities using their skills in industry or politics. A few were at the Border, fighting in the Frontier War. Her brother had written home about seeing one of them, a woman who had some kind of strange metal under her skin in spots, rigid and dark, and how she had risen up barricades during a crucial maneuver. How'd that woman get her start? Fil hadn't said. Even if Sal knew, the witch woman wasn't there. Sal couldn't take her to the medicine man.

Sal walked through the streets, finding herself heading back to her home, the dark and humid night surrounding her like a heavy cloak. She couldn't give up but her family would find her missing soon, wouldn't they? Maybe she could show her face at home and sneak out again, with none to be the wiser. It wouldn't be hard. Sal walked up quietly, seeing the lights of her home.

Her ma and pa were standing in the field, under the moonlight. Her father had his arms wrapped around her mother's waist, Ma standing in front as they looked over the garden and land. Her father buried his face in her mother's hair and must have said something because she laughed, reaching up caress his face. Her mother looked back and kissed her father, longer than their usual kisses and Sal blushed as their hands strayed over each other. Sal didn't know if she should move or say something as her mother turned to her father, the pair of them kissing and embracing under the night sky, their whispers drifting over the wind, their skin seeking the warmth of the other. Sal saw her mother say something to her father and he hesitated before he grinned and took her by the hand, the pair of them rushing into the house. Sal watched as the light in the house flickered and moved into their bedroom.

Sal looked down at the dirt road. She wondered if there'd be a baby in the spring. She thought of Lem and marrying him in the autumn and summer children. He wasn't a bad man, he just wasn't what she wanted, not now. Sal sighed and looked back at the window with the flickering light. The house she'd been born in. A thought formed in Sal's mind and she turned around and walked back down the road, thinking about her mother and father in the room and the medicine man's words.

The caravan was still where it was earlier, of course, the horse asleep, standing on its hooves. The light still glowed from within the caravan and Sal wondered if the medicine man slept at all. Sal knocked on the door more loudly than she intended and her heart thumped in her chest.

After what seemed like too long, the medicine man came out. His shirt was opened, suspenders hanging at his sides, his hat still atop his head. He looked at Sal with blurry eyes. Perhaps he had dozed off.

"I figured it out," Sal said. "I have your payment."

"Do you now?" the medicine man asked, starting to button his shirt. "Well, give it to me, then."

"I'm the payment," she said. "You said something that started out like nothing, only to become something miraculous. I know how I started. As an act between two people. Heat and movement and ten moons later, I came along."

The medicine man laughed. "You think highly of yourself, don't you?"

"I have high hopes," she said, more cheerfully than she thought. She frowned and raised an eyebrow at him. "What does it mean though, me paying you?" Sal wasn't sure, but already she could feel the town shrinking behind her.

"It means," he said, holding a hand out toward her. "You come with me." Sal felt her fingers tingle and then her hand as she stepped closer and reached up. He held her hand in his and led her back into the caravan, the case already sitting it out on the table. Releasing her, he walked over to the case, opening it, the same burnt, ozone smell filling the room.

Sal watched the vial, his hands unable to dampen the light the container emanated. Finally, she reached out toward it and uncorked it. Heat seemed to pour out of the lid and the smell of hot metal tingled in her nose.

Without a hesitation, Sal brought the vial to her lips, heat both comforting and vivacious leaping from the edge of the vessel and filling her mouth. It was like lying in a warm field on a summer day. The life of the earth singing around her, earth at the height of her energy. More poured through Sal, flaring through her limbs. She gulped, the taste of a hundred tastes she'd never had before dancing ecstatically on her tongue, rich and unctuous. Citrus and amber and crushed sunflowers, warm sand and hot roads and lusty thunderstorms raging with the energy of sweltering, humid weather and churning oceans. Memories of the Ravine became singed and the corners of them curled and folded in as fire engulfed them until Sal alone was left, feeling warmer than she had ever felt before. The road lay before her and the medicine man beside her, the sunflowers of the oil fields growing ever smaller behind her.

Tristan J Tarwater is the author of The Valley of Ten Crescents *fantasy series as well as the weird urban noir short story,* Botanica Blues *and the upcoming comic,* The Misadventures of Streetsman Shamsee. *She has contributed to the roleplaying site Troll in the Corner and Pelgrane Press. A fan of speculative fiction herself, the first fantasy book she fell in love with was* The Crystal Cave. *Originally hailing from New York City, she considers Portland, OR her home.*

JUDGMENT

A BODY FOR YOUR BIRTHDAY

By Jennifer Wingard

"NANA, I DON'T HAVE TIME FOR A READING. LET ME get on with the work or you'll end up tripping on one of those gaps in the patio and breaking a hip."

"In the old country, people took the cards seriously, Antony."

"You were born here, Nana. Visiting relatives in Brooklyn is about as 'old country' as it gets for you, you silly old woman." Antony softened the words with a peck on his grandmother's wizened cheek, but it didn't help him escape the sharp pinch from her gnarled fingers.

"Keep it up, Nana, and I'll leave your patio the way it is and you'll end up in the hospital where the only pasta is overcooked macaroni and cheese."

Rosemarie reached out to pinch him again, but he backed away with a grin—one she mirrored when he tripped over the rug and almost landed on the freshly mopped kitchen floor.

⊕ ⊕ ⊕

Rosemarie shrieked in tandem with the slam of the patio door when Antony stalked back into the kitchen an hour and a half later.

"Antony, the cards—"

"No time, Nana. Where'd you put your phone?"

"Same place as usual. Where I'd remember it."

"This is serious, Nana. There's a fucking skeleton under your patio."

Rosemarie's eyes snapped up from the cards she studied, Antony's face white even through streaked grime and sweat. "It's her. I know it's her. The cards."

"If you don't stop yapping about the cards and give me the damn phone, I'm going to track dirt all over your clean floor." Antony ran one shaking hand through his hair, and started again. "Nana, I need you to get the phone for me so I can call the police."

Rosemarie sprung from her chair with speed that belied her seventy-two years and dug the phone from beneath a stack of Sudoku books on the tiny built-in desk.

"Don't bother with the police. They're all but useless. Call him," she said as she waved a wrinkled, yellowing business card, plucked from an address book on the desk, in front of Antony's face.

"Nana, I have to call the police. If we don't call them, we'll both end up in trouble for not reporting this. Someone is dead. The cops have to know."

"Fine. Call them, but it's a waste of time. Tommy Kinter knows more about the case than anyone else, though."

"I have no idea what you're talking about, but if it's that important to you, we'll call him after we call the police."

Ten minutes later, Antony handed the phone back to Rosemarie and continued the conversation as if there hadn't been a lengthy interruption. "Now what's this man and your cards have to do with anything?"

Rosemarie perked up, years dropping from her in her excitement. "Ten years ago, when I was still doing readings at the place over on James, this woman came in for a reading. Even though the room was candlelit thanks to Maria being a dotty fool and wanting to give it a gypsy ambiance—whatever that means—I could see the bruises on this woman. Darly something or other, she said. She looked like she'd been a punching bag for someone, and her questions made me certain the poor thing was in a bad way with a monster of a husband."

"I don't get it, Nana. What's this got to do with your cards and this Kinter person?"

"I'm getting to it, boy." Rosemarie took her seat next to the window and opened the red-checked curtains to get a view of the street. "She asked me about her marriage, should she leave her husband, that sort of thing. This"—Rosemary gestured at the cards before her—"was her spread. The cards never tell the same thing twice, but today, her cards came up. Judgment. Because of this one, I warned her to leave. She needed a new start, a different direction in her life, or things would end badly. I know he killed her. Had to be him. She was in tears when she left me that day. Swore she was leaving before it was too late."

"He? Her husband? And you still haven't told me about Kinter."

"Three days later, this Darly woman was all over the news. Missing person. Her mother appealed to the press, certain her son-in-law murdered her daughter. Kinter was a detective working the case, but he's not your typical cop. He's…special. Sees things. Old country Romas would call it a curse, but, in his line of work I can see how it would come in handy." Rosemarie traced the offending card with one wrinkled finger, tapping the upturned face of the woman pictured before speaking again. "He's not with the police anymore, but he would want to know."

Antony stared at his grandmother, trying to work through her reasoning for thinking this particular body was a missing woman from a decade-old case. "I'm sorry, Nana, but I don't see why you think this is that Darly woman or why Kinter would need to know."

Rosemarie waved him off without bothering to explain further and dialed the number on the card she still clutched.

⊕ ⊕ ⊕

"Ms. DellaPenna—"

"Mrs. DellaPenna," Rosemarie snapped at the young policeman, giving him a look that never failed to make her children quake.

"Uh, sorry. Mrs. DellaPenna, we'll go around the side so there's no need to track in and out of your house. We'll need several hours to have forensics go over the scene and remove the body and the surrounding area. Looks like it's been there a long time, though, so it's not likely we'll find much. If you need counseling, the department has a grief counselor and you can make an appointment—"

Rosemarie interrupted the officer once again, "I'll be fine, young man. I'm no daisy."

"Yes, ma'am, I'm sure you will be fine, but just in case, I'll leave the card with your grandson." Officer Daly handed the card to Antony while Rosemarie rolled her eyes at him.

Antony's disapproving glare was wasted on her as she surged to her feet to greet someone behind him. He turned from the officer to see his grandmother wrapping a man nearly twice her size in a hug.

Officer Daly hissed under his breath, but rose to shake the newcomer's hand. "Kinter. What brings you here?"

Rosemarie turned to the officer, her eyes crinkled at the edges in the way Antony knew meant she was up to no good. "Tommy is an old family friend. I'd feel so much more comfortable with him around while there are strangers on my property." She rested a wrinkled hand on Daly's arm, patting him gently like he was an anxious dog. "It's important for the old and helpless to feel safe, don't you think?"

Daly barely managed to refrain from choking at the absurdity of Rosemarie being helpless, but nodded his agreement before promising to update them later and leaving the room.

"I see you're as feisty as ever, Rosemarie. You must be Antony," Tommy said, extending his hand toward Antony as Rosemarie ushered him to the couch.

"Yes, sir. And you're Mr. Kinter, I suppose."

"Okay, okay. We've had our meet and greet. Let's get on with things." Rosemarie nearly bounced with impatience from her perch on the edge of her seat. "It's Darly whats-her-name. I know it is."

"Yeah, you mentioned that on the phone, but what makes you think it's her?"

Rosemarie waved her hand at the question she deemed unimportant and continued, "Have you kept track of that husband of hers over the years?"

"He's remarried and living on State with the woman he was seeing at the time his wife went missing. Always thought he'd done her, but there was no evidence he abused her, as you thought, let alone killed her." Tommy leaned forward, drumming his fingers on the thick file he carried. "I dug through my old files after you called. Did you know Andrew Marsden's mother owned this house ten years ago?"

Rosemarie's shriek answered the question for him.

"I'm going to call my old partner then head over to see Marsden. Will you be okay here with people tearing your back yard apart?"

"Of course I will," Rosemarie spat. "I want to go with you, though. Want to see the bastard squirm. Maybe you could rough him up just a little."

"Nana!" Antony stared at his grandmother, trying to reconcile the bloodthirsty woman in front of him with the cheek-pincher he'd always known.

Tommy laughed and passed the file off to Antony. "Rosemarie, stay here. You can't leave right now. God knows what they'll do to your house if you're not around to keep them in line. Antony, you keep her occupied. Let her pore over the file until I get back."

Rosemarie and her curses followed Tommy to the door, but he shooed her back to the living room with assurances he'd be back as soon as he saw Marsden.

Tommy punched Jackson's number into the phone as soon as he

left the porch. "Hey, Jackie. It's Tommy. Remember the Marsden case? Missing person, ten years back? I think the remains on Brewster are connected. I'm going to see the husband. Call me."

When he pulled into Andrew Marsden's driveway, the phone rang, Jackson's number at the precinct blazing across the screen. He tossed the phone into the glove box, knowing he'd catch hell for it later if Marsden decided to file a complaint. Three minutes later, he sat in the Marsden's living room opposite a woman more over-improved hooker than suburban housewife.

"I'd like to speak to your husband, Mrs. Marsden. There've been some developments in the case of his first wife's disappearance."

Tanya's face registered her shock, a feat, considering the fresh injection sites on her forehead and cheeks. "Haven't you people put Andy through enough? She's been missing for ten years. She's legally dead, according to the court."

"As it turns out, she may be more than just legally dead. A body was discovered at the house your mother-in-law owned when Darly went missing."

"So? What's that got to do with Andy?" Tommy winced as she leaned so close he choked on the cloud of perfume surrounding her. "If a body was found at his mother's old house, ask his mother about it. Or ask the people who have lived in that shithole since she moved out."

"It's a less shitty neighborhood since she moved out. Nice folks moved in once the trash moved out," he finished with a wink.

"How dare you come into my house and talk to my wife or about my mother like that." The voice from behind Tommy bellowed like the ass he knew it belonged to.

Tommy pointed at the scar along his left temple. "Brain injury. Getting shot in the head fucked my impulse control."

Andrew opened his mouth to respond, but before he could get a word out, a screech reverberated through the house.

"You get her this time," Tanya whined. "She's your mother and I'm tired of hauling her cranky ass around."

"Shut up and get her. I have to deal with this." Andrew's face reddened in anger, but he looked no less thrilled at the thought of his mother joining the conversation than his wife did.

Turning back to Tommy, he said, "I thought this was wrapped up years ago. Why are you here?"

"Well, it is wrapped up. Or something is, at least. There's a body in pieces in your mother's old back yard. They even found a smashed-in skull wrapped up with a sparkly red bow. Know anything about that?"

"Should I?"

"Considering your wife disappeared, you liked to smack her around, you had a stand-in ready, and your mother had the patio put in about three weeks later, I'd say yes."

Tanya re-entered the room, pushing a wheelchair. A sour, wrinkled face looked at Tommy from the squeaky confines of the seat.

"Who are you?" The nails-on-a-chalkboard voice didn't sound any better up close than it had from the top of the stairway. "Why are you harassing my son? Is this about that bitch again?"

"I'm Tommy Kinter. I worked the case when your daughter-in-law disappeared, but I don't believe we ever met. This morning, a body was discovered at the house you lived in when Darly went missing. Don't be concerned, though, ma'am. Your alibi is still on file from ten years ago."

The old woman stared at Tommy for several seconds before responding. "Don't be ridiculous. If your department hadn't been run by someone getting it up the ass from my priest, that bingo alibi would have been thrown out a long time ago. Still can't believe the dumb girl had to say goodbye to me before leaving my Andy—on his birthday, no less."

Three faces gaped at her, but she didn't notice.

"I know you've had to wait a long time, Andy. Really, I thought you'd find your gift much sooner—you were always so good at finding your presents—but you just had to hire someone else to lay my patio instead of doing it yourself. Happy birthday, ten years late."

⊕ ⊕ ⊕

Jennifer lives on Virginia's coast and spends most of her time copy editing for some amazingly talented authors. When not editing for her business, The Independent Pen, she usually writes, sews, or knits in the few minutes she can snatch that aren't filled with homeschooling or chasing the kids and pets. During the summer, she can often be found at one of the many local beaches, books and knitting in tow.

Jennifer is currently at work on a series of novellas, **Brides of Sam,** *and a mystery novel (or series of novels). You can find her here:* **about.me/jenniferwingard.**

THE WORLD

PHOENIX

By Laura Eno

THE ALTAR SHIMMERED WITH CANDLELIGHT, THE MIRROR sitting behind it multiplying the glow. Renae glimpsed her reflection, younger-looking than truth, unhappiness a burden crushing her soul—or it would be if she still had one. Her hand fluttered over a deck of Tarot cards resting between two of the pillared candles, waiting to reveal the answers to her unspoken questions. If she dared to ask.

The only other item on the altar, the only item Renae truly possessed amid the flotsam of trivia collected over the years was an hourglass. No bigger than a bottle of wine, its sands held in stasis, time arrested as it waited for her to finish what she'd begun. She traced the fine woodcarvings cradling the glass in place with one fingertip, feeling the energy swirl through her blood. Calling to her. Wondering if the waiting had come to an end.

She thought maybe it had. The cards would confirm it.

Some would tell you there are no vampires. Don't listen to them. They're real. Maybe not the bloodsucking kind, but others do exist. There are worse things that move through the shadows. Through the light, as well. I'm living proof of that, although living might not be the best description.

Renae picked up the Tarot deck and turned over a card, placing it on the altar in front of her. *Yes, a foolish beginning.*

⊕ ⊕ ⊕

The summer intern job at the UN was a dream come true for Renae. Fresh out of school, the offer of travel lured her away from the familiar and into an exotic landscape normally reserved for those with more experience in avoiding pitfalls. Intoxicated by it all, Renae soon blundered into the wrong situation, collapsing at a party with only vague memories of her time there. Even now, knowing what happened, she had a hard time recalling more than fragments.

I remember the sting of venom coursing through my veins. The fire as it tracked through my belly, forcing me to the edge of death before allowing me to return. The horror of awareness when I awoke, even without realizing what I'd become.

The thirst dogging my every footstep, almost too strong for me to deny. Almost.

She awakened in an elegant bedroom, the dark paneled walls displaying paintings of fair maidens ravished by mythological gods or some such nonsense. The images gave her the creeps so Renae cast about for another distraction while her fogged brain cleared enough to figure out where she was and what had happened.

Her body ached, head throbbed. No answers materialized, only an insatiable thirst irritating her throat, moisture-starved tissue begging for liquid.

The door opened and Renae's breath caught. The man glowed in the light from the doorway, his red hair seeming to catch fire from the sun pouring through the windows behind him. He crossed the floor, coming to stand by the bed. Renae's blood quickened in her veins with each step he took. Suddenly, nothing mattered but him.

"You're awake." He smiled and took her hand in his. She hadn't remembered being so cold before but he exuded a delicious warmth and she didn't want him to let go. The burning in her throat eased as well.

"I am called Fen. Do you remember what happened to you?"

Renae shook her head but images flashed through her mind like tiny explosions threatening to engulf her if she concentrated for too long. Images of this bright man, bathed in darkness, drawing toward her. Cloaked shadows in the background writhing like cobras attuned to his every move. A woman's laugh echoed in her head.

"It's all right. I'm here to help you."

The flashes left and Renae smiled up at him, her stupor increasing into euphoria. His next words didn't mean much at the time. She would come to understand slowly, much later. Not that it mattered. It was already too late.

"You've been reborn to serve me," his voice crooned, clasping Renae in a sexual heat too powerful to resist. "I will teach you, nourish you, provide for you. In return, you will deny me nothing. To betray me would mean your death."

Fen held a hand to her cheek, stroking it as a lover would. His energy fed her until Renae felt strong enough to sit up. As he broke contact and stepped away, the thirst crept back again. Renae felt the lust to drain another human of their energy and stared into Fen's eyes, now lit from within as if a fire blazed there.

"What's wrong with me?" Waves of heat crested within her chest, crashing against her lungs and robbing them of air. She struggled to breathe, the fire in her throat charring each effort.

"It's a glorious day. Come." He offered his hand to her. "I'll show you how to thrive."

I fed off the energy of others to survive but never to the point of killing them. Never to the point of turning them, either. I like to think I have some semblance of humanity left within me. If that ever fails, all hope will be lost.

And so began my descent into hell, accompanied by an unholy angel.

⊕ ⊕ ⊕

Her thoughts reaching outward again, Renae picked another card from the deck and turned it over, her eyes squeezing shut at the sight. *True enough. He wove his decadent magic around my throat like a collar made of velvet but as unbreakable as an iron clamp.*

Renae felt Fen's presence now as he walked through the penthouse. Smelled the scent of another woman's perfume lingering about him like a wisp of fog trying to hide from the rays of the sun. Conjured a mental image of his red hair awash with golden light as he strode down the hallway toward his private rooms in the penthouse, the floor-to-ceiling windows casting a blazing trail in his honor.

Everything seemed to be in his honor. The viper charmed the masses. They gave themselves over to Fen without question. He might soon hold the fate of the world in his hands.

Adulation fed him well enough but a small number of spent bodies weren't uncommon, either. No one noticed the missing. Magic took care of the evidence, turned away the questions.

A few, like her, he kept in servitude, turning them for his private entertainment. His private soldiers. His private worshippers.

She'd even married him, a disgrace Renae would never be able to overcome, much less explain. He needed an image. She gave him her soul.

Twisting and tumbling along the road of this insane odyssey with a man poised to inherit the political world, Renae happened upon a splinter of hope from an unlikely source, in a place where no hope had any right to exist. A turn of fortune materialized during a chance encounter in New Orleans five months ago.

The mirror mocked her now, daring her to draw the next card. Renae held her breath, her fingers tingling as they hovered over the backs of the Tarot cards. How many times had she gotten the wrong answer in the months since? She touched the deck and pleaded with any spirit listening. *Let it be today.*

A whoosh of breath escaped her lips as she pulled the card. Yes. Renae felt the wheel spin as she dropped the card down on the altar in front of her.

⊕ ⊕ ⊕

The tiny shop sat back from the alley in a rundown section of town, a place where you know the voodoo is authentic and sane people don't venture into the shadows.

No one's accused me of being sane lately. The very idea tickled Renae's long-forgotten sense of humor. A joke at her expense. The thought appealed to herThe shop door stood open, inviting Renae in along with the humidity of the summer day. An old woman appraised her from behind the back counter, a smile touching the corners of her mouth enough to give her a benign countenance. Renae didn't believe it for one moment. She felt the power rolling off this dangerous woman. The prospect excited her.

"You be far from home, needing more help than you've a right to ask for." The Cajun queen laughed, her voice sounding like textured silk rasping against sand. Eyes snapping with black fire burned their way into Renae's mind, leaving her feeling as if she had a gaping hole in her forehead. "You know who you be tied to? He rise from the ashes. Fortune don't play no role for him."

"Please. There must be some way. I know you can help me. I can feel it." Renae knew she'd give this woman anything she had, plead for as long as it took.

"Maybe. No telling how fate might twist the intent. Just so you know. I may have something to ease the pain."

A raucous sound rolled from the woman, more like gathering spirits to do her bidding than anything resembling a laugh. The air around the Cajun spun, her black hair whipping upwards in a funnel, snakelike, twisting into an emotion fraught with seduction and easy magic lying there for the taking.

Renae blinked and the room around her settled into a shop once more, the seething energies held back in an uneasy truce. Her spine crawled with unaccustomed trepidation but she stood her ground, refusing to look away from the obsidian eyes staring her down, the mouth curved as if ready for trouble.

The woman sauntered over to a shelf at the back of the shop, plucking an hourglass from it and spinning back to Renae in one quick movement. She tapped the hourglass three times in rapid succession. Something inside the sand repeated the beat like an echo, the color of the granules turning from a vibrant blue to that which was found on a stroll along the beach.

Renae kept her unease to herself. After all, she had asked for help and only the strongest magic had any hope of succeeding. Still, the wrongness pounded a drumbeat of doom within her, the message intoxicating at the same time. The lure of the darkness ready to savage the unwary.

The Cajun queen held the relic aloft, away from her body, and studied Renae for a few moments before speaking. "When the time arrives for you, the cycle will end. Your journey comes to a close, and a new beginning spreads before you. Rebirth is possible if you do not waiver. There's only one escape, one chance. You await the world. To move before the moment of clarity brings you nothing."

Renae nodded her understanding.

My chance at redemption.

⊕ ⊕ ⊕

One card to go. Then she'd know for sure. Trembling fingers slid along one card to the next before coming to rest on what Renae hoped was her redemption. A tear formed in her eye as she laid it above the others. This was her card, the answer to her question.

The World.

Renae picked up the hourglass, careful to keep it away from her body as the energy vibrated down her arm, restlessly seeking what the voodoo woman called "an awakening." She walked past the windows in the hallway, the sunlight dimming now as storm clouds gathered outside. The soft carpet beneath her bare feet beckoned to Renae to lay down her burden and rest. Forget her plans. It would all work out if she kept quiet.

Only the pull of the hourglass held in front of her kept Renae going, the energy contained within jumping with a frenzy of kinetic activity. The sand still didn't move between the two chambers but rather surged in place, as if experiencing a tidal pull inside the glass. The motion drew her eye and she quickened her steps. The sooner she got rid of this dark magic, the better.

Fen lay on the wide bed asleep, his chest bare, his hair a tousle of flaming color against the pillow. Renae almost wept at the thought of destroying such beauty. Only the knowledge of his blackened depths drove her on.

She placed the hourglass on Fen's chest, directly over his heart, hoping the Cajun queen's knowledge held true. The voodoo woman had said the object would hold him in stasis. If not, Renae had no doubt these would be the last moments of her life.

Better to die trying than not to try at all.

His body trembled but he didn't wake. Renae let go of the breath she held and watched in terror as fangs appeared in the sand for a brief moment before sinking back down again.

Inside the hourglass, the sand turned red in a blaze of glowing fire, as if kissed by the sunset. Fen's body jerked several times in spasms, then stilled, his breath fading as his lungs ceased to function.

There would be recriminations. Wars could start over his death as factions accused each other of conspiracy. Renae might be blamed as well—only fitting as it would be the truth—but standing aside and doing nothing to stop his intentions would have been a far greater evil. Even if she were the only one who could see it. The only one who knew him for what he truly was. The only one capable of stopping him before he destroyed free will.

Her pulse gave a savage kick as Fen's body crumbled to dust, a desiccated wasteland lying on the mattress, the room eerily silent but for a gentle hissing sound emanating from the sand in the hourglass. Renae wondered for a moment what those fangs belonged to before deciding she didn't want to know. The sand itself started moving again, its new color causing each grain to seem like a tiny drop of blood dripping into a pool of the stuff. She tore her gaze away from the sight as her stomach did a slow flip, holding the offensive timepiece away from her body with a straight arm as she made her way back to the altar.

Whatever happened, it was the end of the threat. The world could re-group, start anew. So could she, even if it was from inside a jail cell. At least she'd know she made the right decision.

The candlelight sputtered and flared as she knelt in front of the altar and stared into the mirror once more. The flames briefly consumed her image before settling back down, as if something in the aether called out to the fire, giving it renewed life. The smell of cinnamon filled the room, turning sweet, cloying, combining with a burnt stench, which assaulted Renae's nose.

Something in her peripheral vision moved, a shadow sending chills to roll along her spine. She turned her head with reluctance, afraid of what she'd find.

Nothing but empty space. *I'm alone in the room.* The realization surprised her.

When she turned back, the mirror had iced over, its surface showing jagged cracks within the white. It caught Renae in a trance, the cold numbing all movement. Casting out all reason. Tightening the grip of fear.

The moisture heated again to room temperature, melting in rivulets along the length of the mirror. It seemed to be crying fat tears, showing the tracks on Renae's reflected cheeks. Cheeks no longer under her control.

The face in the mirror is still mine but belongs to Fen now. I'm floating somewhere behind him, off to his left, insubstantial and helpless. A wraith, nothing more.

The reflected image dissolved, re-emerged as Fen once more. Like the Phoenix, he had emerged from the ashes to start anew. The perfect ruler. Feared as the antichrist by some, adored by many more. Free to steal their will, their power, their lives.

And I helped him do it.

He smiles as if he can sense me drifting over his shoulder. Perhaps he can.

The sound of a Cajun queen's laughter fills my mind as fear of this new existence extinguishes all hope.

Welcome to eternity.

Laura Eno. Speculative Fiction wordsmith. Author of fifteen novels and novellas ranging from fantasy to romance to horror, she also has stories included in nineteen published anthologies.

The secret to her stories? Spread lies, blend in truths, add a pinch of snark and a dash of tears. Escape into her world. She left the porch light on so you can find your way down the rabbit hole.

Find her here: **lauraeno.com**

AFTERWARDS
FROM THE EDITOR

"Let me explain. No, there is too much. Let me sum up." (To quote one of my favorite movies.)

Putting together this anthology has been one of the most amazing experiences of my life. Right from the very beginning, this whole crazy idea clicked so hard I'd swear it registered 10.0 on the Richter scale.

I had the idea for an anthology based on the Major Arcana of the Tarot for months. I wasn't quite sure how to pull it off, but after much thinking and losing sleep, the idea just wouldn't go away. I figured it this way—it was never going to happen if I didn't make it happen.

I know and work with some of the most amazing writers on the planet. I can never express my gratitude for the way this group pulled together and supported the concept. From donations to working the social media platforms to help with funding; from services to ideas and getting their stories in on time...it's just been a dream come true.

And the STORIES! The talent of these writers just blew my socks clean off. I can't say I was surprised, because I know them and their work, but as one fiction freak to another, let me just say I am so proud of each and every writer in this anthology I can hardly contain myself.

If you like what you read, please consider reviewing and spreading the word. Support your favorite authors by visiting their websites, and don't be shy! We all love hearing from our readers, because YOU are the reason we do this.

In other words, THIS FICTION IS FOR YOU. I hope you love it.

~Netta the Editah

THANKS AND GRATITUDE

Thanks to Mr. X for his donation of time and our beautiful website at **allegoriesofthetarot.com**.

Thank you to Eden Baylee for her unflagging efforts as the Twitter Queen and the force behind **@AllegoriesTarot**.

Much appreciation to Badass Marketing for the push for launch and the blog tour.

Thanks to Clive Aryn Arnold for the use of his lovely artwork and to Valerie Bellamy for her mad formatting skills and who took this book to a higher level. Not to mention her unflagging patience.

Thank you, Kris Austen Radcliffe for taking my vision of the cover and making it real.

Much love and thanks beyond measure to every author in the anthology who supported, shared, tweeted, Facebooked, Tumblred, and hosted many an interview or shout-out on their own blogs.

Special thanks to Jennifer Wingard, who has eagle eyes and misses nothing.

Words cannot express my love and gratitude to the writers involved for your belief and support, and all the shits and giggles. This book is truly a labor of love, and evidence of what a team of outstanding indie writers can do when they pull together. I AM SO PROUD OF YOU.

For the supporters of the Indiegogo campaign to get this off the ground, thank you! You made this possible.

Eternal thanks to:
Laura Eno
Steven Grant
Kirstin Lund
Kelly Kiernan Sampson
Lisa Perez
Melissa Jensen
Lynn Siperelle
Grant Kearney
Valerie Bellamy
Janet Sked
M Aja Martinez
Nita Fortune
Eternal Elf Creations
Bridget McKenna
Lauren Stark
Stuart Ashen
Gil Cantrell
Charmaine Murmer
Kevin McKay
Alexis Latshaw
Tracey McDonald
Pete Williams
Renee Laprise
Patti Larsen
Denise Battista
Sue Goldberg

Michael Swift

Hilary Melton Butcher

Christine Ludwick

Janet Hinkel

Carol Romanella

Kathy Walsh

Loren Kleinman

Justin Kalinay

Julie Devin Dodd

Helen Yee

Donna McCoy

Lon Prater

Susan Haines

Andrei Tretyakov

Jennifer Wingard

Hal Lewis

Joy-Anne Whiteside

Ashely Penno

Kimberly Kinrade

Lisa Perez

Catherine Dickson

Brett Laughlin

We couldn't have done it without you. Thank you for your support!